BELOVED NIGHT

WORLD WHISPERER BOOK 5

RACHEL DEVENISH FORD

SMALL SEED PRESS

First published in 2020

Copyright © 2020 Rachel Devenish Ford

Small Seed Press LLC

racheldevenishford.com

This book is for Gale and Joy. I love you.

And for Kenya, the daughter of my dreams.

CHAPTER 1

Herrith hurried along the narrow alley in the bottom tier of the city, head down. On either side of him, the buildings rose up, two or three stories of red stone, crammed full of the lives of people. Their washing hung out of the windows or along strings that stretched from one side of the alley to the other. On the walls of the slippery street, Herrith could see the prints of many hands, blackened and shiny over time. He heard babies crying in the heat, women calling out or laughing. The scents of dinner wafted through the air, and at least once, Herrith heard the muttered words, "Red Robe."

He paid no attention to the muttering. All his concentration was directed toward the slight figure of a woman in front of him. She had slipped out of the palace just before Herrith, and the guard, a Circle member, had pointed her out.

"She's acting suspiciously," he had murmured. "I don't know who she is, either."

Herrith was instantly on the alert. There shouldn't be

anyone in the palace that the guard didn't know. He needed to make sure the woman wasn't up to anything dangerous.

He paused and put his hand on the building beside him, feeling old and a little shaky. The woman was moving swiftly. After a few breaths, Herrith followed her again. Work at the palace was growing ever more tense. Gavi told Herrith that he was almost certain the kitchen staff had been seeded with spies from the king. The Circle—the little group of resistance fighters in the Desert City—was trying to decide whether Gavi should go or stay. The boy desperately wanted to stay close to Aria, but she was so heavily guarded that few of them ever saw her.

They all needed to know: what would the king's next move be? Gavi asked Herrith every day if he knew anything, and Herrith had to restrain himself from snapping at the boy. Didn't Gavi know Herrith would share the information with him just as soon as he heard? Herrith had lived a life of danger, a spy and member of the resistance who had existed in the king's aware-ness since he was a young boy, and still these days vibrated with more tension than ever before.

King Ikajo had stopped confiding in Herrith, his cousin, the Red Robe who had been with him the longest, and Herrith knew that the king could easily, without a second thought, decide to end Herrith's life. There didn't seem to be anything remotely like loyalty within the king's soul. The only person Ikajo had ever seemed to love, even remotely, was Isika, his hope. Ikajo's father had stolen the Maweel queen, so Ikajo could father a Warrior Whisperer with Amani, her daughter. Now that the daughter, Isika, had rejected the king, Ikajo was dangerous in a way that terrified Herrith and everyone around him. Isika had the potential to be the most powerful person alive because of the combination of strengths within her, and she wanted nothing to do with Ikajo's plan to subdue the lands around them. The king's dream was dying.

Herrith was shocked and dismayed by the king's way of thinking. Did he really believe Nenyi, the Shaper, the Uncreated One, was so easily manipulated? That she could be tricked into creating a weapon for Mugunta, the evil one, from a combination of bloodlines? The king had been so sure. Maybe he knew something Herrith didn't.

Herrith nearly lost the woman as she turned a corner, so he sped up, clutching at a pain in his side. There she was. She was slight in figure, swathed in layers of clothing. As Herrith watched, she clutched her cloak more tightly around her, clinging to the shadows as she sped along the narrow alley. Her hands were covered, no part of her body visible. She looked like a drift of clothing, scudding along the narrow street, hardly touching the ground. Goosebumps broke out along Herrith's body, and he cursed his superstitious mind. The thought had come to him, briefly, that he was following a ghost.

The fragrances of a city evening continued to shower Herrith's senses as he hurried after the woman. He smelled heady night-blooming flowers, dough and rich spices frying in hot oil, an old woman's cigar. Herrith's stomach rumbled. Mara's food waited for him at the Circle meeting, but he was stuck following this woman, who now seemed to be traveling erratically, zigzagging through the alleys, apparently searching for something.

He almost missed seeing her stop and had to regain his balance as he skidded to a halt. The woman stood gazing into a large window, large enough that Herrith could see into the room from where he stood, hiding in the shadows a little further down the street. What was she doing? Was she a spy? But there was nothing significant about the old weaver she watched. He sat, unknowing, at his loom, lit by magic stones in a sconce on the wall. The rhythm of his shuttle moving back and forth, back and forth, seemed to entrance the woman for some time. Finally, she hurried down the alley.

Herrith paused in front of the window to see if he had missed something, but no, the room was bare and simple, with one weaver working in the low light. Herrith watched for a moment, then, with a brief shake of his head and anxiety starting to pinch his gut, followed the woman again.

The woman had begun to cling more closely to the shadows, as though she suspected she was being followed. She looked back over her shoulder from time to time, and Herrith held his breath and kept himself very still. He couldn't see her face with the hood of her desert cloak pulled all the way forward. Once or twice, it seemed that she would turn and go back the way she had come, but each time she stood, head down, clinging to a wall with a gloved hand, and then continued into the lowest tier of the city. Other than the zigzags, she was heading in the same direction as Herrith, toward Circle headquarters.

He grew more afraid, anxiety turning in his stomach, trickling into his limbs until he trembled. The king watched them all so closely ever since Isika had infiltrated the City, releasing hundreds of people destined for slavery and nearly killing the King.

Aria was guarded like a rare diamond, marched from her rooms to sit near the king and attend him, then taken back to her rooms when he was tired of her. Herrith was rarely close enough to her to talk to Aria. When he did manage to be in her vicinity, he was careful not to look at Aria for too long. He felt the king's eyes on his every move, the king's awareness spreading out to draw all of them into a tighter grip than ever.

The woman stopped again, gazing into another window. This one didn't even have glass. It was merely a few bars crossing a small squarish hole on a dilapidated building. She stood, swaying slightly, for several breaths, seemingly transfixed. Herrith couldn't see what she was looking at, but when she finally moved on, he hurried closer to peer in.

A small family sat on the floor, eating from a single pot. Light came from a few candles. This meant the family couldn't afford the magic lighting of the city, and the weak light barely illuminated a mother feeding her toddler bits of rice. Nearby were a small boy and girl, eating quietly from the pot. They took turns without fighting, but as soon as the food was in their hands, they quickly shoved it into their mouths, as though it would disappear. Herrith felt tears sting his eyes, watching them, and made a mental note of their location. The mother smiled down at the toddler in her lap.

A suspicion began to form in Herrith's mind.

He turned to look for the woman and couldn't see her through a group of laughing people crowding the narrow alley. His stomach felt as though it would drop out of his body. He knew where the woman was going. She wasn't safe. None of them were safe. Panic rose as he rushed through the crowd, pushing past people even when they protested his rough treatment, scowling at him and shoving him back.

He caught sight of the woman just before she lifted her hand to rap on the blue door with the etched symbol of the broken circle. He drew near her as Mara opened the door, and without hesitating, caught her elbow, plowing past Mara into the room, slamming the door behind them.

"Herrith!" Mara exclaimed.

Gavi was on his feet. "Who is this?" he demanded. "We're supposed to tell each other before bringing anyone new."

Herrith ignored them. "Well?" he inquired, staring at the covered woman. "Are you going to show yourself?"

She reached up and pulled back her hood, then unwound the cloth that covered her face. Very expensive fabrics, Herrith noted now, crossing his arms over his chest.

Gavi glanced at Herrith, his face confused, but Herrith shook his head, keeping his attention on the girl who emerged from the billow of cloth, looking back on him defiantly.

"Aria!" Gavi said with a rush of breath, moving close to hug her. She blinked up at him, smiling slightly. The smile turned to a confused frown for a moment, then she shook herself. Herrith felt a pang of love. This girl, ensnared by her father's poison most of the time, was like a daughter to Herrith. He took her elbow more gently and led her over to some cushions. She sank onto them, seeming weary to the core.

"Are you trying to get yourself killed?" he asked. He couldn't quite keep the fearful anger out of his voice.

Her face shifted through a strange mix of emotions. Herrith was used to this. Aria was really only half herself, these days, with the king's poison arrow still lodged inside her. The fact that there was anything of her left at all was astonishing, and Herrith felt a deep pride in the resilience of Amani's daughter. He didn't know of even one other person who could have withstood the king's poison for this long.

Herrith sometimes wondered if Aria really was the most powerful person in the world, resisting the king's enslavement as she did. She should have withered and died long ago.

But at this moment, Herrith was more concerned with the

fact that Aria had broken out of the palace. She knew what was at stake. The king watched her closely, with guards and spies in place to follow her. She had put herself in danger. She had put them all in danger. She could have easily been followed.

Gavi scooted close to Aria, keeping his eyes trained on her face. She smiled back at him. Mara approached with a cup of tea for the girl, and only then did Herrith look around to see who else was witnessing this. Enfa, Abbas's sister was in the corner of the room with two other Karee circle members. An old friend of Mara's sat at the table, bent over a bowl of soup in the dim lighting. That was all. Herrith exhaled.

"I had to come," Aria said in a soft voice after taking a gulp of tea. She paused and closed her eyes. They waited for many breaths before Aria opened her eyes again. "I'm sorry," she said, "he's angry that I'm gone and trying to work out what to do about it."

All around the room, there were gasps and muffled exclamations. Abbas's sister sat forward.

"Does he know you are here?"

"No," Aria whispered.

Herrith leaned forward to hear her better.

"He can't tell where I am. He thinks I'm hiding somewhere in the palace."

There were more exclamations and whispers from the Karee in the corner. Herrith held his breath for a moment.

"But how would he think that? Unless..." he felt a jolt of understanding, "Aria, are you altering his awareness?"

She nodded and closed her eyes again. Herrith nearly staggered. Aria had layers of curses on her, guards set to watch her, and was physically frail. Despite all this, she could read and alter the king's mind.

7

Herrith met Gavi's eyes and saw the same shock that must be visible on his own face.

Aria took a shuddering breath. "I came because you must be aware of his plans. They are...dangerous. For all of us."

"Tell us," Gavi said gently. His face was very still, and every muscle in his body seemed rigid. Beside him, Mara was wringing her hands.

Aria took a few more moments to answer, then forced the words out. "He will go to the seas and fight from the water." It seemed as though she was fighting for every word, her eyes shut tight, her face raw and pained.

Gavi leaned closer and laid his hand gently on her shoulder. He let his breath out in a hiss. Herrith flinched, knowing that Gavi was feeling Aria's pain, part of his gift as a healer.

She spoke again, biting out each word, with long pauses between some of them.

"The king will attack the Hadem. He plans to destroy them to draw Isika to himself. Then, he will either turn her or kill her and go through the Hadem lands through Maween to the city of Azariyah. Without the protective magic of the Hadem, the Maweel will be greatly weakened and will fall. Forever."

She got the last word out and then slumped over. Gavi caught her, keeping her head from hitting the ground.

He opened bloodshot eyes and whispered, "Give her a moment, and then we need to get her back to the palace grounds. We can leave her in the garden...they can assume she just wanted to be outside."

"What's wrong, Gavi?" Mara asked. "Why did she collapse?"

Gavi's eyes filled with tears. "He's torturing her. We have to fix this, find something to cut the bond between them, or she isn't going to make it. She'll die. I can feel the despair within her.

She's the strongest person I've ever known, but no one can take this much torment.

Herrith moved closer to stroke Aria's hair. His eyes were stinging. He blinked back tears.

"How can he do this to her?" he murmured.

"He's a monster," Enfa said.

"That's the problem," Herrith said. "He's not a monster, he's a man. How can a man harm his own child like this?"

Herrith had the tiniest flicker of hope, then. Maybe, after so many years of frustration, he was finding the reason he was here. Maybe he would be the one to rid the world of this evil, to finally take the life of the king.

CHAPTER 2

"Hey, hey, hey," Jabari murmured from where he stood in the horse stables. "It's okay. You don't need to buck like a crazy beast." In animal speech, he added, *I thought we were friends.*

Wind, Isika's horse, showed the whites of his eyes and kicked at the wall behind him. *Friends is a word for people,* he replied.

Jabari sighed, clutching the reins tightly with one hand and wiping sweat off his chin with the other. He was irritated beyond measure, and the last thing he needed was a horse educating him on human and animal word choice.

Okay then, but you have to admit that we've been through a lot together, he said. *No need to kick at me.*

They stood at a standstill, Jabari trying to encourage the horse to lift his foot so Jabari could check it, and Wind flatly refusing. At the other end of the stables, someone strode in. It was Bara, the horse keeper. She walked to the door of Wind's stall and crossed her arms, looking at Jabari with barely concealed amusement.

"What's this?" she asked. "Arguing with the horses again?"

Jabari gritted his teeth. "He won't listen to me," he muttered.

She continued to watch him, arms crossed, narrowing her eyes as she surveyed him. She wore her tightly coiled hair short and natural, and her tunic was sleeveless, showing dark brown arms that were muscled from years of hard work.

"I don't get it," she finally said after several long breaths where Jabari tried not to snap at her for staring. "Isn't this one of your giftings? Why is it so hard for you?"

Jabari blew a short, impatient breath. "If I knew that, I wouldn't be here."

Ivram, second elder, had grown increasingly frustrated with Jabari over the previous months and finally assigned him to spend time in every place where he had a gift but wasn't "performing to potential," whatever that meant.

Jabari leaned his elbow on the side of the stall and considered the horse, who tossed his head and refused to look at him.

This wasn't even his fault. The thought came unbidden, insistent, though he didn't want it. Jabari had no strength because their Whisperer was weak.

And you wonder why the horse does not want to cooperate with you, said a familiar and alarming voice in his head. The horses in the stable began to protest, neighing loudly, shaking their heads, shuddering their coats, and pawing at the ground with their hooves. The stable was suddenly full of dust, and Bara whirled around to see what had happened.

Jabari already knew, even before she turned back and pointed an accusatory finger at him.

"Get them out of here! What are you thinking?"

Jabari hurried out toward the door, shooing the huge cats

out of the stables as he went, but turned back to call, "They go where they want! Not my fault!"

Are you crazy? he demanded, looking back and forth at the two Palipa, giant silver cats who had put the horses into a panic. As he and the cats passed by the horses in their stables, the horses reared and whinnied. *I'm here to improve my gathering gift and animal speech. You've set me back weeks!*

They arrived at the yard, and Jabari could see Bara letting the horses out from the other side of the stable. The horses ran as fast as they could, out to the far end of the long meadow, tossing their heads and working out the jitters they couldn't help feeling in the presence of the large cats. Jabari shook his head. They wouldn't trust Jabari anytime soon.

He turned to face the Palipa, the heat of the midday sun blazing down on his head. Hera, the mother cat, sat looking at him impassively. Her head reached the middle of his arm, nearly his shoulder. Her grown cub sat beside her, washing his paws and ignoring Jabari.

What's that supposed to mean about the horses not wanting to cooperate with me? Jabari asked.

Hera narrowed her eyes into slits. *Why would they? We all serve the World Whisperer. As long as she is loyal to Nenyi, we have unwavering loyalty to her. Even creatures as stupid as horses can feel that you blame her for your weakness.*

Jabari frowned. He stood without answering for a long moment, then realized he was clenching his fists. He forced himself to relax them.

"What are you talking about?" he asked aloud. The Ancient Ones could understand human speech, and he momentarily lost the ability to ask nicely in his head. "I love Isika. Even before I knew I loved her, I was loyal to her."

The silver cat's eyes were steady on Jabari's face, and he forced himself not to flinch or look away.

You believe, Son of Andar, that something about Isika and her place as World Whisperer is causing the problems with your own gifting. It is ugly to shift blame to her, young one. You show that you do not understand Isika, her power, or your own.

The younger cat stopped washing his paws and blinked. *Humans are stupid when they blame.*

Jabari could not really believe that he was standing in a stable yard being castigated by creatures on four legs. *I don't blame her,* he insisted. But the words weren't convincing, not even to him. He didn't want to blame her. The thoughts came without his permission. He knew they weren't rational. He didn't know how to stop them.

We came for another reason, said the younger cat. He went back to washing his paws.

We did, Hera said. She stood and stretched, then settled back down. Jabari waited.

The elders are together in the meeting space, preparing to call Isika in. We don't think you should miss what they are planning. It would be helpful for you to go and hear what they have to say.

Jabari squinted at the cat. She settled back on her haunches. He wasn't sure what she meant by her cryptic words, but they seemed to be all she would offer. He took a moment to absorb the shift in his plans, then turned to gather his things.

Don't follow me back in here, he warned as he went toward the stable. He felt their flickers of amusement, and, glancing back, saw them stand and fluidly lope away, the sunlight flashing on their silver hides.

Bara was still in the stable. Jabari walked to the hook on the back wall to take off his apron. Bara eyed him without saying anything, still clearly annoyed.

"They should know better," he said. "Especially Wind. When we went into the Desert City, the Palipa used their magic to make Wind, Night, and a few of the other horses invisible. They should be used to the scent of their magic."

"I'm not sure anything could get horses used to the scent of a large predator," Bara said. "Even these ones, who love Isika enough to allow large cats to cover them in magic."

Jabari nodded, dropping the apron onto the hook and winding his *ser* onto his head.

"Something came up, and I have to go back to the palace. I'll try to check Wind's shoes another time. If he'll ever let me get close to him again."

He picked up his pack and swung it over his shoulder, looking at the older woman.

"What do you think is stopping me from progressing?" he asked, feeling desperate, suddenly, for an answer.

She considered him. "You are arrogant," she said finally. "And also somehow afraid of your strength. Animals don't like that. You need to command love from them the way Isika does."

"You don't think Isika is arrogant?" he asked. "And I mean that in the best way."

"Isika is brave and sure of herself," Bara replied. "It's not the same thing. I'm shocked that you would think it is." She turned away, shaking her head, and he flinched at the pity that had flashed in her eyes. "You have a lot of work to do, little brother."

The dry grass crunched under Jabari's feet as he headed up the hill to the castle. Underneath everything else he had picked up from the horses that day had been a single-minded ground note of fear. Fear of hunger. The drought went on and on, and like all grazers, they were afraid of drought. Their fear made them skittish. That wasn't his fault.

He looked up at the sky, a brittle, faded blue. Not a single cloud drifted overhead. There should be rain now, cooling the earth. Every year, without fail, Maween experienced three to four months of rain that made them miserable indoors but was provision for the rest of the year. The rest of the seasons had brief storms, but the wet season was the basis of life in their region. Last year's wet season had been meager, and this year again, there was nothing. No rain.

The people of Azariyah had begun walking around with a furrow between their eyes, chewing their lips, wringing their hands. The land could not survive without rain for another cycle. They knew why it was happening, but they didn't know how to stop it.

The Desert King had pulled Maween into his net of authority. He had weakened their Whisperer and taken her sister. Their protection was breached, and he could pelt them with curses. They were vulnerable to him.

Jabari knew, deep within himself, that someone with his power should be able to counteract this curse, shift the weather and change the course of events for the rainy season. So in a way, it was Jabari's fault. But in a way, it was everyone's fault and no one's fault.

Humans waste time thinking about fault, Jabari heard Hera say from a distance.

It was a waste of time. Jabari needed to focus. Their impossible task was to find a way to break the betrayal magic that kept them tethered to the malevolence of the Great Waste and Mugunta's power. Betrayal magic tied them down and prevented them from being the strong kingdom they had been during and before Queen Azariyah's reign.

They had their World Whisperer, and she was powerful. Ivram thought she was perhaps mightier in her power than even Azariyah had been. But the betrayal magic had crippled her. Jabari felt frustrated, powerless, and above all, irritated.

The door to the conference room was ajar, so Jabari nodded at the guard and stepped in quietly. He wanted to hear the last fragments of conversation before they noticed him.

"We can do it the week after next," Jabari's father was saying.

Jabari blinked and took in the room. Light streamed in from the high windows, illuminating the rugs and cushions around a low table, where the four elders sat or reclined.

"Not soon enough. We need it to take effect immediately, before we have to send our animals away to find pasture." That was Ivram, his voice low and troubled.

"We could send gatherers with them to protect them," Laylit, Jabari's mother, suggested.

Ivram shook his grizzled head. "We need all our gatherers here," he said. "The coronation must happen next week."

Jabari had been following until then, but at these words, he blinked and nearly staggered. He stepped farther into the room, so they couldn't help but notice him.

"Coronation?" he asked.

A multitude of emotions crossed over their faces as he watched. All four elders, elegant in their robes, were striking. His parents, Andar and Laylit, beautiful in their bright colors that highlighted the same deep black skin Jabari had inherited. And then Ivram with his dark skin, wise eyes, and graying head, and his wife Karah, pale-skinned with long red hair tied back in a hundred braids.

At the moment, though, their faces were a combination of irritated, exasperated, or angry.

"I have it on good authority that your faces might stay that way if you keep looking at me like that," Jabari said, winking at his mother, who had threatened him with that outcome many times when he was a boy. He crossed the room in a few long strides and collapsed onto one of the cushions, reaching for flatbread and soft cheese. His stomach growled, and he realized with surprise that he hadn't eaten anything that day. Too busy with the horses, who now would hate him forever because of the wretched Palipa. He spread cheese on a piece of bread and then looked up to find everyone still watching him. Ivram had his head in his hand.

"You were not invited to this conversation," Andar said mildly.

Jabari felt a flash of anger. "I thought you must have forgotten to invite me since I'm sure I just heard you planning an event that you wouldn't dream of without consulting Isika, or even me."

Laylit sat forward. "Isika is on her way," she said. "But why would we consult you?"

Jabari gaped at his mother. "She is my friend and beloved," he said. "This is about our future!"

His father scoffed. "This from a person who 'allowed' Gavi to stay in the Desert City without consulting any of us."

"I didn't realize it was only Gavi's influence that kept you civil, Jabari," his mother added. She was trying to speak lightly, but her voice broke.

Jabari stared at a pattern in his woven cushion. So that was why they had grown more close-mouthed around him. He had noticed that where they might once have included him to train him for eldership, they were now holding more meetings behind closed doors. He and Ivy, Ivram and Karah's daughter, had often flowed in and out of meetings without being stopped, but now they were left out of important conversations.

The pieces were coming together. The elders didn't trust him because Gavi had chosen to stay in the Desert City with Aria, and Jabari and Ivy hadn't stopped him.

"Gavi made his own choice," he said, trying to keep his voice controlled. "It hurts me as well, but he is my brother and equal. How should I have stopped him?"

He spread his hands on his knees and looked at them. What a mess they were all in. He didn't even want to look at the elders. He was disappointed in their response to Gavi's absence. Disappointed in himself for not being able to change anything. Of course, he had tried to change Gavi's mind about staying in the Desert City. He missed Gavi like he was sure he would miss his arm if it was gone.

"Isika should be here to hear this, though, don't you think?" he asked when the silence grew thick enough to be deeply uncomfortable.

"I should be where?"

Isika's voice was clear and musical, and Jabari turned so quickly that he felt a twinge in his neck. She was the most beautiful creature on the earth, he thought again as he saw her. He shifted to get up, but she widened her eyes at him, just a fraction, and he stayed where he was. She stood looking at them all, hands loose at her sides, head cocked to one side. She looked like a queen already. Jabari thought that he might be the only one who could tell that she was nervous. He could see it in her jaw.

The silence grew, then Laylit sat forward.

"We want to hold the coronation ceremony," she said.

Isika's face was faintly puzzled. "Well, yes, I knew that," she said.

"Next week," Laylit added.

There were two, maybe three heartbeats before Jabari lunged, just as Isika's knees gave out and she crumpled to the floor.

CHAPTER 3

Isika blinked, and the world slowly began to come back into focus. Beside her, Jabari shifted so that his hands were on her shoulders. What had happened? Ah, yes, the elders had told her she would be queen next week, and she had fainted. Wonderful. Could Isika pretend that she had simply decided to sit down fast? She looked into the many concerned faces around her. Too late.

Had she heard correctly? Did the elders really mean they thought Isika should be crowned queen next week? She stifled a laugh. The thought was making her woozy.

Beside her, Jabari shifted and spoke.

"She's not ready. Whatever you think is happening to the country is not going to be solved by making Isika queen if she's not up for it!"

Isika frowned. Wait, why was Jabari speaking for her? She held out a hand.

"Slow down, please," she said. "I haven't even heard the full idea. Let me take a breath or two and hear for myself."

A servant drew near with a glass of water, and Isika

accepted it gratefully, smiling into the man's worried eyes. She took a long swallow and felt better immediately, sitting up and shrugging Jabari's hands off her shoulders.

"We've always planned that I would become queen—" she started.

Jabari interrupted. "Yes. When you're at least eighteen."

There were murmurs of disapproval. Jabari had spoken over her, and the elders didn't like it. If Isika wasn't mistaken, even a couple of the servants had made annoyed growls. Isika stared at Jabari, her friend, and dearest love.

"It's unlike you to be so attached to the rules, my love."

He gazed back at her, his face set and angry.

Ivram broke in. "She's right, young one, it's unlike you. You can't change your essence just because you love Isika. Your strength, your gifts, lie in your ability to take risks. You'll cut your feet off if you allow worry to stifle this gift."

Isika glanced at the older man in surprise. It was an odd thing to say, but she sensed the truth in his words. The other elders looked tense and unhappy, watching Ivram and Jabari. Isika let out a long breath. She could see the weight of years sitting on the elders—their hopes for Isika, their yearning for their true lost queen, their sorrow over Gavi.

I lost them all too! she wanted to shout. *I lost my grandmother and mother, my sister.*

Where were the Othra? Their calming presence was needed at this meeting.

Keethior! she called.

What? the Ancient One responded.

Isika closed her eyes briefly, hiding a smile. Keethior was the servant of the World Whisperer, bound to her, but this fact didn't mean he was controllable or even polite.

I need you. Will you come, please?

Jabari threw Isika a glance, and she knew that he had heard her. She hadn't bothered to shield her animal speech from him. He sat with his arms crossed, silent and upset. Isika smiled at him. He was so beautiful to her—everything about him—from his scowl to his long, dark brown hands. Now that they were really together, really in love, she often let herself look at him for as long as she wanted. She liked the flare of his nostrils and the line of his jaw. Even now, when she was genuinely annoyed with him.

"Please don't speak for me," she said in a low voice.

The angry look disappeared, and Jabari looked startled, but Isika was not about to discuss her request. She turned to speak to the others, not waiting for Keethior to arrive because there was no question, really, about her answer. She looked around at all of them, sitting tall, or reclining against cushions—Ivram, with his kind eyes, Laylit, frowning slightly. Andar, impassive but with a clenched jaw, and Karah leaning forward, calm as always. Karah's expression flickered as her daughter, Ivy, burst into the room. Isika glanced once at Ivy, then said what she needed to say.

"Of course, we can hold the coronation next week if you think it is necessary."

The ensuing clamor swirled around Isika almost without involving her, so she simply observed. No less than four Othra flew into the room in a flurry of feathers. Ivy stood with her hands on her hips, shouting that no one ever told her anything, and did anyone remember she had a place in this palace too? Uncle Dawit, on guard at the door, had choked and sat down on a chair amid a coughing fit. Isika nearly went to him but saw he was all right when he held up a hand, imploring her silently to stay where she was. Jabari didn't do or say anything. He sat gazing at Isika, while the elders remonstrated with Ivy.

This was alarming in itself. Isika stared back at him.

We knew this would happen, she told him in the inner speech they shared.

Yes, but not yet, he said. *You don't know what it means to be queen.*

You weren't alive during my grandmother's reign, either. I know as much as you do.

My parents are elders. I know that they never run off for swims in the waterfall or climb trees with their best friends.

She smiled into his worried eyes. *Oh, but I'm World Whisperer,* she said. *I have to do those things, or my power will wither. Don't worry, Yab. It won't be terrible. It could even be good.*

But you'll still be in too much danger. We haven't figured out what to do about Aria or the deep betrayal poison.

But, Jabari, friend of my heart, she said, holding his gaze, *we're all in danger. The sun is burning holes into the ground. Something has to change. You can't keep trying to protect me, no, listen.* She put up a hand. *I will be queen. I will always be in danger.*

It dawned gradually on Isika that the hubbub in the room had quieted. The room was silent. Every bird and human watched while Isika and Jabari stared at each other, communicating silently.

"It's creepy when you do that," Ivy said. She was seated now, leaning back, one elbow on a cushion.

"Do what?" Jabari asked, his face pure innocence. They had never actually told anyone that they could communicate in their minds, but more than one pair of eyes narrowed at his response.

"Do we look stupid to you?" Laylit asked.

This started a back-and-forth argument between mother and son. Ivy jumped in as soon as there was space to speak, and Isika tuned it out, going somewhere far away in her mind, thinking about what being crowned would actually mean. She felt a lot more afraid than she acted. Worse, she suspected Jabari knew.

* * *

Isika told her family about the decision as they gathered around the table at home for the evening meal. Abbas and Jerutha had come over as well, bringing little Mesu with them. They came over often, keeping the connection between their homes full of life. Jerutha and Abbas had married after Abbas came home from the Karee camp, bringing his father and mother to witness the ceremony.

Abbas was a prince, and Jerutha had grown up in a poor Worker home, but they loved each other fiercely. Jerutha's belly was beginning to grow round with her second child, and Isika sometimes wondered if Abbas could love another new baby any more than Mesu. Abbas doted on the little boy. Both Auntie and Isika loved to see Jerutha's face rounding out with her pregnancy, now that she was away from the Worker village and ate enough to feed herself and the baby she carried.

Ibba was also at the table, her attitude letting them all know that it was torture for her to be there. She hated to be away from her apprenticeship at the palace gardens. She had changed a lot over the last year, gaining confidence, growing assertive—a bit too assertive, Isika sometimes thought—and spending almost all her time with plants and animals. She didn't have nearly as much interest in people as she did in the dozens of varieties of mushrooms the gatherers grew in great caves in the mountains.

Kital was at the table, too. He was still sweet, still the boy of Isika's heart, but he was getting long-limbed, and he was more serious, often deep in thought. He liked to spend evenings talking about the *why* of everything with Uncle Dawit. Isika would sometimes try to join in, but she lost focus quickly. She cared more about *what* than *why*, she realized.

"I have something to tell you all," she said, taking a deep breath and placing her hands on either side of her bowl.

"I wondered when you would say something," Benayeem said.

"What's that supposed to mean?" Isika demanded, turning to look at him.

He shrugged. "Your music is out of control, so I figured you must have something you were planning to say."

"Is this something appropriate for everyone at the table?" Auntie Teru asked. She looked pointedly at Mesu and Kital, one eyebrow raised.

Isika stared at her, widening her eyes. "What do you think I'm about to say? Of course, it's appropriate."

"Okay, honey, just checking."

Dawit cleared his throat. "Now, just before Isika says anything, let me say that what she has to tell us will change things for us, in good ways and...not so good ways."

Now, Auntie had her arms crossed, and Jerutha was frowning. "You know?" Auntie said. "How do you know? I'm practically her mother, and I don't know what she's about to tell us, but you know?"

"I'm also practically her mother," Jerutha inserted, sitting forward in her chair, and when Auntie turned as though to argue with Jerutha, Isika took another breath and rushed to speak.

"I'm going to be crowned queen next week," she said.

There was a sudden hush. No one said a word, which suited Isika, because she had been wondering whether they had all lost their minds.

The silence went on and on. Isika began to wish that she had invited Jabari to dinner. She would have liked to squeeze his hand under the table.

Finally, Auntie spoke. "I don't know what I thought you were going to say, but that wasn't it."

"Guard duty," Dawit said, his voice defensive. "No need to get mad at *me.*"

"Sorry, honey," Auntie said, patting his hand.

There was another silence. Jerutha dipped a piece of flatbread in the curry and took a bite. Abbas wiped Mesu's mouth. Auntie looked at the ceiling. Isika's siblings were all staring at her.

"Well," Auntie said. Isika saw that she was blinking back tears. Isika realized she was holding her breath, that she had been waiting all day to hear what Auntie would say. "I think making you queen is the smartest idea those elders ever had, Isika, because if anyone can save us, it's you."

Isika's chair clattered to the floor as she leaped up and ran around the table, throwing her arms around her foster mother, the woman who had taken her and all her complications into her home so many years ago. Soon others joined in on the hug, and Isika felt the warmth of their confidence seeping into her as they murmured and patted her arms and hair. There were tears in Isika's eyes, but they weren't tears of desperation or loneliness. More than almost anything else, this, right here, made her believe she could be what the Maweel needed her to be.

* * *

ON THE MORNING of the coronation, Isika was still thinking about that moment and Auntie's words. She left the house at first light, running to the forest to walk in the shelter of the trees. It was dark and calm in the woods, and Isika felt her racing heart slow into a steady beat, echoing the pulse of life in the trees.

Isika didn't know if she believed Auntie's words: that she was the one who could save Maween. She did know that ever since the day she met Gavi and Jabari on that beach, back when she was still a scared girl with no idea of her true identity, she had been taking one step after another, each one leading her inexorably to this moment. She walked slowly, gently laying a palm on the trees she passed. Some were heavy with bloom, others covered in vines. They offered her nourishment as she went, humming with life song. She was the Whisperer, and she was a friend of the trees. She knew them, with their individual life songs that they offered up with openness, not guarded, the way people were. Isika felt honored by the trees that morning as she walked in their shade—*hoona* and *silverwood*, flowering *burda*. As she walked, she saw visions, ghost pictures behind her eyes: dancing light on her crown; Aria curled on the floor, crying; Herrith looking at something with desperate eyes: the Hadem dancing in lines; a tall ship. Isika blinked. What was that? But it was gone. It had lasted only a breath.

Then she heard the pounding rhythm of the drums. It was time.

"Thank you, friends," she whispered.

For a moment, Isika caught sight of a tall man, striding along between the trees, his skin like the night full of stars, and smiled. *Nenyi*.

THE CORONATION WAS MORE spectacular than any event Isika had ever seen in Azariyah, which was saying a lot. The Maweel loved to celebrate—to dress up, dance, and sing until the valley rang with the sound of thousands of voices. And the food! The people of Maween loved food and life, and Isika could barely believe she was going to be their queen. She felt undeserving and small, and very, very honored.

A coronation was a rare event, and it held all of the profound sacredness of Maweel customs, as well as an excellent reason to celebrate.

The ceremony began with the choir singing the song of loss for Queen Azariyah.

BLACK AS BELOVED NIGHT, *eyes like stars,*
Her smile the sudden glimpse of
a crescent moon.
A line to the Uncreated One,
a thread into heaven's heart,
Tied to the whirling sky,
the planets, the stars, the mountain peaks.
Protected by her love
The Shaper's hand among us
Light all around us
we were brought in and encircled

Loved and surrounded

FROM HER BELLY sprung
  A child of light and promise
  A child strong from the first
  Their love the sun rising
  The sight of them love itself
  But hearts break and the Great Waste
  Moved against us
  Thieves, they wanted her,
  They took our queen
  she was gone and her baby with her
  we wailed to the heavens,
  but the grasp of the cruel was strong,
  the Great Waste didn't give her up to us.
  Still, we search,
  Still, we search
  Still, we search.

ISIKA SAW many people wiping away tears, and found that she was crying as well, hit with fresh grief for the mother she had known and the grandmother she had never met, whose place she was stepping into now. She decided, standing there, that she would ask the singers to write a song for Amani. Their mother should have a song—without her protection, Isika wouldn't be here at all.

The grove was filled with floating lights and flowers as the ceremony went on into the evening. Colored cloth had been woven between the trees. The branches met overhead. Isika had

her circlet on as she stepped closer to the elders for the ceremony. She felt apprehensive about giving it up for a new crown,
as though she knew it, and it knew her. She felt the circlet grow
warm on her forehead as solemn words were spoken. She
walked to stand beneath the tallest tree at the far end of the
meadow.

The people roared as Ivram bent down to kiss her forehead.
They sang and ululated, leaping in pure joy. Isika grinned and
waved, singing back to them, and they shouted louder. The
sound filled the air, ringing from the nearby hills. It continued
in that way as the ceremony went on. The choir did its best to
sing the ancient coronation songs, but at times the people were
so overwhelmed with joy that their shouts and ululations
drowned out the sounds of the singing.

Isika's face ached from smiling at her people, but she found
tears on her twice during the ceremony. Once was when a long
list of missing people was sung out to be recorded, and she wept
when she heard Aria and Gavi's names. "Herrith and Mara,"
she whispered under her breath, wiping away tears.

And she cried when the elders gathered around her and
sang to her, each touching her forehead in blessing. She could
feel the gift of each person in their gentle hands on her head,
each of them esteemed and formed by the Shaper. Her senses
seemed raw and heightened, it was almost too much, and tears
streamed down her cheeks.

But Isika was dry-eyed when she looked out at the sea of
people—overflowing from the meadow, hanging off the palace
roof, perching in the trees, on the roofs of nearby homes. Ivram
stood before her. His eyes were wise and kind as he held her
staff out and touched her circlet with it. The staff flashed so

brightly Isika was blinded for a moment, and heat flared in the circlet, followed by intense cold. She shuddered.

She reached up and found that her circlet had changed, growing branches and loops until it swooped up, taller and broader, away from her head. It was the crown of a queen. The Palipa pressed close on every side, and Isika could hear Keerza hooves thundering in the distance, while Keethior, Eemia, Nirral, and Efir flew in high circles overhead. Peel after peel of thunder roared, and every leaf on every tree shook, though there was only a slight breeze. There was a long silence from the people until as one they roared, and the sound of their voices was like the ocean waves breaking. They began to ululate and jump, and the noise they made was like nothing ever heard in Azariyah. The Maweel had a queen again. They had suffered and waited for so long, and their love for Queen Isika could not be contained.

CHAPTER 4

Benayeem stood with the other singers in the coronation ceremony, thinking about his sister. He had hardly seen Isika in the days leading up to her coronation. She stayed still for only moments at a time, landing to eat and then fluttering off for robe fittings, lessons on coronation rituals, and a whole series of cleansing baths and preparations. When the two of them were together, she was often somewhere else in her mind, and if Jabari was with them, Benayeem might as well have been invisible.

It drove Ben crazy to be ignored, partly because of the fact that he couldn't help noticing everyone, all the time. It would be such a luxury to forget that someone else was in the room. At all times, always, Ben's gift called out to him with the songs and sounds of the people around him. He could muffle what he heard only with great effort. So it was an affront to Ben that people could simply forget that he was there.

That morning, though, as the family sat at the breakfast table, Ben caught Isika's eye and felt that she really saw him. She reached over and squeezed his hand.

"Nervous?" she asked him.

"Shouldn't I be asking you that?" he replied, smiling.

"Well, obviously, I'm nervous," she said, "but you have some big parts in the singing ceremony."

Auntie Teru clicked her tongue as she heaped more food on Ben's plate. "There is nothing to be nervous about, Daughter," she said.

Both Ben and Isika turned to stare at their foster mother.

"Auntie," Ben said, "Isika is being crowned queen of a country today. They're still arguing over whether she has to move into the palace."

"Over my dead body will she move into the palace before she is eighteen," Auntie said calmly, gesturing with her serving spoon. "But she doesn't need to be *nervous*. What use are nerves? What will happen, will happen. Worry is like tightening a thread and fearing what will arise when the two edges of cloth meet."

"I wish my stomach was easy to convince," Isika said. She smiled at all of them. "It's time. I'm going to the forest. I'll see you all later."

Benayeem hadn't seen his sister again until the ceremony started, and even then, he hadn't realized he was looking at her. Sometime during the preparation song, which was complicated and sung in eight-part harmony, Ben realized that the woman he had seen—and assumed was a delegate from another land—was actually his sister in her royal robes.

She looked like a queen. Her night blue dress stood out from her body, cascading to her feet. She wore a stiff cape of a deep, vibrant red that swept up to stand like a halo behind her head and shoulders. Her head was bare, with her hair tied in several long braids that flowed down her dress. As jewelry, she wore only her circlet, a thin silver thread shining against the rich brown of her forehead.

Benayeem had a flashback to the day they had run from the Worker village despite their fear and uncertainty. His sister had been impossibly thin, dressed in faded ugly colors, with wild, matted hair and cuts on her face. A different person stood in the center of the glade now. And yet, she was the same.

"She will make a great queen," Deto said when the song was finished.

Ben nodded.

Brigid had asked Ben recently whether he was jealous that Isika would be queen, and not him. Ben had merely looked at his friend until she started to laugh. Benayeem was not jealous. He had no desire to rule anything more substantial than his own mind, which was enough of an effort sometimes. Ben wanted simple things. He wanted to sing in the choir, he wanted Aria to come home, and he longed for peace. He was thrilled that Isika was the one in line for the throne and not him.

He sang for the remainder of the ceremony as the people called out and roared their approval. He was first singer for two of the songs and felt his gift radiate through him as he sang, lifting all that was there into a sacred, joyous place. The people were caught up in the rightness of the coronation, and the joy of having a queen once again.

As the afternoon went on, though, moving through the speeches and blessings of various elders and leaders from the countryside and villages surrounding Azariyah, Ben began to feel uneasy.

Something was wrong. He felt worry heat his chest and neck. He waited for someone else to say something about the problem, but no one appeared to notice what Ben could sense.

The celebration went on and on, the people oblivious to the glaring issue, full of joy and bliss.

At the feast, Ben and Brigid were seated together on cushions around a low table. Brigid was one of Isika's dearest friends, but recently she and Benayeem had become closer, especially as the approaching coronation and Jabari had taken up all of Isika's spare moments. Brigid was an excellent friend, seeming to know intuitively when to speak and when to wait.

As they ate, Brigid kept glancing at Ben between bites of food, seemingly aware of his distress. Finally, she said something.

"What's going on?" she asked.

He looked at her. How much should he tell her? He knew he could trust her. It was just that he didn't even like to say the words, didn't even like to *think* them. He sighed. It would all be obvious enough eventually.

"Something is not right," he said, his voice low. "The coronation is not...taking."

She inhaled, her gray eyes on his face. "What? Not taking? What does that mean?"

"She's queen, no doubt of that. I can hear her new song, and it is the song of a ruler, intertwined with the land, the Whisperer's song, but stronger."

Brigid smiled, her eyes drifting to Isika, who sat in conversation with Jerutha at a nearby table. "That's beautiful," Brigid said.

"Yes, but there are gaps in the song—huge holes. And in those gaps, there are...other songs."

The new queen song was loud and stirring, with drum beats that made Ben feel like he wanted to get up, run somewhere fast, or jump higher than anyone had ever jumped before. But the gaps in it taunted him, pulling the rhythm of the queen song down, slowing and distorting it.

Brigid stared at him, stricken, her food forgotten. "What other songs?" she whispered. "Are you sure?"

Ben wished he were wrong. He longed for what he felt to be false. But he recognized these songs, the same way he recognized Brigid's sweet, innocent music as she sat across the table from him.

His voice was a cracked whisper. "The Desert King's song," he said, "and Aria's music. They're still tangled in there, they didn't go anywhere, and it means this plan—to make her queen and fix all of this, to bring the rain—didn't work."

Brigid's face fell. She looked across the table at Ivy and Deto. Ben noticed they were very still, listening. He wondered how much they had heard.

"I worried about something like this," Brigid said, her own voice low. "I could sense that the plan wouldn't work, but I hoped it would be wrong. I couldn't see its exact downfall."

The pale-skinned rescued girl had a gift of foresight, often knowing something was off before any of the others did. Her gift was vague, though, and often frustrated her, offering hints of future peril without clarity.

"What do we do?" Deto asked, sitting up from his cushion. Apparently, he had heard everything.

Ivy's face was troubled. "Maybe we should wait," she said. "Let's not bring too much attention to this right now."

Ben looked over at Isika, seeing his sister's face, transformed by the brilliance of her smile, and agreed.

* * *

* * *

THE NEXT DAY, Ben and Brigid went to speak to Abbas during training. Ben told Abbas a little of what he had heard during the ceremony and after.

"Did you notice anything off?" Brigid asked.

Abbas rubbed at his chin, staring off into the distance. They sat on the little hill where they often ate lunch together during training season. Brigid was there every day with Ben. She had finally settled on training to be a Ranger, like Ben, rather than becoming a Weaver like her family.

"I can't settle into a life of weaving after all we've been through," she had told Ben. "I will weave when I can and continue my learning, but I want to be a Ranger. There is so much to be done, so much poison and malice in the world. And my sisters are weavers, so my family's work can continue."

Brigid was growing stronger through her training, Ben thought as they waited for Abbas to speak. Her arms were corded with muscle, and she could spar with him in a nearly even match. She was still a little absent-minded and dreamy, but he thought she would be able to hold her own as a Ranger.

"The Karee people have something similar to what you have," Abbas said finally, turning to look at them. Abbas was a Karee prince who had come to serve Isika and live among the Maweel. Benayeem had noticed that he still worked things out in his head by thinking back to Karee customs.

"Similar to what?" Brigid asked, swinging her braid over her shoulder as she scooted closer.

"It's a kind of mantle of power that settles on the king, allowing him to keep his people and lands healthy. We have no lands now, so my father's power is not as strong as it would be if he had the blend of his magic and land. He cannot protect us as well as he could if he had his full power. Maybe it is similar to what you are feeling?"

Ben nodded slowly.

"Yes," he replied, "but it is not that Isika is not tied to the land. It's that all of it is mixed, somehow, with the king and Aria, and the poison of betrayal. It's that same bitter problem. We are linked to the betrayal of the past, and we don't know how to get free."

"What will you do with what you know?" Abbas asked. His gaze was direct.

"I suppose I should tell the elders," Ben said. He felt a twist in his gut as he said it. "Ivy thinks we should keep it quiet. I don't know what to do. I don't know what they have already sensed for themselves. It would be embarrassing to tell them something they already know, and if they don't know, it might hurt Isika to have it come from me."

Brigid was nodding beside him, but Abbas shook his head.

"I think we are past the luxury of worrying about those sorts of things," he said, gesturing at the brittle yellow grasses in the fields. "If we are going to save this land, we need to act."

Brigid met Ben's eyes, her face full of compassion. He nodded slowly. "I will tell them," he said. "But give me another day. Let's give her one day of being happy without reserve."

* * *

THAT NIGHT, Benayeem heard music in his dreams. All evening, he had been listening hard to the space where Isika's queen music was ragged at the edges, and Aria's song, poisoned by the Desert King, was woven between the notes.

38

When he went to sleep that night, the rhythms were still traveling through his mind, and he fell asleep in their ebb and flow.

In Ben's dream, Aria's music rose and fell, rose and fell. After some time, Ben recognized the music of the sea—the sound of water and the cries of a boat crew mingled with the calls of sea birds and the clinking of chains, the dipping and lifting of many oars.

Embedded in this sea music were the heart cries of chained creatures and the distress of sea animals straining against poison. It was a ship, Ben heard in his dream, rowed by slaves. And all entwined, Aria's music rose and fell, rose and fell.

Ben woke with a start. She was at sea.

"When can I talk to you and the elders about something serious?" he asked Isika as they ate the morning meal. She blinked at him, still sleepy. It was strange to see his older sister in her housedress and know that she was a queen who happened to live in his house.

Auntie had put her foot down, saying she would only give her blessing to the coronation if Isika stayed in the house until her eighteenth birthday. Isika, in turn, had refused to be crowned if Auntie didn't give her blessing. The elders gritted their teeth and acquiesced, though they sent a ranger who would be Isika's personal guard from now on, a woman with short graying locs named Nat. She lived in a hastily constructed cottage outside the house. She had swiftly become excellent friends with Auntie and Ibba and now sat at the table with the family.

"Petitions is a good time," Isika said, stifling a yawn. She looked at him for a moment, her face concerned. "Is everything okay?"

Ben shrugged. "I just want to tell you something I'm hearing," he said. "But, I don't want everyone at Petitions to hear."

"Come at the end, then. After the day's requests, I sit with the elders, and we talk over the different issues. Come then."

He did as she said, waiting until the long shadows of the afternoon told him that Petitions must be drawing to a close. He brought Brigid and Abbas with him and assured himself that it wasn't that he didn't trust his sister. In a way, Isika sat on a different side from him now, on the side of power along with the elders. Ben wanted his friends to be present.

As they drew close to the throne room, Ben listened to the music of the people who governed their lands. He relaxed as he heard the peaceful sounds. Their talk seemed to be going well, and their music didn't seem anxious or angry. Then he winced as he realized that what he came to tell them would end the ease of their songs. Ben turned to walk back down the corridor and out of the palace, but Abbas put a hand on his shoulder and gently turned him back around. Ben allowed himself to be led, taking a deep breath as he walked into the large room to face Isika and the elders.

They greeted each other and chatted for a while, settling onto the cushions around tables that held fruit, flatbread, different kinds of cheese, and cold tea. Ben could sense the curious music coming from the elders, so after preparing himself, he jumped in.

"I need to tell you something," he said.

"Go ahead," Isika replied, nodding her head toward him.

"I can hear a problem with Isika's music. The magic of her coronation has not exactly settled in perfectly. I think it hasn't gone as we hoped it would. She doesn't have the full power a queen and whisperer should have."

His words were met with silence. Abbas shot Ben a concerned look. They waited for the elders to say something.

Isika stared at the ground, suddenly looking years younger, and if Ben hadn't been watching her, he would have missed the tear she quickly swiped away. He should have warned her. He sighed. He could be so stupid.

Finally, Karah spoke. "What makes you think that the magic hasn't settled?" she asked gently.

Ben didn't want to say another thing. He had made his sister cry. But Brigid squeezed his shoulder, and Ben realized she was letting him know he was on the right track. Her own gift was telling her something.

"I hear music pulling Isika's queen song out of tune," he said. "It is Aria's song, poisoned by the music of the Desert King, and it occupies these...gaps...in Isika's queen music. I believe it is keeping the full authority of her queen magic from resting on her."

Silence again. Ben could barely comprehend what it was like for people not to hear music at all hours of the day, the way he did, but he did sense that his words were hard for them to understand.

Isika cleared her throat. "Thank you, brother," she said softly. "I thank you for your honesty. I had wondered myself why I didn't feel more."

"There is something else," Ben interjected before he ran out of courage. "I hear Aria. And I think she is sending me music to tell me she is at sea. She is warning me that the Desert King will attack from the sea."

CHAPTER 5

The royal caravan traveled for days before it reached the harbor. Aria faded in and out of the stupor that had surrounded her ever she arrived in Dhahara, the Desert City. She couldn't help flickering in the poison haze, but when she was lucid, she did her best to pay attention, to see and remember.

The caravan was ostentatious and opulent. Ikajo would settle for nothing less. Drohmeds, cattle, and no-beasts trundled through the hot sand as the large group of travelers rode or walked through the desert. Herrith and Aria rode with the king in the spacious wagon pulled by two bad-tempered drohmeds who occasionally rebelled from their servitude. When one or the other tried to pull away from the yoke, the carriage would lurch, causing Aria to briefly snap out of her fog. Once, after a particularly rocky bump, she noticed Herrith looking at her with concern on his kind face. She smiled to reassure him, but he didn't seem reassured.

All I need is to have this camel jolt me as often as possible, she thought. Could she wake herself up on her own?

She pinched her arm, hard. Immediately she was wide awake, and she saw it all clearly—the long train of people walking behind their carriage, the shadows on Herrith's eyes, the dangerous insanity in her father's eyes. Aria looked away from her father quickly, afraid of his gaze.

She leaned out of the carriage window to look more closely at the line of people that stretched behind them. The no-beasts moaned as they walked. Hunting dogs nipped at their heels. The canvas above Aria's head blocked out much of the sun, but still, she could feel its heat. Many travelers carried shade covering on poles above their heads, but the sun beat mercilessly on the enslaved. They walked chained together in two lines, behind everyone else and without any shade covering at all.

Aria twisted to see in front of the carriage, past the lumbering drohmeds. Her heart thudded as she recognized where they were. That was the shelter where Isika had called water out of the earth when she had rescued Jerutha from Batta. It felt like a lifetime ago.

"We're going to the Worker village?" Aria gasped.

Her father swiveled his head slowly toward her. "You remember this place?" he asked in his silky, dangerous voice.

Beside the king, Herrith widened his eyes at Aria. In them, Aria read the terrible future in store for the Workers of the village if the king knew that they had mistreated Aria and her siblings. He didn't know. Herrith had kept it from him. Aria was shocked that she hadn't already handed him that knowledge, the way she had given him everything else of importance in her many hazy moments.

"Yes," she said. "I remember." She didn't elaborate. But as she remembered, she began to tremble.

It was here that Aria had been sent over when she was eight

years old, pushed out into the sea in a tiny boat by her own step-father. They hadn't meant for her to survive. The sleeping tea had worn off quickly, so Aria had sobbed in the boat for hours, wet, shaking with cold, and terrified. She still remembered holding her arms out to the Rescuers when they found her. They brought Aria to her new life in Maween.

She had come back to the Worker village only once—when she and Jabari and the other Seekers were searching for Isika and Ben, and Isika and Ben were searching for Jerutha. That time, Aria was pierced with arrows meant for Isika. Now she was trapped with her father by the arrow's poison, trapped like an animal no matter how badly she wanted to get back to her sister.

This place had not been good to her.

Aria was shaking hard now. She noticed her father's brow crease the instant before he held one hand out toward her.

Nothing...she knew nothing for a long while.

Aria didn't know how much time passed, but when she came to, Herrith was gripping her arm. The caravan had halted at the harbor. The king was not in the carriage.

"Ikajo doesn't know this village means anything to you. You can't let him know. Keep anything you love or hate close to your heart; neither is safe. He already knows that you love Isika and that she loves you. Now you are his weapon against her."

Aria figured it wasn't the right time to tell Herrith that she had been sending Benayeem dreams. That Isika would soon be on her way.

Herrith watched her face closely, as though trying to see her more clearly.

"This is not good," he said. "You look...faded. Whatever he's doing to you is starting to hurt you badly."

It hurt her to see the bleakness in his face. So even though she had decided not to say anything, she couldn't help herself.

"I'm sending Ben dreams," she blurted, "to tell him where we are. Our people need to have time to prepare a defense from his attack. And also, I'm hoping Isika has figured out how to free me by now. Maybe I can finally be free."

"Or, the king will discover you are sending dreams to Benayeem and find a way to stop it," Herrith said. Aria could feel her face falling, but Herrith shook his head and smiled.

"You are very brave, little bird," he said, using Gavi's nickname for her. "I hope your plan works."

The stillness around the carriage was interrupted by shouts and the sounds of a scuffle. Aria poked her head out of the carriage. Ikajo had bypassed the village, directing the caravan around it, but now a group of villagers stumbled out of the sea gate, gesturing and shouting at the travelers.

Aria felt a wave of despair. She missed her family. She missed Isika and Ben. She missed her mother worst of all. She didn't want to face whatever was going to happen alone.

She heard a woman screaming.

"Give him to me! Give me back my son!" the woman shrieked. Aria tried to see her, but the crowd blocked her view.

She pinched herself as her vision began to fade again. The gray water lapped at the shore. Aria remembered the day of her sending so clearly. It came to her at strange moments, often while she was dreaming. She had been so so small and thin that the boat barely rocked from her weight, but she was too tall for it because ordinarily, two-year-olds were sent over.

She remembered her mothers' screams as Aria was taken from the house. Those screams sounded like the despair of the woman who was wailing now. Aria looked around. Herrith wasn't beside her anymore, but she didn't remember him leaving. She hated the unreliability of her mind, how it faded in and out. She left the carriage and took a step toward the scuffle, then one more, until she saw a woman on her knees in the dust, holding her hands over her face.

"Sister," she called. "They have all been rescued. Your children are well."

Herrith was beside Aria almost before the words had left her mouth, putting an arm around her, guiding her back to the carriage. A familiar, tall figure ran forward, stooping down beside the woman and placing a gentle hand on her shoulder.

"What is your son's name?" he asked.

"Gadian," she said.

The young man, who was Gavi, of course, stared at the woman.

For a moment, it looked to Aria as though he stared into an older, more feminine reflection of himself. She put a hand over her mouth. What were the chances that Gavi's mother would run out looking for her son? Gavi was very likely the only other person in the caravan who was from the Worker village.

It did not happen by chance, she heard a voice say.

Aria recognized Nirral's voice. When she looked up, she saw the Othra flying high above them, a speck in the sky. Normally, to hear the Othra, Aria would have to be close enough that they could speak audibly to her.

"But Herrith, I don't have animal speech," she whispered, and then went quiet and fuzzy again, for a long time.

The next time she was aware, she found herself standing between Herrith and the king, watching a procession pass by. Person after person boarded the hundreds of boats that filled the harbor, then rowed out to a string of ships on the horizon.

After the initial moments of realizing she was lucid and checking for injuries, it dawned on Aria that she was watching a procession of enslaved people. She caught her breath in horror as people of all ages walked by her, many of them emaciated or limping. Some looked like workers, some like people of the North, some like the Maweel. Others were from even more distant places. As they passed, most kept their eyes on the ground, but some caught her eye and stared back at her. She saw desperation in the looks they gave her.

Me? she thought. *What can I do? I'm his slave too.*

After the slaves, the servants filled the boats, rowing out to the ships. Aria spotted Gavi among them and caught a glimpse of Mara. She blinked.

"Won't he recognize Mara?" she whispered to Herrith.

"Shhhh," he responded. When the king's attention was elsewhere, he answered her. "He hasn't seen her for many years. And she will be veiled."

"Oh," Aria murmured. She felt better, knowing Mara would be on the ship. Gavi too.

Finally, after the whole caravan had boarded, it was time for the king and his red robes to follow.

"Why do we go last, Father?" Aria asked, genuinely curious. It wasn't like him to wait for anything.

He glanced at her and smiled one of his rare smiles.

"Good question, daughter. They go first to make the ship presentable for us. These are ships of the sea people, who will captain them and guide us. But they do not live at our standards. It gives our people some time to clean the ship."

The sun burned down on the sea. Aria tried to imagine running around the ship cleaning frantically before the king boarded, knowing he had killed people for a drop of spilled soup. She shuddered.

A man with the tattoos of a slave rowed them out to the ship. Aria watched him for a while, then turned back to her father.

"And why do we have slaves to row the ship?" she asked. "What about the sails?"

The king looked at her sharply. "You are full of questions today, beloved." His voice was velvety and terrifying. "But I am pleased by this question. We have slaves because Mugunta's magic is stronger when it rests on the toils of working people. It would be a waste to allow the wind to fill our sails. We are much more powerful this way."

Before Aria could cry out at this new horror, Herrith squeezed her elbow, hard. But Ikajo saw the look on her face anyway.

"You will get used to these realities one day when you are not so soft," he said. "The ways to achieve power are varied and many. And the Maweel only use the weakest ones."

Remember, Nirral called to her. And a picture came to Aria, the last Circle meeting before the caravan left the city.

"What is my job?" she had asked, as they outlined plans in a huddled group.

"You have one job," said Gavi. "To keep the king happy and unaware of what we are doing."

He shook his head at her protests. "I know it is hard, little bird, but think of how much more valuable it will be if we can take him by surprise and beat him when he least expects it. If you can keep him content, he will not look for us."

Remember, the bird repeated.

But I don't have animal speech, she thought back at him. Then she took a deep breath.

"I would like to learn about the strongest kinds of magic, Father," Aria replied, struggling not to wince at the malice in his answering smile.

Then Aria was distracted by a shadow over their small rowboat. When she looked up, the tallest, largest ship she had ever seen in her life loomed over them like a mountain. It was terrifying to look at, with a mast carved to look like a human skeleton and ravenous beasts carved along the hull.

"Our home on the seas!" the King cried, and Aria mustered every bit of strength she had to smile in response.

After they climbed the rope ladder and clambered over the edge, Herrith bent close and squeezed Aria's hand, softly this time.

"Very good, little bird," he whispered, and tears sprang to Aria's eyes. She missed hearing the name spoken with Gavi's voice. Her friend felt so far away.

As they walked along the main deck, the ship's captain approached. He was tall and had a mass of hair, broken teeth, and the patched clothes of the sea people. Aria inhaled. She thought she knew him, the captain who had been possessed by the goddess when Kital was taken. He stilled served the Great Waste? But why?

"Brilliance," he said. "I am so honored by your presence..." He seemed ready to go on, but the king interjected.

"'That's enough," he said. "Give me a tour."

The captain led them over the ship's many decks, pointing out the kitchens, the eating area, the rows of seats, and the crew already in full work mode, lifting the anchor and preparing to leave.

"And this is the princess's room," the captain said, opening a door. "I have given her my best handmaiden to watch after her while she is at sea."

"Oh, she has her own maid," Herrith started to say, pointing at the maid who followed them, but he fell silent at a brief, surreptitious signal from the woman, who stood quietly, her head lowered.

"One can never too many servants," Ikajo quipped, and Aria was struck anew by fresh hatred for him.

The men talked for a while longer, then left Aria to get settled. When she was finally alone in the room with her maids, she walked toward the new woman, who lifted her veil.

"Mara," breathed Aria. "How?"

"This captain is easily bribed," Mara said, matter-of-factly. "And that is good for us, my sisters. We have a long fight ahead, and we can use all the help we can get."

CHAPTER 6

"No, you may not sleep in my room," Isika told Hera for the seventeenth time. "Auntie is going to retire from feeding our family if there are people-sized beasts everywhere. You can sleep in the garden like a regular cat."

Not a regular cat. Hera told her. *Ancient one. Royal guardian.*

The huge silver cat regarded Isika through half-lidded eyes. She stood on her hind legs outside Isika's bedroom window, front paws resting on the sill. Behind her, stars were coming out in the evening sky. The Palipa looked as though she was readying herself to jump anyway, but just then, the door to Isika's room burst open, and Auntie Teru stalked in, wielding a broom.

"Shoo!" she said, shaking the broom at Hera's face.

"Auntie, is the broom necessary?" Isika asked.

"They do not listen to you or to me," Auntie muttered, glowering. "I do what I must do."

Hera gave Auntie and the broom a long, slow blink. She did not seem at all worried.

Please give her a break, Isika pleaded with the cat, using animal speech in her mind. *She's had a lot of upheaval in the last weeks.*

Being crowned is not upheaval, the cat said.

It is for Auntie, Isika replied.

Hera gave a disdainful glance that encompassed both women and the broom, then disappeared from the window.

Auntie Teru turned to Isika. "See?" she said. "The broom always works."

"It certainly does," Isika said, holding back a smile.

"How are you, young one?" Auntie asked.

Isika sat on her bed and patted it for Auntie to have a seat beside her. The new moon peeked through the open window, and the cool air of the evening was a relief for Isika's troubled mind.

"Thank you for asking," she said. "I'm tired. It was a long day of talking." Isika thought of the many conversations, some of them simple, some of them much more complicated. It was not always easy to see eye to eye with the elders. She buttoned up her housedress. Hera had interrupted her while she prepared for bed. "But it seems wrong to complain about being Queen."

Auntie settled herself against the wall at the end of Isika's bed. "If you can't complain to your Auntie, who can you complain to?" she asked, pulling a pillow into her lap. "Here, let me help with some of that tiredness."

Isika put her head on the pillow, closing her eyes as Auntie used her finger-pads to massage the tension out of her forehead and temples. She felt tears forming.

"Thank you," she whispered. As always, whenever anyone

cared for Isika, longing for her late mother pierced her heart, making it hard to breathe.

Auntie hummed under her breath, kneading stress out of Isika's forehead and face. When she spoke, her voice was soft.

"What has your forehead so tense, young one?"

Isika considered the question, opening her eyes to look at the black branches of a silverwood tree against the night sky.

"All the talking," she said. "Sometimes it goes on and on, and all I want is to climb a tree or run to the waterfall to clear my head. Besides the talking at Petitions, there is the constant chatter of the Othra, the horses, and the Palipa. They're always telling me things or trying to get in on the conversation. Sometimes it feels like everything is closing on me. Today..."

Isika sighed, remembering.

"What happened?"

"Today, Ben came and told us more things he's heard. Some seem reliable. He has complete faith in his gift. But then there were conflicting stories, and he refused to see that one of them must be wrong. He was so stubborn, Auntie. He's been hearing these things from Aria, ocean song, and the song of the Hadem. And we've been using that as information. But then today, he started hearing other things about the Karee and the desert, and he got really confused, but he refused to pick one."

Auntie stroked Isika's hair away from her face, and Isika wished she knew her grandmother. She needed someone who knew what it was like to be the queen of these gifted people who also loved to argue. She glanced up and saw Auntie smiling at her.

"You brave girl," Auntie said. "You grow smarter and more beautiful by the day. Are you sure you want to settle for the son of Andar?"

Isika burst out laughing.

Auntie went on. "Oh, he's handsome, there's no doubt that he is a beautiful young man. But I'm not sure he is good enough for you." Isika snorted and turned onto her side to laugh some more. Poor Jabari. She squeezed Auntie's hand, sitting up slowly.

"Thank you," she said. "And yes, I do want Jabari. There is more to him than you know."

Auntie sniffed. "If you're sure. But what will you do about Ben?"

Isika frowned, her troubles flooding back to her. "We meet to talk it over again tomorrow," she said. "Soon, we will travel to face whatever force the Desert King is sending, so we need to decide which way to go. Hadem or Karee? I think we will choose to go to the Hadem. I don't know where Ben's new impressions are coming from, but I'm inclined to believe his first ones."

Auntie leaned over and kissed Isika on the forehead, then stood. "Get some sleep," she said. "Sounds like tomorrow will be a big day."

Isika slept dreamlessly until the very cusp of dawn, and then she dreamed with startling clarity.

"Stop sending him messages!" the Desert King was screaming at her, but when she looked down, she saw thin dark brown fingers that weren't her own. She was Aria, and the King was screaming at her. And one thing was sure. The floor beneath her was pitching back and forth. She was on a boat.

She woke, gasping for breath.

Dressed in her best robes, Isika faced the elders and many of her people from her throne later that morning. Keethior was perched on his pedestal just behind her, and Hera and the other

Palipa sat at her feet. Isika knew that she looked impressive on the throne with the Ancient Ones around her. She was glad for the help. In so many ways, she still felt like a young girl.

"We will travel to the Hadem village," she declared. "To find out what they know, and to use their ships, since we don't have any." She frowned at Ivram.

"We have smaller boats," he said, holding his hands out. "And we did have ships, but they have not been maintained since Queen Azariyah disappeared."

"As you said," Isika replied. It seemed like an enormous misjudgment to her.

"They're falling apart," Olumi said. Isika hid a smile.

Ben started to speak, but Isika held up a hand. "I believe that you were right in your first hearing, Benayeem. I think the Desert King is sending you false messages now. But our delegation will go soon, and we will find out what there is to know. I will form a group of my own choosing. Yes, Jabari, you will be part of that group." The last sentence was meant to keep Jabari from interjecting. He had stepped forward as soon as Isika spoke of a delegation.

"That's not what I was going to say," Jabari replied.

He held her eyes, and for a moment, it felt as though they were the only people in the room. She smiled into his face, which was awash in frustration. His hair had grown, and she liked how he wore it now, natural and jagged with tight curls. She loved everything about his face, especially his smile. He wasn't smiling at her now, though.

"You shouldn't go," he said. "You should send a delegation, certainly, but you shouldn't be part of it. You are our queen now, and we need to protect you."

"Jabari!" Andar thundered. "You are out of line!"

Laylit put a hand on Andar's arm and sat forward.

"Is the Desert King set on starting an outright war?" she asked. "If he has taken to the seas, it seems that he is preparing to attack the Hadem, and through that breach, to attack us."

"That is what I am worried about, yes," Isika said. Behind her, Keethior stirred.

That is what he is doing, he said. *Tell them.*

"Every animal I speak with confirms this," Isika said. "And I am an active queen, not only some monarch on a throne. I am World Whisperer." She took a breath. "And I am Warrior. I must go and see how I can help our allies."

She looked into Jabari's burning eyes.

"I'm sorry, my love, but I will not stay at home to be protected. You can come with me, though."

Jabari stared at her for several breaths, then bowed his head.

"Excuse me," he said to the room, and left quickly, not bothering to gather his things. Isika heard his footsteps quicken and knew he would leave the palace and run into the forest. He would run and run. She wished she could go with him, even if he was mad at her right now. She bit her lip and looked at her younger brother.

He sat with his head bowed, staring at the palms of his hands. Isika knew that he was questioning himself and his discernment gift. She silently cursed the Desert King, but she knew that none could be truly free of his interference until they took care of their immense problem. They were held by the entanglement and power King Ikajo had over Aria, the way he could reach them because of the power of betrayal magic, a long line that stretched back to Queen Azariyah.

"Don't worry, Ben," she said. "This is just another way the king is trying to hurt us. But we will find a way to rid ourselves of him and take back our power. Right now, we need to protect the Hadem. This is our first challenge. We leave in a week. I will tell you who will come when I know, but I know that you will accompany us, brother."

Ben nodded, and the elders bowed their heads. Isika excused herself. As soon as she could, she changed into her traveling clothes and reached out for Jabari in her mind. He didn't answer her. She narrowed her eyes.

Where is he, Keethior?

The waterfall, Keethior said.

I'm surprised you are helping me, she said. *I know how you feel about Jabari.*

There's no accounting for taste, the bird told her.

Isika frowned. She had more questions, but she didn't need to get into it with him now. She told Nat, her guard, where she was going, and that she needed to be alone. Nat agreed to give her some time, waiting at the forest's edge. Isika ran through the trees, exulting in their life force. She found Jabari at the waterfall, as Keethior had said. He was diving to pick up rocks in the pool, pulling them out and tossing them to the side. He didn't acknowledge her, but Isika felt him notice her, and she could tell he wasn't angry anymore. She sat and watched as he dove and surfaced, dove and surfaced. The stones clacked loudly against other stones when he threw them, and Isika felt the buzz of the earth around her. She let it wash through her, cleansing her of impatience, frustration at needing to travel again so soon, her ever-present anger at the Desert King.

When she felt the sense again of a great expanse, of a sky without limit and endless possibility, she reached her hands above her head and launched herself into the water in a long dive.

Jabari met her in the water and hugged her tight for a moment, before letting go and swimming away to climb onto the widest boulder. She let him go and did her own swimming. When she was cool and calm, she climbed onto the flat rock and waited for him to speak.

He turned on his side to look at her.

"I'm sorry," he said.

She watched his eyes. "You can't do that," she said. "Or, I guess you can do whatever you want, but don't you think it would be better if we were strong together?"

"I feel like I can't watch you do this. You're so much more of a target now."

"You can do it. Come on, Jabari. Don't you get it? Every person I have ever loved has been a target. My mother died, I watched Aria being sent over, I watched Kital being sent over. We rescued Jerutha from Batta. Aria is still locked in the king's influence. I've seen Ben beaten more times than I can count. The Great Waste holds a particular malevolence for my family."

"Gavi's in a terrible place, too."

"Exactly. You can't try to protect me." She held his eyes with hers, willing him to understand. "You can't, Yab. We'll be so much weaker if you do. If you can't accept that I will be in constant danger, at least until we figure this thing out with my father, then we can't be together. I can't have you making me weaker. I can't protect Maween if you do."

He blinked, and she saw she had wounded him. She lifted his hand to her face and kissed it. A few hot tears fell on his hand, and he wiped at her face with his thumb. Nothing in her wanted to hurt him. But she couldn't let go of what Nenyi asked.

She looked into his eyes again. She saw him, then, saw how

different he was because of the way he had grown up in safety, saw his hurt at Gavi leaving, how he didn't understand the new world they lived in. But she also saw him reaching for understanding.

"We could be amazing," she said. "We could be the most powerful couple, with strength like ours. No one will be able to get past us when we fight together. I am Queen of the Maweel, Jabari. Please stand with me. I need your strength." Her voice broke on the last word, and she covered her face.

Something changed, and understanding flooded Jabari's eyes.

"I get it," he said. "I see it now. I'm sorry, my love."

When he kissed her, she cried again, but mostly because she was filled with relief.

CHAPTER 7

The ship's kitchens were hotter than Gavi could have imagined. He drank as much water as was allowed, but he couldn't eat in this kind of heat, and he could tell he was losing weight. The magicians on board removed salt from the seawater for drinking, but water was still rationed because it took time to work the magic. Also, the ship didn't have enough containers to hold enough drinking water. Gavi was certain that Ikajo drank as much as his belly could take and didn't spare a thought for his overheated kitchen staff.

Gavi adjusted to life at sea, at least after the first three terrible days, when his seasickness almost made him lose the will to live. He was embarrassed when Mara laughed at him and told him that Aria hadn't been seasick at all. After the sickness passed, he perked up and went to work.

He had managed to get himself a job aboard the ship because he was known as the only person who could make food Aria would eat. Hiding from the king in an even smaller space than the palace, he had grown his hair long and now kept it braided. Sometimes when he saw the wiry, tired, toughened young man who looked back at him from the mirror, Gavi barely recognized himself. He had always been the huskier one of the two brothers, with a big smile and an amiable personality. So much had changed since Isika had come into their lives.

He shrugged off his sadness at being so drastically changed. Nothing mattered more than staying close to Aria. His job in the kitchens kept him too busy to think about it much anyway.

Late one evening, he put the dough aside to rise, shoved the beans to the back burner to soak for the night, and ladled Aria's soup into a deep bowl, handing it to Mara on a tray.

"All well with our girl?" he asked the older woman.

"She's fine. In and out of wakefulness, but she remains alert when she can."

"And you, Auntie?" he asked.

"I'm fine. Though I wouldn't mind seeing land. This sea just goes on and on, doesn't it?"

He smiled at her. "It does."

As soon as the head cook would allow, Gavi wiped his face and slipped up to an upper deck, lying in a shadowed spot where no one could see him. The moon hadn't yet risen, so he could see stars behind stars. A gentle breeze danced over him, and he sighed.

Even though he missed the person he had been, the strapping younger Gavi, the companion for all of Jabari's plots, Gavi suspected he would never find that person again. Even if he made it back to Azariyah, how could he ever rest, now that he knew how other people lived? He wanted to change everything in the Desert City, to release people from their suffering, to help them know what a free life could be. The face of the woman he had seen at the Worker village swam in front of him. He remembered all that the Desert King had done to her and the others while he had been powerless to stop it. He groaned and shrugged the memory away.

"Nenyi," he breathed toward the sky. "What do we do? Shaper? Are you still with us? How long will we suffer?" There was no answer, but the stars were very bright. He missed his brother, his parents. He missed *beauty*. But Aria would die if they didn't find a way to remove the parasite of her father's magic from her thoughts and emotions. Gavi would not cease looking for a way to save her.

After the beauty of the night, the close quarters of the crew were stifling. But Gavi knew it was worse in the section where the enslaved rowers were kept, so he sighed a prayer of blessing for others who were worse off than him and tried to get comfortable in his hammock. As he drifted into sleep, he thought of Aria, alone in her berth, isolated in her suffering. What magic could break the spell she was under? There *must* be something they hadn't thought of yet.

Morning came with a chorus of groans from the other crew members as everyone stretched and prepared to get up for their shifts. Gavi didn't have to work first thing until later in the day, and he had plans for how he would spend his free time. He brushed and rebraided his hair, tying a leather cord around the plait.

"When did they say we were setting anchor?" he asked a man in a neighboring hammock. Gavi badly needed to bathe.

"A quarter moon longer," his bunkmate said. Gavi sighed and splashed some water on his face at the bucket in the corner. The king could bathe, yet his crew slept in the heat and rose in the heat without enough water to refresh themselves.

He covered his head to sneak around the ship. It had occurred to Gavi recently that his ability to explore without being noticed might be part of his gifting. There had been times when Gavi was stuck in the open, sure he would be discovered by a guard or crew member, but then the guard would look right past him, and Gavi continued, undetected. It was almost as though he were invisible.

He went first to the top deck, where Aria and the king slept in different cabins. Gavi had come to hate the king so much that he frequently wanted to kill the horrible man. When he had violent urges to take the older man's life, he grieved the loss of his younger self. The old Gavi would not have thought of killing a human, no matter how horrible the person was. The old Gavi whispered thanks to every desert lizard he hunted for food.

He was awash in memories as he snuck along the corridor, hoping for a glimpse of Aria. Memories of running along Maween roads, side by side with Jabari, sleeping outside and being lighthearted, rather than heavy with grief. Now he moved like an old man, his shoulders so weighed down that he had to force himself to get up in the morning.

He didn't find Aria. But as he stood behind a post in the corridor, he caught sight of Herrith. He froze, waiting for Herrith to notice him, and when the older man looked as though he would pass by without looking his way, Gavi had to say something.

"Herrith," he whispered.

The Red Robe jumped nearly out of his skin. He turned and saw Gavi standing behind the post.

"Ah, Gavi...how do you do that?"

Gavi examined Herrith's face. Even on the ship, Herrith wore the long red robes of the closest servants and advisors to King Ikajo. They were also the men in the most danger of being on the receiving end of his cruel whims. Anyone who spent a lot of time in the wrathful king's presence was in peril of death daily. And somehow, against all odds, as Herrith himself often said, the older man was still alive. He had lived the longest. All the king's advisors were men, all related somehow, distant or close, and Herrith was a close cousin of the king. All the other cousins had died.

Herrith's eyes were shadowed, and there were new lines on his forehead.

"Any news?" Gavi whispered. He barely dared breathe, this close to the king's chambers.

"He will drop anchor in a cove soon, not far from the Hadem, to get fresh supplies. He's planning to attack before they are aware of us."

Gavi felt the blood leave his face. "What do we do?" he asked.

"Aria has been sending her brother music that she hopes will tell him what is happening. The king has learned of it and stopped the messages, though, and I fear he may have sent them mixed signals. I have tried calling the magical birds."

"Othra," Gavi said.

"Aria swears she has seen one, but it's hard to know how much of what she sees is real. These days, it's hard to know anything." He pinched the top of his nose and took a breath. "You can try calling them too," he went on. "They may listen better to you. Other than that, it is our job to protect Aria."

"I will try to call the Othra," Gavi said. He paused. "Herrith, is there something we are overlooking? Some kind of magic that the King has no access to? Something that can undo this terrible hold he has on her?"

Herrith looked out to sea, and Gavi followed his gaze. The

ocean was still comforting. It went on and on, sunlight sparkling across its surface, oblivious to their troubles.

"If there is, I've never met it," Herrith said, "but the Uncreated One has many ideas that we have never even dreamed of. He has endless ways of forming magic, limitless ways to bring freedom. We only have to locate the way that will help us now."

Gavi nodded. Herrith reached out and put a hand on his shoulder.

"Go now," he said. "Ikajo is angry. He won't hesitate to kill you if he finds you here."

"He hasn't found me yet."

"Yes, you are shielded in some way. I am glad for it," Herrith said. He looked old and tired. "We need it now, as we try to halt the king's destruction. Go."

So Gavi slipped away without seeing Aria. Without knowing why, he made his way down to the lowest deck, where the slaves rowed the ship. Maybe he wanted to jar himself into action. If the King were permitted to attack the Hadem, he would wipe out the leaders and take the rest of the people as slaves. These slaves would be put to work in his kingdom or sold to the emperor on the next continent. Gavi smacked the side of the stairwell, feeling sudden rage. *Think, Gavi!* They had to stop the attack on the Hadem before it started.

And they needed to find a way to set all these slaves free, Gavi thought as he entered the rowing chamber. Here in the bowels of the ship, it was even hotter, and most of the slaves were rowing endlessly. They had a sort of tuneless chant that they used as they rowed, and the overseers kept time by beating canes against the sides of the ship. Canes that they would use to beat the slaves over the head if anyone got too slow. Gavi sat down in a corner, unseen. Every once in a while, the singers would burst out of the slow rowing chant into a different song. The overseer would allow it for some time before beating his cane on the side of the ship, a signal for the slaves to come back to the work chant.

Gavi listened to this cycle for some time. The song that emerged from the chant, as though it could not be held back, was heart-stirring and full of lament. But as he listened, Gavi realized it was not only lament that he heard. The song was full of magic. He let his eyes drift out of focus. To his shock, he saw that the singing was building a web of power, a shimmering net. When the supervisor put a stop to the singing, the web remained, so that every time the rowers sang the song, the net grew more extensive.

Gavi looked around. His shift would start soon, and he didn't have much time. He wanted to talk to someone but didn't want to get any of the rowers in trouble for talking. He noticed a doorway to another room and shrugged. Might as well try it. He went to it quickly and silently.

When he ducked through the doorway, Gavi found himself in a large room filled with other enslaved people. They were sitting, sleeping, or eating, taking a break from rowing. The room also seemed to be a space where the children were watched, and the elderly rested. In the corner, children played some kind of game together, and against a wall, several elderly people sat quietly talking and watching over them.

They watched as Gavi entered, but no one said anything. They didn't seem concerned or afraid. Gavi felt drawn to one man who looked older than the rest. He looked like he was from the northern mountains, with wide cheekbones and long, dark eyes that swept into wrinkles at the corners. His long silver hair was braided in a thick plait. The man and gestured for Gavi to come closer.

"You have a question?" he asked.

"Yes, Uncle," Gavi said, "I do. What are the people doing out there? When they sing, and the magical web is spun?"

"Ah, you can see that," the old man said. "Of course, you would be able to."

Gavi stared at him. "What do you mean?" he asked.

"We know who you are," the man said, his eyes crinkling in a smile. "You are one of the unlike twins."

"I don't understand how everyone knows that," Gavi said. He found it unsettling.

"Don't worry," the man said. "The enslaved talk quickly, like trees murmur to each other. Everyone knows everything. We have to. No one values our lives. Staying on this earth depends on us knowing everything all the time. We know about the unlike twins and about the good they do in the world, despite their shortcomings. But to answer your question: We are building strength. The web can become many things. Water, if we are thirsty. Food, if we are hungry. Peace, if there is discord among us. We sing and store the magic for what we will need."

Gavi stared at him.

"I've never heard of this type of magic before."

"You wouldn't, where you are. Nenyi offers this to the suffering. The gift fills the container. If the container is very empty, more of the gift flows in. We wait to become free. But instead of only making us wait, Nenyi offers us a way to take our own power."

"What about Aria?"

The man exhaled. "Ah, that one. Yes, she has suffered terribly."

"Do you think she might have this power too?"

"She might. But she doesn't have anyone to teach her how to use it."

"Maybe you can teach her," Gavi said. He felt goosebumps erupt on his body. Maybe Aria could find a new kind of magic, one that might help her fight back.

CHAPTER 8

Ben walked somewhere in the middle of the group of seekers and rangers Isika had picked to journey to the Hadem. They were several days into their journey, and he was deep in thought, reliving a conversation between Auntie Teru and Isika.

"This is getting to be so familiar," Auntie had said, washing dishes one night before they left.

"What is?" Isika asked, drying a cup with a hand towel.

"You, leaving on dangerous journeys. Me, waiting for word."

Isika stopped drying the cup and flung her arms around Auntie Teru, burying her face in the older woman's neck. Ben averted his eyes, looking back at the table he was wiping.

"I'm sorry," Isika said. "This will all be over one day, I hope."

"Oh, don't listen to me," Auntie said, but Ben could hear the tears in her voice. "I'm only waiting, but you're the one who has to march out there and be brave. I shouldn't be feeling sorry for myself. It does no good at all. Shaper's heart, we'll be through this hard patch soon."

"And Aria will be with us," said a clear voice from the door to the garden.

Ben glanced up, but he didn't need to look to see who it was. Kital's song had preceded him. He held his arms out to his little brother, and Kital ran over and hugged him around the waist. Then Ibba came into the room, and her song was like a picnic or a sunny day. It was hard to leave them again.

It was hard to leave Auntie too. Benayeem knew that her worry for them was heavy with the memory of the son who had never come back. Ben wished his life and the lives of his siblings weren't pursued by the evils of the Great Waste. Auntie Teru needed a good long time when she could have her family surrounding her with no worries to keep her up at night.

Ben needed time with his younger brother and sister—no more goodbyes. He also needed to learn more control over his gift, which grew more potent by the week. Lately, it meant that he could identify people before they entered his range of vision. It seemed an unfair advantage—something the Desert King would exploit if he had it. Ben didn't know how to live in the world fairly, with such a gift.

These were the thoughts pinging around inside his skull as he walked with the others. Once again, they were on a journey, once again a strange procession. Now that they traveled with a queen, they carried her banner—a vivid crimson swathe of fabric, stamped with a flying Othra and separating into two tails snapping in the wind.

Ben had snorted with laughter when he heard the waves of pride coming from Keethior at the impression of an Othra on the queen's standard. The flag had been hidden away for decades now. Pulling it out carried such meaning that the entire land vibrated with it as the party walked away.

Isika refused to ride in any kind of contraption, though.

"We are a running people," she said, grinning at Jabari. Ben remembered that day, the first time they had heard that the Maweel ran everywhere, and how it had been so hard to keep up at first. And then, the health of their own land had restored them. He felt a flash of pain as he thought of Aria, poisoned by the arrow, separated from her land, under the king's spell. He wanted her to be healthy, too, like the rest of them. *Enough*, he thought. *It has to end.*

Isika had asked a few of the younger elders to come, and Abbas was with them again. They walked with Isika's trusted friends and many rangers, surrounded by the Palipa and accompanied by four Othra. The horses came along, though the company walked. They carried supplies and seemed proud of being on the journey, though Ben often heard spikes of nervousness from the horses when the big cats got too near. Isika said she wanted Wind and Night there, in any case.

Isika herself walked with a swinging stride, close to the front of the party, head high, staff in hand, and the circlet of the queen on her forehead. Two Palipa walked close enough to her that they were in danger of tripping her. Nat walked not far behind her. Only Isika's song was an indicator of her nervousness, and Ben thought again that it wasn't fair to know as much as he did.

He felt a light punch on his shoulder. It was Brigid, narrowing her eyes at him, though she couldn't quite hide a smile. Benayeem faked a scowl at her.

"You're doing it again," Brigid said.

"What?" he asked.

"Going in circles. Don't do it. It doesn't do any good."

Not many people could understand what Ben's mind was

like, how many sounds or thoughts intruded at any given minute, but Brigid had the tiniest idea. She had visions that came when she least expected them, brilliant flashes of light or tunneled vision, accompanied by pictures that were only sometimes readable.

"All right," he said. "I'll try not to."

Isika turned back and caught his attention, pointing off to one side.

He knew what she meant without needing to ask. They were walking near the Worker village, in the distance to the south. They had decided not to travel too close to it. They wanted to get to the Hadem village as quickly as possible, so there was no time to engage.

A sound like a thunderous clap came and went in Ben's mind as he looked toward the Worker village. He staggered to a halt.

Something was very wrong.

Distantly, Ben heard the sounds of his traveling companions calling to one another, but he was caught in the depths of what he heard, a silence so ringing it was almost like sound. Only one thin, wavering voice came from the village, and it was a voice of doom, a wordless, cracked sound of endless fear.

Isika was in front of him with her hands on his face, Jabari at her side. Ben came back like crawling up a mountain.

"What is it?" she asked. Her circlet flared with light.

"Something at the Worker village. I don't know what exactly."

"Try to listen," she said, frowning.

"There's nothing. I can only hear one weak sound, and other than that, it is silent. I've never even heard silence like that before. The forest has song. The ocean, even the desert... but there is nothing but fear and silence coming from the village. Something terrible has happened."

"Are they dead?"

"I don't know."

Isika called a discussion with the rangers and elders. It grew heated as many of the rangers didn't see the point of stopping to help the workers. It was an old argument, but after a relatively short amount of time, Isika won.

Ben's eyebrows shot up as he heard her declare, "We're going, and that's the end of it."

She fell into step beside him, and Jabari walked on Ben's other side. Ben knew they were there in case he stumbled again, but he welcomed the company.

"There are advantages to being queen," she said quietly.

"Yes," Jabari said. "But you'll want to limit how often you strong-arm them. They'll stop trusting you."

Ben heard Isika's angry music flare up, and he sighed. If they were going to argue, he would change his mind about wanting their company. After a moment, though, Isika's angry music died down, replaced by worry. He reached over and squeezed her hand.

They hadn't been happy in the Worker village, but it was part of their past, and they knew more now about the terrible pressure on these people. Mugunta, in the guise of the four goddesses, was not kind to the Workers, and they didn't even know they were at the bottom of the Desert King's rule. Ben had a sudden thought.

"Do you think he came this way?" he asked.

"Who?" Isika asked.

"The Desert King," Jabari interjected. "That's what I wondered too, Ben, when you said something had gone really wrong. Maybe he did something to them if he came through here."

"Let's take the horses," Isika said abruptly.

"The Elders won't like it if you go ahead," Jabari said.

"That wouldn't have stopped you before," she said, whirling to look at him.

He gazed at her for a minute, then turned and shouted for horses. Ben, Jabari, and Isika mounted horses along with Nat and three other rangers. They galloped for the Worker village, leaving the rest of the party to run in their wake.

Ben heard the danger an instant before they stepped into it, immediately before the walls of the Worker village. The silence was not merely silence, and in a moment, they had crossed from the everyday world into the sticky, bent world of the four goddesses. It was a kind of magic Ben had not heard or tasted since they had gone to Batta to rescue Jerutha.

He was stuck. He could hear and see, but he couldn't move. There was nothing to hear anyway, except the same wavering, doddery old song, winding all around like a thread of disease.

He saw that all of them were stuck, frozen in place on their horses where they stood, the horses caught mid-leap, some frozen already trying to leap away from the threat, half twisted.

But there! Ben caught sight of movement. One of the Palipa moved closer to Isika inch by inch, so slowly, it was barely perceptible. It was Hera, battling the magic with all her might.

Go, thought Ben. Go!

After what seemed like an age, the great, silver cat got close enough to place her head under Isika's hand. As she did, movement returned to Isika's hand and arm. Isika moved her hand slowly, so slowly, toward her head, reaching for her circlet, and when she finally touched it with her fingers, there was a brilliant, blinding flash of light. They fell out of the glue that held them, the horses landing with loud whinnies. Ben felt the air leave his lungs as he fell on his hands and knees. He pressed his face to the ground. Then he sat up.

"They're awake," he said. "Or back. I can hear them."

The gates to the village were flung open, and a red-headed woman ran out.

"Isika!" she called. She tore closer, clearly wobbly on her feet, but determined. Ben recognized Faiza just before she fell on the ground in front of Isika. Nat moved closer but didn't interfere.

"I knew you would come," Faiza said.

Behind her, the villagers clustered, not as close as Faiza, but not unfriendly. Ben felt prickles move up and down his arms. This was new behavior for the Worker village. They were usually suspicious and distant.

After a few moments, the rest of the travelers arrived, and they all went into the village together. Jabari tested for poison first, but nothing had been left to attack them.

A small group of villagers shuffled toward them, and Ben saw that they had a priest, bound with ropes. Ben's jaw dropped, and when he turned to look at his sister, her eyes were huge in her face.

"Faiza," she said. "Can you explain what is happening here?"

"It is a long story."

"Tell us as much as you can."

"We have been...restless...for a while now. When we realized that our children were being rescued rather than sacrificed, that nothing was even happening when we gave them over, we decided to stop the sacrifices. But the priest tightened his grip on us and began punishing us in other ways." She sighed. She looked so weary and underfed. Ben shuddered as he remembered life in the Worker village. The priests were smart to keep the people weakened with hunger and fear.

Faiza continued. "Then, the Desert King came and acted as though he would pass by without even acknowledging us. We had heard rumors of a powerful man who controlled the priests, but then there he was in front of us. I don't know, so much became clear. We have followed simply because we were told what to think. Dark-skinned people were called dangerous. The goddesses were our masters. The priests were our keepers.

And then one woman found her son in the crowd. And we grew even more impatient. The king took all of our boats. He set fire to them so we couldn't follow him.

And the priest told him of our unrest. He was very angry.

He uttered one command, and all of us were frozen. I was able to think, see, and fear, but unable to breathe, eat, or move. We were suspended. Until you came."

CHAPTER 9

Jabari watched, his eyes narrowed, as the priest stood with his head bowed in the center of the group of people who had captured him. He heard the words of Isika's friend with only part of his brain. Something wasn't right. He was sure that worker priests were too powerful to be captured by a ragged band of workers. What was going on?

Then, a flash. A blast of power lifted him off his feet and set him back down. He felt disoriented, and when he tried to open his eyes, he realized they were already open. The sky was black with an impenetrable darkness, though he had been standing in bright daylight a moment ago. He felt all around himself and found a feathery shape—an Othra.

Which one are you? he asked.

You can't tell? The bird sounded offended.

Jabari sighed. *Hi Keethior,* he said, his voice dry even in his head. *What is this? What is happening?*

This is the priest's work. He found his strength. You must fight this.

Keethior flapped his giant wings, and as he did so, a trail of light moved through the air, following the shape of his wings. Jabari saw his friends standing close by, but he couldn't see Isika. *What on earth?* Rage shook him as he stooped and put his hands on the earth, using all his protector magic in an attempt to disintegrate the strange power that had overtaken the village.

Light spread from his hands to the ground, illuminating every dry crack, traveling like lightning, until every fissure was aglow. But it didn't do anything to stop the untimely night that had fallen.

Jabari! Isika called in his mind.

His head shot up, and he looked around for her, finally seeing her a long distance away, surrounded by the silver cats. They glowed with their own light.

There you are, he said. At the sight of her, Jabari's heart began to slow from its panicked racing.

We need to find the priest, she said. *He will be in the temple. That's where he will have the most power.*

She pointed in the direction of the temple. Jabari hesitated, and in the eerie glow that came from the earth, he saw her smile.

I've been there many times, she said. *There's nothing to be afraid of. The goddesses only have the power we give them.*

Jabari wasn't sure he agreed. Years ago, he had been there when Isika fought a sea person possessed by a powerful goddess, but he shut his mouth and went to her.

He walked through the darkness, leaving the others, ignoring the rustles and hushed calls around them. Ben caught at Jabari's arm as he walked past.

"Where are you going?" Ben asked.

"The temple."

78

Ben shuddered. "I'll stay here," he said. "I can collect the others and keep us together until you get back."

"Be careful," Jabari warned him. In the dim light, he saw Ben's face turn thoughtful.

"I don't think anyone here wants to hurt us," he said. "I think we may only have one enemy in this place."

"What do you hear from the workers?"

Ben paused for a moment. Jabari glanced at Isika, who had given up on waiting and was striding on ahead. He was going to have to run to catch her.

"I hear curiosity... and longing," Ben said.

Jabari tried to puzzle that one out as he ran after Isika and the cats, but soon enough, his mind was filled with other things. The temple, a red cube with gold highlights, was before them, which was not unexpected. But it was floating five feet above the ground! The air around it radiated with malice. Jabari caught up to Isika and took her hand.

"Do you feel that?" he asked.

"Yes," she breathed, frowning at the building. "How is that little priest doing that?"

Jabari didn't know. He had never seen such a thing.

"That doesn't seem like something that only has power because we give it power," he said.

She glanced over at him.

"No, Mugunta has immense power. But he only has power in this village because they have given themselves to evil over and over again, sacrificing their children. They have given themselves up to those who oppress them. So Mugunta and the goddesses have power here."

She smiled at him. "But they don't have power over us, my love."

Jabari felt a surge of love for Isika and a familiar longing to find his own power. Isika was tethered to Nenyi—Jabari knew that was how she reached her magic. But what was Jabari's way? How would he find his power?

Nenyi? he called. *We need you now.*

They ran toward the floating temple, and as they ran, Isika cried out and jammed her staff into the dirt. When the staff made contact, a light flashed, and Isika and Jabari rose, still running, as though the ground was still beneath them. The temple rose higher, and they rose with it until they were running through the doorway, Isika's staff glowing so brightly that Jabari couldn't look at it. Her circlet was bright with light as well, illuminating the contents of the room. They paused in the doorway.

Again, Jabari could sense that the room was filled with malice. Isika grabbed his hand, and his magic pooled with hers until they were both glowing. Jabari felt a grin spread across his face.

He strode forward, still holding Isika's hand, and found the man who cowered behind the statue of the four goddesses. With that much power in him, all it took was reaching out and grabbing the man by the arm.

Immediately there was a crack, a great tearing, and wailing of the earth, and the darkness was gone. Jabari blinked. The temple was on the ground, they were in the ordinary light of midday, and he held a whimpering man by one arm.

Jabari was no longer glowing, but the man didn't fight back as Jabari pulled him along behind him, out of the temple. Isika followed, pulling the temple door closed behind her. It sealed shut with a puff of air, and when Jabari turned to look, she held her hands up.

"I don't know either. I didn't do it. But I don't think the goddesses want us back in there."

The priest wailed.

"Be quiet," Isika said. "You're embarrassing yourself."

Jabari tightened his grip and continued to pull the man along. Back in the square, groups of Workers were milling around, staring at the company of travelers. Nat caught sight of them and relief bloomed on her face. She walked over to them swiftly with Ivy beside her.

"You're going to give me a heart attack," she told Isika.

"I'm not an easy queen to guard," Isika said. Nat just shook her head.

"What are the Workers doing?" Jabari asked Ivy.

"They know about the rescues," Ivy answered. "I think they are looking for their children."

Jabari had a funny feeling in the pit of his stomach. This was a possibility he hadn't foreseen. Looking for their children? They had given their children up. They had put them in boats and sent them out into unforgiving waters. Jabari was thankful the workers had decided to stop the ritual. But they couldn't have their children back. The rescued ones weren't workers anymore. They were Maweel.

He saw Brigid standing like a statue as people walked by her, staring at her and murmuring, clutching each other's arms.

Jabari turned his attention back to the man trying to wiggle out of his grip.

"I don't think so," he said.

"Let me take care of it," Isika said. She drew a chair under a shaded awning, gesturing for the man to sit. When she did, branches unfolded from the chair and attached themselves to the man's legs. Faiza came and stood nearby.

"Please tell us what you know about the king's plans," Isika said.

"Oh, do you mean your illustrious father?" the priest demanded slyly. He sat back for a moment, then frowned when the only person who seemed startled was Faiza.

"I don't call him that," Isika said.

"You mean you know?" the priest asked Jabari. "And you allowed scum like her to become queen?"

Jabari stood and walked toward the priest with his fists clenched, but Isika turned and shook her head at him. He gritted his teeth and sat back down.

"Tell me what he is planning," she said again.

"Of course," the man said, but his voice started to come like a hiss.

"He is going to wipe the Hadem off the face of the earth," the priest hissed, his voice growing increasingly raspy, his eyes starting to bulge. "He will attack them and form a large doorway that will lead all the way to you— the ungrateful, the pretentious, the ones who refused to bow. You will bow. You will bow as your loved ones are killed. After all, you were too stubborn to see what needed to be done, you put yourselves before anyone else. You will bow because you are old and horrifying, because you are old and broken, because Mugunta's might cannot be stopped..."

Jabari jumped up and pulled Isika back. There was a sound of shrieking and rumbling that seemed to come from beneath them, and the earth opened and swallowed the priest, pulling him under and snapping closed behind him.

They stared at the spot where he had been, moments before.

"Well," Jabari said, feeling shaky but keeping his voice light.

"I guess that solves the problem of what to do with him."

Isika shot him a look. "Insensitive even for you," she said.

"He's not dead," Ivy said softly. She bent down and touched the spot where the priest had disappeared.

Faiza looked horror-stricken. "Did your...did your goddess do this?"

Isika was shaking her head even as Jabari answered.

"This was not the Shaper," he said. "Some magic of the king was protecting the priest in case he was captured. Who knows what will happen to him now? But he made a choice to follow power, and power got him."

Isika stood, her face fierce. "And in the meantime, we know what he is up to," she said. "We cannot allow him to attack the Hadem."

"Ben, you were right," Jabari said. He looked up to find Ben and realized that he was nowhere to be seen. "Where is every-one?" he asked.

"That way," Ivy said, pointing toward the village.

Isika looked worried.

"Let's go find them," Jabari said, taking her hand. They walked to the village and in through the gates with the others. Once inside, he looked around the little village with new eyes. "What do you think they'll do, now that they don't have a priest?" he asked, taking in the walls and gates, the houses that were shuttered even in the daytime, and the lack of green spaces, the lack of beauty.

Isika looked around too, her face solemn. "I don't know," she said, "they've been following the priests for a long time. Too long to remember anything else."

"There he is," Jabari said with relief as he caught sight of Benayeem. The last time he had seen Ben was in the strange night of the priest's magic, and in the shock of the priest's disappearance, Jabari had feared that more than just one man had gone into the earth. A silly fear. But it was good to see Ben anyway.

Ben was standing beside Brigid, who looked pale and stunned. Ben's face was drawn with sadness. Jabari and Isika went to them, and it was only as they drew close that Jabari realized Brigid was crying.

"What's wrong?" Isika asked.

"They touched my face," Brigid said. "They had no right to touch me. How dare they call me *daughter*?"

"Who?" Jabari asked. Isika and Ben gave him a look.

"Who do you think?" Ben asked. "The Workers who cast her away."

"They are not my parents," Brigid said. "My parents don't look like them. My parents wear colorful robes and dance in the evenings. My parents are weavers, and these people would have called my parents black outsiders, like they did to you, Ben," she sobbed. "I can't believe they dared to ask me to stay. I don't ever want to see them again."

Isika reached out and pulled Brigid into a hug. She wound her arms around the shorter girl, and Brigid rested her head on Isika's shoulder.

"You are Maweel," Isika said. "Through and through. The Maweel found you and claimed you. That is forever."

Jabari voiced his agreement, but as Isika met his eyes over Brigid's head, he had to wonder what they were going to do if all the workers started wanting their children back. Life grew more complicated by the day.

After a short conference with the elders, Isika decided that the company should stay in the village for the night. The workers broke into the stores behind the priest's house to find enough food to feed the travelers. They rested and chatted for the remainder of the afternoon, helping with the cooking in the village square. It all felt oddly surreal. Jabari was exhausted. All he wanted was to lay out his bedroll and close his eyes. He waited for the sun to set. He wanted morning to come so they could get away from this place. It troubled him.

He sat and ate with the others. The food was not good, but Jabari was the son of elders and knew how to be polite. Also, he was famished. Isika and Ben looked somewhat stunned and kept glancing over their shoulders. Jabari thought they couldn't leave this place too soon.

As he was scraping his plate clean, a Worker couple approached. Jabari was thinking of how the woman's hair was exactly the same color as Gavi's when they spoke.

"Are you the brother prince of our son?" the man asked. "We saw him earlier, we spoke to him. But we have heard of you also."

Jabari couldn't get words out for several breaths. "Gavi is my brother," he finally said, swallowing around a lump in his throat. "But we are not princes."

He exchanged a few more words with the couple and then abruptly stood up and walked away.

He was...he couldn't believe what had just happened. Those people could not lay claim to Gavi. They had cast him away.

Jabari couldn't breathe. He didn't want any kind of separation to exist between him and the brother he had loved for as long as he could remember. It was already hard enough that Gavi had claimed allegiance to some group of outcasts and rescued that he had said Jabari could not understand.

These people couldn't have a piece of him too.

CHAPTER 10

The king had established a meeting room on the ship and spent most of his time there, issuing orders and considering the best way to wipe the Hadem off the face of the earth. A few days went by, cloaked in tension that seemed unbearable.

One morning, Herrith stood in attendance, straining to see Aria's face. The lights were dim, and everything looked blurrier than it should. Herrith wanted to read what state Aria was in, but there was a sort of sparkling fog around her, and he couldn't see her face clearly.

"Herrith!" Ikajo barked. Herrith nearly jumped but caught himself in time, holding himself very still.

"Yes, Brilliance?"

"Are you following me? You're meant to be writing this down."

"Yes, Brilliance. I am following. You were speaking of what you will do to...Isika...when we find her."

"Don't use her name!" the king exclaimed.

"To the Maweel woman."

"The Maweel *girl*." The king paced in the small space until Herrith felt dizzy. Everything glittered strangely, hurting his eyes and head. This was some sort of foul magic.

"You said you could possibly still turn her," Herrith said.

Better that the king imagine Isika could be turned, Herrith thought. If not, he might just kill her on sight. The king looked at Herrith sharply, though, at these words.

"I knew you weren't listening, Red Robe," the king snarled. "I said she most likely cannot be turned. We will have to kill her."

Don't move, don't move, Herrith begged Aria internally, but he saw her flinch. The fog cleared a little when she moved. It was okay, though. The king was too wound up to notice.

"What do your years of research tell you, Herrith?" he demanded. "If I kill the eldest, will this one become the next Whisperer?"

Alarm flooded Herrith. What could he say to diffuse this terrible weight? The other Red Robe, standing beside him, spoke up.

"I too have researched, Brilliance," he said. "And it is likely, but also the title of Whisperer could go to the brother."

The king turned, frowning. "Did I give you permission to speak?" he asked softly in his dangerous silky voice.

"No, Bright One," the man said, bowing his head.

Herrith shifted, trying to force his terror down. To risk being killed for the interruption, the Red Robe surely knew how valuable that information was. Herrith had hoped the king would not gain the knowledge that Ben could be Whisperer.

"Yet," the king continued. "That is useful. Has there ever been a male Whisperer?"

"Not for four hundred years, Brilliance," Herrith murmured.

"And there is no assurance that the title passes with the magic through the bloodline."

"But there are examples of it happening," the other Red Robe whispered.

Now Herrith had to think carefully. While this stupid man fed information to the king, Herrith couldn't keep lying to him without Ikajo discovering his deception. That meant carefully offering the king only a little bit of knowledge—not true, but not blatantly false.

He bowed his head, trying to think of what to say. If only his headache would ease. If only he could think!

"What is it you want to know, Father?"

Aria's clear voice echoed in the room. Herrith closed his eyes.

"Daughter?"

"Why do you want to know about the Whisperer title?"

The king stared at Aria, and as he did, the fog lifted a little. Herrith could see Aria's eyes. They were perfectly clear. She was aware and well. Was this her magic? Was she pulling the fog around herself to hide from the king? She was speaking now to stop the king from focusing his attention on Herrith, he realized, as she glanced at him for a fraction of a second. *Don't do it, Aria,* he tried to communicate with his eyes. But her attempt at distraction didn't work.

"Why don't you explain to Aria why we are interested in this line of thought?" the king said to Herrith, his voice still dangerously soft.

Herrith took a breath. He walked over to the wall, where a map of the known world had been fastened. The map showed the great desert running to the plains, and then down to the sea. At the shoulders of the plains, the green hills of Maween sweeping up to the northern mountains. Tiny, all of it. Across the sea was the vast expanse of the distant continent. Cities, mountains, caves. Creatures that guarded the shores of the other landmass. Aria stood, moving closer to the map.

"This..." she held a hand out, "this is us?" she pointed at the small piece of land that was their continent.

"Yes," Herrith said.

"What? How? I thought..." she turned to the king.

"Watch what you say," Herrith whispered quickly, urgently to her.

"I thought you were ruler of all," Aria said, her voice clear and brave in the small, close room. The ship pitched a little, and Herrith closed his eyes again. If the king was angry... Herrith held his breath. Finally, the king chuckled.

"Oh my beloved, how kind of you. No." There was immense bitterness in the king's tone. "I am not the ruler of the world. The emperor is the ruler of the world. Do you not wonder why we send ships full of slaves to him, daughter? Tribute, all tribute. Payment for him not wiping us out. He is a cruel ally."

Aria stared at her father, then turned to look at Herrith. He shook his head very slightly.

"I didn't know," she finally breathed.

"This is it, daughter, this is the reason. Do you think my father enacted this plan of joining Warrior and Whisperer only to wipe out the Maweel? Your tiny lands? No... not at all. With you, my Warrior-Whisperer, we will take the continent. I will become emperor and pay no more tribute, no more food or wine or slaves. No more taxes."

"We may yet turn Isika," Herrith couldn't help saying to the king. Thankfully, the king didn't seem to notice just how much Herrith was harping on that fact.

"We may. Either way, no emperor will be a match for a fully-fledged Warrior-Whisperer."

"Have you ever been there?" Aria asked, still gazing at the map.

"Once," the king said, after a moment. "As a mission of diplomacy. Terrible creatures are guarding the coast. It is impossible to invade."

"Creatures?"

The king started pacing again. "I am weary of this conversation," he said. "And I have no desire to speak of these things anymore. What we need is to turn Isika or kill her. The first step is to secure this continent. Later, we worry about the other one. Later..." The king's chin sank onto his chest as he went deep into his thoughts. Aria and Herrith remained near the map.

"You never told me," Aria whispered under her breath.

Herrith sighed a tiny, inaudible sigh. He let his shoulders slump. "The things I've seen," he breathed. "The things I know. I tell you what I must. It's too much for anyone to take."

"Too much for you, too?" she asked. She turned slightly so that her elbow bumped Herrith's. He felt the weight of all the years of his life, the hiding and secrets passed down, always serving the Shaper but never catching a glimpse of the Uncreated One, years of failure and sorrow, all so heavy that Herrith feared they might press him into the earth.

"Too much for me, too," he said.

"What are we going to do?" she asked.

"We're going to press on. We're going to wait for the others, and we're going to find a way to help you overcome his poison. What have you been working on?"

"A lot of things," she said. "Mara has been giving me ideas. But it's not enough. I need more strength, and I am no Whisperer, not yet. I can't pull it from the sea, and Nenyi hasn't seen fit to hand the power to me." Aria's voice was bitter.

Herrith lifted his hand, acting as though he was pointing out the continent's various ports and cities to Aria. Out of the corner of his eye, he saw the king nod in approval.

"Yes, she must learn, if she is to be our warrior whisperer," Ikajo said. "Come," the king said to the other Red Robe. The two of them strode from the room. As soon as they were gone, Herrith pulled Aria into a hug. He let her go after a moment, staring into the girl's face. Her skin, richly black like the night sky, was so much like her mother's. In the time Herrith had known Aria, she had become like a daughter to him.

"You must believe," he told her. "If Nenyi does not reveal himself, it is for your good."

She gazed back at him, tears filling her eyes.

"You can't know that," she said.

"I do, I believe it with all my heart," he said. "There is something, daughter of my heart, something that will change everything. We don't yet know what it is, but it will heal you."

"I am not your daughter," she said, crying openly now. "I am the daughter of a monster."

Herrith felt something break inside of him. He remembered an old story his father had told him. The memory was a breath of life and healing right now. He barely thought before he spoke, telling Aria the idea that had first come from this story from Herrith's own father.

"I would claim you as my daughter if you would have me as a father. It is old magic that might lift a little of the pressure of the king's poison. Maybe it will help you to gain more strength."

Aria stared at him through her tears. "You can do that?"

"Yes. It is risky. If the king notices..."

"Try it," she said.

Herrith felt his heart beating fast as he pulled off his hood and lifted his graying braid over his shoulder. He unwrapped the gold cord he had worn tied around his hair his whole life, tearing a small piece off. He took a small section of Aria's hair and tied the cord around it, whispering the words his father had taught him.

The effect was immediate. The arrow that was hurting Aria pierced Herrith's heart. He gasped and nearly fell. The gold cord gleamed for a moment. Aria looked at him, startled, moving close to grab his arm.

"I didn't know it would hurt you," she said as she began to cry again.

"I can help you hold it," Herrith said, forcing the words out through the pain. "That's what a parent does."

She hid her face in her hands, weeping. "It does feel better, but will it make you weaker?"

"Shhh," he said. "That's not your worry. I'm honored to be your father, Aria. I'm so sorry, now that I feel what you have been feeling. I knew, but I didn't know how bad it was." There were tears in his own eyes. He touched her hair. "Wash your face, and keep hiding. This will give you the strength to look for a way. I'll be fine. This is strong magic from the Shaper. I feel pain, but I am also stronger, now that I am your father."

He tucked the gold cord under her halo of curly hair.

"The king can never see this," Herrith told Aria. "You must begin wrapping your hair, so it doesn't fall out."

She hugged him and buried her face on his shoulder again.

"Thank you, Herrith," she said. "I feel like I can breathe." They stood like that for a moment. Then she said, "Thank you...

Baba." He felt a wave of love and also pain as the arrow dug deeper into his heart.

What had he done? The consequences of this choice began to sink in. He had undoubtedly weakened his chances of surviving. The king may find out or kill him just because he sensed his new weakness. But Herrith knew he would do it again, immediately, if he could.

Pain, he could live with. Watching Aria suffer alone was impossible.

CHAPTER 11

Aria stared at the map for a long time after Herrith left the room. For the first time since the arrow had pierced her, she felt like the old Aria. Well, not exactly, but at least a wisp of the old Aria was dancing around within her.

The short ceremony with Herrith had changed something big within her. She had felt the moment things shifted at the same time that pain had rushed over Herrith's lined face. The arrow had pierced him too. A tiny ray of hope burst into her heart. For so long, Aria had heard that betrayal was the worst kind of poison, that there was almost nothing that could be done to overcome it. But Herrith had not overcome it. He had shared it. It was something she had never imagined possible. She knew he could only do this because he loved her like a daughter. Herrith had loved her mother, and he loved her. The sense of loneliness that followed Aria everywhere released its grip somewhat. She breathed in and out, marveling.

She put a hand on the map, over the continent where Maween and the Desert City existed. Then she moved her hand outward, over the sweeping ocean to the unknown shores King Ikajo had spoken of, the lands that stretched out, nearly four times the size of their own continent. And this was only the known world? What about other places in the world? Other islands, other lands? She stared at the words on the map.

Fierce beasts guarded those shores. What were they?

But then she shook her head. Did it matter? The Desert King wanted to conquer them. Worse, he wanted to turn Isika to his cause. Aria knew this could never happen. So then, he planned to kill Isika and use Aria to conquer the other continent. She pulled her hand away from the map and stared at her open palm. If the Desert King succeeded at killing Isika, would Aria become Whisperer? Would she, because of her weakness and the arrow's poison within her, become of a tool of the king? An instrument of destruction stronger than any other human? She could not let it happen. She did not want to be used. She wanted to be loved.

But she could hardly ever think clearly. She was so scarred by the magic that had struck her down. She began to panic, realizing her times of lucid thinking were always so short, that even this one was nearly up. The king could do anything he wanted with her.

Aria forced herself to breathe. She was on a ship, about to be part of a battle for the wrong side. But she was not alone. She had other members of the Circle here. She had Herrith, her new adopted father. Even thinking the words gave Aria a feeling like the faint dreams she still had of her mother, Amani, stroking her face to help her sleep. Aria had Mara, too, and Gavi.

Gavi. She needed to find Gavi and tell him about King Ikajo's plans.

Aria left the room and looked around with unblurred vision.

She could see clearly. She looked closer at her surroundings. The corridors were dirty from years of work at sea. The floor beneath her feet was iron, covered with rubber mats. Her feet didn't make a sound as she tiptoed along the corridor. She put a hand under her hair, touched the gold cord, and then pulled her hood up to hide her face.

She hurried. It was only a matter of time before they noticed she was gone, and she didn't only want to find Gavi. She wanted to see the whole ship. She wanted to see her surroundings, really see them and be in them, rather than trapped in a room.

She walked quickly until she came to the end of the corridor, then stopped in amazement. The passageway ended in another open walkway, protected by iron railings. On the other side of the iron railings was the sea, the most beautiful thing Aria had ever seen.

She could see nothing but ocean, reaching into the distance. The water went on and on, bigger and more expansive than the prison she had found herself in. It filled her with joy. She wanted to dive in, to swim away, and just keep going. She leaned over the railing, looking farther, and then she heard the faint sound of singing. But where was it coming from? She listened for a little while longer but didn't hear it again.

Aria reluctantly turned away from the sight of the ocean and went to look for the kitchens, where she knew Gavi would be. But where were the kitchens? She slipped down more corridors, glancing in all directions, scanning for some hint of where she should go. People hurried by on various errands, not pausing to look at her. Oh, she didn't have *time* for this! She had a moment of desperation, but then she caught a whiff of food.

Aria followed her nose down a set of stairs, deeper into the ship, noticing as she went that the air got hotter and louder with the sounds of talk and clatter of dishes. After a few moments of walking along narrow corridors, keeping her head down, Aria found a door with kitchen sounds pouring out of it. She peered inside. People shuffled around a small, hot space amidst sizzling pans, chopping boards, and the scents of garlic and flatbread baking. They wore white clothes, but none of them looked particularly clean. Aria spotted a familiar blond head, towering over the people beside him. She started to walk into the room, but was stopped by a thick arm blocking her way.

"Only kitchen workers in here, girl," a man spit out. He wasn't from the Desert City, by his accent, and he wasn't wearing white. She stared up at him, trying to figure out what to say, but Gavi turned to see what was happening and spotted her. His eyes widened, and he moved quickly toward the door, chef's knife still in hand. At the door, he handed the knife to the man who had blocked her way.

"You have a message for me?" he asked Aria. "It's okay," he said, speaking to the man. "She's a messenger. King's business. Can you carry on chopping?"

"Do I look like a prep cook?" the man snarled.

"If you want to work in the kitchen, you will help chop like everyone else," Gavi said, his voice like steel.

The man looked like he wanted to burn holes into Gavi's face with his eyes. "Boy, if I ever discover what made you higher than me in the chain, I'll find a way to pull you down."

"Try being able to cook," Gavi suggested mildly, grasping Aria by the elbow and steering her down the corridor ahead of him. Aria drew in a breath, but the big man didn't follow, and they hurried along until they came to a short set of stairs that led farther down into the ship. Gavi let go of her and walked down the stairs. Aria followed him into a room filled with sacks of grain and other dry foods. The room was hot and airless, so Aria pulled off her hood, looking up to find Gavi staring at her.

"What happened to you?" he breathed. "How are you...how are you doing this?"

She was startled to see that he had tears in his eyes.

"What?" she whispered. "You can tell?"

"Yes...this is the first time I've seen your eyes clearly, I mean your eyes, not his eyes, not only the pain." He moved forward and hugged her. After a moment, she put her arms around him and closed her eyes, relaxing into the feeling of being held. She could hear his heart beating under her cheek. A few hot teardrops landed on her head. Then he put his hands on her shoulders to look at her. She looked into his familiar face, the bright blue eyes, tanned skin from so much sun. His hair, like wheat or sunlight, now bleached even more from days of walking in the desert. His hair was long now, tied back in a braid. She liked it.

She reached under her own hair and found the cord, pulling it out to show it to Gavi.

"Do you know what this is?" she asked.

He shook his head, reaching out to touch the cord.

"No," he said, frowning. He inhaled sharply. "But the magic in it is powerful."

"Herrith asked me today...if I wanted him to be my father. I said yes, not even knowing what he meant. And he tied this in my hair. I felt..." she reached for words to describe what had happened. "I felt like someone very tall had crouched beside me, and when they stood, they lifted the heavy blocks off my shoulders. I felt like he had reached into me and taken pieces of the arrow away. And I saw his face, Gavi. It hurt him badly. It was like he took part of the pain away. He said it's what parents do."

Gavi's eyes were on hers, grave and intent. He let go of the cord after a moment and sat on a stack of grain sacks.

"This is what I mean," he murmured. "There are just so many kinds of magic that we know nothing about. I've never heard of something so strong. Did you feel anything like this with your parents in Maween?"

She shook her head. "No. I mean, I feel the love and warmth of family with them. I know they love me, and they are my home. But this magic...I've never felt anything like this before."

Gavi crossed his arms over his chest.

"I haven't either," he said. "I'm so glad it exists. I'm...I can't believe you're feeling so much better."

She hunched her shoulders and balled her fists at her sides.

"But that's just it, isn't it? We're happy that I can function. I'm going to need to do so much more than *function* if we're going to rid the world of Ikajo's poison. If we're ever going to be reunited with our families."

He nodded, looking down at his hands, which were balled into fists.

"Do you think they're coming?" she asked him.

"What do you think?" he asked back.

"I sent songs to Benayeem," she said.

"Yes, Herrith told me. If he got them, they're coming," he told her, a slight smile on his face.

"Do you think I will always be like this?" she asked him. "Scarred and poisoned? It feels like our world is so far from the world we used to know. Will they even know us when they see us?"

He smiled again, but his eyes were sad. "I ask myself the same questions," he said. "I think healing will come to us. But you're right. Nothing will ever be the same." His eyes grew sad.

Aria went to him and sat beside him, grabbing onto his hand and bringing it to her cheek.

"I'm thankful I'm not alone here," she said.

"How did you get down here, anyway?" he asked, tightening his fingers around hers.

"You doubt my sneaking abilities?"

He smiled, his eyes crinkling. "I think they're looking for you," he said, pointing at the ceiling. For the first time, Aria noticed a lot of thudding and shouts overhead.

"Can't he just tell where I am?" she asked, almost to herself.

"We're not in his palace anymore. He loses power away from his city, where he has a strong connection with the Great Waste. Let's talk, quickly, and then you need to follow me."

"I want to tell you what he is planning," Aria said.

"And I want to tell you what I've been thinking about," he responded. "You first."

Aria told Gavi about the plan to turn Isika or kill her, so Aria would be Whisperer and conquer the other continent. Partway through telling him, Aria realized she was still holding Gavi's hand and dropped it, feeling heat rise to her face. She looked at him when she was finished. She could almost see him thinking. He stared down at the floor for a few minutes, then lifted his eyes to her face.

"You've had a very eventful day," he said.

She gave a short laugh. "Yes, I suppose I have," she said.

"I don't have as much to tell. Only that I've been learning about other kinds of magic as well. Nothing bad," he said, as she flinched. "Just that Nenyi offers a different way of being gifted to those who have suffered a lot. There are waves of magic coming from the laborers who row the ship. I think they may be able to teach you."

"Why would they want to teach the heir of the person who enslaved them?" she asked.

"For freedom," he said, his eyes growing hard.

"Would they believe us if we promised it?"

"I don't think anyone has ever even offered it to them before. It's not like Ikajo cares about them enough to offer them anything. He treats them like animals." His face grew bleak, and he put his face in his hands, then blew out a short sigh. "Maybe...maybe they can help. I don't know, but I know that we have to try to help them get to freedom. You should meet go down to the rowing level and meet the enslaved people, but not right now."

The noise overhead grew more frantic, and Aria and Gavi looked at each other. Aria knew their time was up.

"Follow me," Gavi said.

They left the room and ran down a corridor to a place where the passageway turned sharply or went straight. "I'm going to run this way," Gavi told Aria. "You go that way, and then slowly find a staircase and make your way back up. You'll need to do your best acting, pretend you got lost. The king needs to believe you're still under his spell."

"Oh, I am," Aria said bitterly. "I'm just the tiniest bit unclouded."

"Well, convince him that you're all the way clouded," Gavi said, smiling at her, a wistful look on his face. He leaned over quickly, kissed her on the forehead, and then turned the corner, his hand lifted in a wave.

Aria stood, briefly stunned, then sighed and made her face blank. She trudged down the other corridor, waiting to be found.

CHAPTER 12

L ater that day, Gavi searched the ship for Herrith. The decks were busy with preparation as the king got ready to meet with the captains of six other vessels. Crews of slaves cleaned the poop deck and put out tables for feasts they would never taste, sailors tied down sails, and set anchor. Gavi kept his head down as he slipped between the many busy people. He found Herrith just outside the king's chambers. The older man looked alarmed to see Gavi, then gestured irritably for him to follow as he walked away from the room.

"You and Aria are going to be the death of me," Herrith grumbled, his red robe flapping as he walked. He shot a sharp glance at Gavi. "And when was the last time you bathed? I can smell you from here."

"You know we have no place to bathe on this ship," Gavi retorted. "There are rumors that we'll be allowed to swim tomorrow. Will the enslaved people in the bottom of the ship be allowed?"

Herrith sighed. "I never know what the king will allow. Of

course, I will encourage it." He paused. They had reached the ship railing, and they both leaned against it, looking out to sea. Herrith tapped on the iron post idly. "I suppose I have you to blame for the furor of searching for Aria today," he said.

Gavi snorted. "Aria does what she wants," he said. He let a few beats pass. The sea was lovely in a way that hurt him because of how much ugliness surrounded them. Created things were perfect. The moon could bring him to tears. The heat and sweat of people who were unloved and exploited was blasphemy. It contrasted sharply with the great tide of beauty from the Uncreated One.

"She told me what you did," Gavi said finally. "And I could feel how much it helped her. How did you do it?"

"Ah, yes, I wondered when you would ask," Herrith said. "I'm guessing your adoption ceremonies don't have quite as drastic a result in Maween?"

"No," Gavi answered. "Not even close."

Herrith held out a hand, and Gavi touched the older man's palm lightly with his fingertips. He felt it then, the sharp poison of the arrow that had pierced Aria. Herrith held it in his own body. Gavi drew in a breath. He recognized the poison from all the times he had pulled it out of Aria, offering temporary relief.

But now it was in Herrith's bloodstream, hindering his power. Gavi stared at Herrith, really looking at him, seeing him clearly, maybe for the first time. The older man looked a lot like King Ikajo—tall with long curling hair that he kept tied back in a braid, rich brown skin, a prominent nose, and deep-set eyes. He had more lines on his face than Ikajo, fanning out around his eyes and mouth. There were streaks of gray in his hair.

"Why would you do this?" Gavi asked. "Won't it make you weaker?"

Herrith stared down at his hand, a small smile on his face. "It will certainly make me weaker. But it is an honor to share her pain, to lift it a little. You asked how I did this. It is ancient magic from farther back than the divide between Maween and Karee, back in the time of the Dancers and Singers. I was taught by my father, who learned from his father. Our line is long. We are an ancient people, though our rulers have given up the life-giving ways." Herrith looked at Gavi intently. "When a person truly wants to take a child into their heart, to hold their pain and keep it close, to walk in every circumstance with the child, powerful healing takes place. I only wish it would work all the way. If your friend, Ben, were here, he would hear my song in Aria and her song in me."

Gavi gripped the railing and stared at the water in shock. "Will the king be able to hear it?"

Herrith laughed a short laugh. "Not normally," he answered. "But if it comes to pass that I am in great distress, it will become clear. So I will be careful not to be in great distress. Don't worry, Son of Andar." He gestured for them to begin walking again. They passed a group of slaves carrying boxes of goods onto the ship from boats that had pulled up alongside the larger vessel.

"Do you know anything about the magic of the enslaved?" Gavi asked. Herrith swiveled to look at him.

"Magic of the enslaved?" he asked. "What do you mean by that?"

"They have a working magical system," Gavi said. "Do you or anyone in the Circle know anything about it?"

Herrith walked faster, slightly bent, robes swirling, hands clasped behind him.

"Not really, no," he said. "I am surprised. I have never noticed it in the palace slaves."

"Maybe they are too close to the King," Gavi said. "Too much poison."

"Maybe. You could ask Mara. She spent time in a large colony of slaves when she was being punished for Amani's disappearance."

Horror washed through Gavi's stomach like heat. He swallowed down nausea.

"They punished her?" he asked.

Herrith looked at him gravely. "Yes," he said. "They punished all of us."

* * *

GAVI WENT BACK to the kitchen to prepare a meal for the meeting between the ship captains. All were sea people, pledged to the King, and called to support him for this battle. If Gavi wasn't mistaken, he picked up some reluctance on the part of the sea people. He wasn't sure that they really wanted to fight. The different captains had their own fleets of ships. Family structures, tribes, and clans branched from the central leader. Gavi sensed they would choose independence from the Desert King if they could. He wondered what the king held over them, to make them submit.

Gavi carried hunks of roasted meat from the ovens to large platters, oversaw loaves of flatbread being pounded, rolled, and cooked on the stovetops, and made the spicy curry the king loved. Gavi had brought some of his own recipes to the Desert City. He was conflicted about feeding Maween's enemies, but his main goal was serving Aria. Nothing was as important as keeping her safe. Keeping himself useful by cooking to the best of his ability meant that he could work where she was. So he would do it.

"Gavi," the head cook barked. "One of the ships has brought dried ginger. We need it for the sauce. Take two men and go. Retrieve anything else they have for us as well."

Gavi kept his face still, nodding once. Inside, he was elated at the chance to board one of the other ships. He wanted to see everything. Every bit of knowledge would help as they grew closer to this horrible battle.

He felt a flurry of anguish at the thought of the king actually fighting the Hadem. Where was Jabari? Was he on his way, ready to show up at any moment? Or was it all in vain—Gavi, Herrith, and Mara trying to support Aria while the king plotted the death of an entire village?

Ah. The other men were staring at him. He had stopped amid these painful thoughts and was staring at the ship's ladder with his hands balled into fists. He grimaced and slipped down the ladder and into the transfer boat. The man guiding the boat had no oars. After a moment, the man raised his hands, and the boat began to move, shooting forward at an incredible speed. Like the captain of Gavi's own ship, the man had a mess of black hair, bound with strings and beads. He grinned at the look on Gavi's face, and Gavi glimpsed several gold teeth.

"We are sea people," he said in response to Gavi's unspoken question. "We have sea magic."

"But from what source?" Gavi asked.

The man glanced at him. "We are allies of the king's," he said. "Our power is from the mighty Mugunta."

Gavi sat back in the boat as it glided to another ship. He knew that the Workers and Hadem were two branches from the same tree. Also, the Gariah and the Karee. Was there a branch of sea people who were loyal to the Shaper? It was worth some research.

He and the other two crew members boarded the ship without incident, and the captain—a woman, Gavi saw with surprise—led them to the storeroom to see the king's tribute.

He cleared his throat. "I didn't think the king allowed women to be leaders."

The captain laughed a rough laugh. "The king doesn't. The sea people do." She gestured to the room full of boxes. "Isn't it nice?" she asked, her voice dripping with sarcasm. "The king can have all this ginger that he didn't pay for, plant, or harvest. Wonderful to be a king."

Gavi's eyebrows shot up. But he got his face under control, hoping that the woman would keep talking. His hunch had been right. Not all of the sea people were happy about serving King Ikajo.

It was a shortcoming in his own education, he realized with a pang. Gavi and Jabari had learned about Maween's enemies, but not enough about how they had been conquered. He bent to pick up a box.

"No, no," the captain said, her voice full of scorn. "You're only here to oversee the handoff and make sure we are not cheating the king. The slaves will carry the boxes."

He straightened and swiveled to look at her.

"All three of us?" he asked. "You need three of us to oversee the handoff?"

She shrugged. "The king requires it."

He stared, suddenly not caring whether he blew his cover. "Why do you enslave people?" he asked. "If you can control the seas and move your boats without work?"

She laughed at him. "Don't you understand the ways of the world? Who are you, anyway? Where is Hol?"

"Hol sent me." Gavi crossed his arms. He wanted answers. A line of laborers ran into the storeroom, and he was shuffled out of the way as they began picking up boxes and running back out with them, muscles straining at the heavy cargo. "And no, I don't understand. Enlighten me."

She had to look up at him, but she managed to convey scorn nonetheless. "Slaves are for power, not for work. Exerting control and keeping it means holding other lands in fear. If they fear for their people, their children being stolen, they will be quiet, like tame beasts. If they have no fear, they are unruly, like wild beasts."

"Wild beasts only to those who want to control them," Gavi said, anger starting a drumbeat in his heart. "To each other and themselves, they will have autonomy, which isn't the same as wildness."

"You are a strange servant," the woman said, crossing her own arms. Her matted black hair was tied around her head in the same way as the other man's had been. Her eyes were rimmed with kohl, stark and dark against her pale face. "Where did you say you were from?"

"I didn't," he responded. "But I am from the Desert City."

Her eyes narrowed, and Gavi realized that he had gone too far.

"We're done here," he said. "Thank you for your tribute, Captain."

The others had left with the boxes, so he followed, glancing around once to see her still looking at him. Whoops. He sighed. He had revealed far too much. Then he froze. He could feel it here also. The magical system of the enslaved.

Holding, deceiving, strengthening, sustaining. A web of protection.

Back on the ship, Gavi finished his cooking and then slipped down into the ship's lower reaches to talk with the laborers. He went to the resting room to find the elder he had spoken to the day before. The man smiled at Gavi and lifted a hand.

"I have more questions," Gavi said.

"Of course you do," the old man replied. "In curiosity, you are like this one," and he gestured at a small child who sat nearby, playing with a small pile of wooden disks.

"What is your name?" Gavi asked, feeling shy now that he was sitting with the elder.

"I am Rema," the elder said. "And you are Gavi. But that is not your real question."

"Where does your power come from, Rema?" Gavi asked. "And is it ever wielded by anyone other than the enslaved?"

The man smiled. "I know why you keep asking these questions," he said. He was silent for a long while, and Gavi thought maybe he wouldn't speak again. "You don't need to be enslaved to wield this power," he said. "It is for the oppressed: For those in strange lands, those without water, for the ones who roam, no lands to call their own. And yes, for those who are enslaved, forced to work against their will. Nenyi suffers with us, you know. And this power creates a great web of care around us. We are at the mercy of those who want to exploit us. Nothing will change that except our freedom. But within these evil bounds, we draw from the water of the suffering of the Uncreated One. That connection, that bond is a powerful one. Mugunta could never offer this power because Mugunta is not connected, the Great Waste does not care. Nenyi is connected to her creation. Mugunta only offers power to power."

They sat in silence for a while more. Gavi watched the child stack the wooden disks into a tall tower, then knock them down. He suddenly realized he was looking at pieces of one of the overseer's canes—the ones used to beat the walls or people. It had been chopped into a toy for this young one. Gavi smiled. He needed to bring Aria to meet these people. She would like them.

CHAPTER 13

The white stone arches on the outskirts of the Hadem village came into view, and Isika breathed a sigh. The intricate carvings in the village's white stone glowed with the crimson, saffron, and mauve of the sunset, and as soon as she was under the first carved arches, Isika stopped walking and leaned on her staff to soak it in. Her heart felt bruised by the ugliness that had happened back in the Worker village, and the beauty was balm to her spirit.

She touched one section of the stone, tracing the dancing carvings that looped and spiraled into waves, trees, and stars.

Jabari came to her, and Isika leaned her head on his shoulder.

"I feel too old and dusty to be here," she said. "It's so beautiful."

"We can remedy that," Jabari said. "The sea is right over there."

"I think we need to greet *them* first," Ben said from behind them.

Isika lifted her head to see a procession approaching. It

111

looked remarkably formal. She bit back a groan and glanced around to check on her fellow travelers. The cats sprawled on the ground, tongues out, and the horses stood with their heads down. Brigid sat on a stone with her head on her arms. Ivy leaned against one of the white carvings, and Deto was fully prostrate, lying in the dust with his head in his hands. Even the rangers seemed wilted, though Nat held her position, scanning the horizon for possible threats. Isika and her companions weren't in great shape. The scuffle at the village had sapped the last of their strength, and it had been several days of hard travel since then.

"Collect yourselves, everyone," she said. "Get it together for at least a little while more. I'm sure they have food and beds for us."

"Beds?" Jabari asked, his voice dry.

"Fine, then, mats on the ground," Isika said. There were groans all around, but Isika's company pulled themselves to their feet and dusted themselves off. The procession kept coming. As they got closer, Isika squinted. The Hadem villagers were undulating across the sand. Jabari squeezed Isika's shoulder.

"They're dancing," he said. "This looks like a greeting for a queen. They must have heard about the coronation."

Isika blinked. She hadn't thought of this possibility. But it was true, the pale-skinned Hadem were dancing their way toward the Maweel travelers, wearing their colorful traditional clothing. There were bits of ribbon tied into their hair, they wore beads and scarves and face paint. They looked like the wind through a flower field or a group of colorful birds. Unexpectedly, Isika felt tears prickle behind her eyes.

Vitalker, the high elder of the village, was at the front of the procession. Isika felt a brief moment of worry that Vita would bow, but she remained standing, gazing at Isika with a wide smile on her face. The Hadem, the dancers of Nenyi's peoples, were from the same branch as the Workers, but they couldn't have ended up less alike. The Workers condemned dancing and were superstitious about any kind of community event, even banning the practice of visiting one another's "home ground."

In contrast, the Dancers, the Hadem, could hear communal music that linked them in an inexplicable way. Their pale skin was tanned from the outdoors, their limbs salt-stained and mostly uncovered. They did not resemble the Workers with their long sleeves and terror of the sun.

Vita seemed to be waiting for Isika to speak first.

"Thank you for this welcome, Elder," Isika said to the older woman. Vitalker was much shorter than Isika, her wrinkles a latticework of pale lines in the deep tan of her face. Her pale blue eyes were sharp, though.

"Queen Isika," Vita said softly, and though she did not bow, she inclined her head, as did the people behind her. "We welcome you."

Isika felt heat rise to her face, but she held eye contact with the Elder and tried to behave as though she knew what a queen was supposed to do.

"Thank you," she said, placing a hand over her heart.

"We have a ritual for those who are becoming elders or leaders," Vita went on. "We would like to offer this to you."

"What kind of ritual?" Jabari asked, and Isika turned to shoot him a look.

Don't speak for me, she said in her mind.

The cats stirred, and Hera turned her head lazily in Jabari's direction.

Would you like me to teach the arrogant one a lesson, Whisperer? she asked.

That won't be necessary, Hera, but thanks anyway, Isika said, fighting a smile.

Jabari gripped his bow and reached as though to grab an arrow. *I'd like to see you try,* he said. The cat unsheathed her claws as though by accident.

Enough, you two! Isika said. *Now is not the time.* The moment felt officially ruined. She glared at Jabari and Hera in turn. *I won't bring either of you next time.*

Vita stood waiting for an answer.

"I would be honored," Isika said, hoping that whatever the ritual was, it wouldn't be too painful. She didn't see any scarring or branding on Vitalker's body—that seemed like a good sign. "My friends are tired and hungry, though. Can they attend to their needs?"

"I will have people take care of your friends," Vita said. "And you can choose one or two female attendants for your ritual."

Brigid and Ivy stepped forward, and Isika nodded at them. Nat shifted, and Isika turned to look at her.

"We're safe here," she murmured. "You can go rest."

After a moment of searching Isika's face, Nat nodded and appeared to relax.

The procession of Hadem people turned and began to walk back to the camp, ducking at every other step so that the line of them rippled in the sunlight, their colors and ribbons waving in the breeze. Isika smelled the salt of the open sea, catching her breath at the beauty of the quiet, dancing people. She felt a stab of rage at the Desert King's plan to attack the Hadem. Then came a wave of fear at the thought of Aria being dragged into that in any way. Isika held out hope that Aria would be completely restored, but how hard would healing be if Aria was involved in an attack against innocent people?

The procession entered the village through the last arch just as the sunset reflected its brightest red against the cliffs. Jabari took Isika's hand, interlacing her fingers with his, and she smiled up at him.

His face was starkly handsome against the white stone, a deep brown that glowed in the evening light, all angles and high cheekbones. She loved his beautiful jawline. Isika knew she was feeling the effects of the villagers' magic, but she was grateful for it. It was nice to feel peace without having to fight for it. The magic felt a little like the effect of the Othra, actually. She looked up to see Keethior, Eemia, and Nirral flying overhead.

It's only partly us, Keethior told her. *The Hadem hold this magic as well. They can offer peace through the simplicity of their dance and their harmony. The Maweel have this too, in their communion with their voices, their songs, and their unity with the earth.*

Vita spoke. "Come this way with your attendants, Isika. The others can go with my son for food, bathing, and rest."

Isika let go of Jabari's hand somewhat reluctantly. He leaned in and kissed her gently on the cheek. She let her eyes drift closed for a moment.

"Don't let them tattoo you," he whispered. Isika's eyes flew open. His laughing eyes were very close.

"I'll decide. Depends on how beautiful the design is," she said, lifting an eyebrow.

"All right, you two," Ivy said. "Let's not keep them waiting."

Isika, Ivy, and Brigid followed Vita and a group of women. They walked through corridors of white stone that twisted through the hills surrounding the Hadem village. Every passage was carved in patterns of flowers, trees, ocean waves, clouds, and birds. Isika felt as though she was in a beautiful dream.

"We didn't see any of this last time," Ivy murmured.

"I guess we didn't have much time for exploring."

"Do you think it's okay that they're coming with us?" Brigid asked.

Isika turned to see over her shoulder. Hera and the other cats padded after them. After a moment, Isika also noticed Keethior flying overhead. She grinned, shaking her head.

"I don't think we can stop them," she said.

From somewhere ahead, they heard Vita's voice wafting back to them. "The companions of the World Whisperer are welcome."

They emerged into a secluded cove. Isika gasped audibly. The sea was the color of turquoise, whipped into tiny waves by the wind. The white stone cliffs surrounded a small curve of beach covered with thousands of bright pebbles. There were pools formed by large divots in the stone. A few canvas tents were scattered around the cove.

"This is our space," Vita said. "A place for women. We use it for birth blessings and coming of age, or for becoming elders. Today, we will have our very first queen ritual."

"It's beautiful," Ivy exclaimed.

Isika felt teary, honored by the fact that the Hadem elders had allowed her into this special place.

"There are robes in the tent," Vita said. "Put them on and meet us back here."

Isika, Brigid, and Ivy grinned at each other. Isika felt a wave of happiness, some more magic linked to this place. She scampered to the canvas tent with her friends. Inside was a space with mats on the floor and three robes hanging from a pole. Isika undressed quickly, thankful to be out of her dusty clothes. She put the robe on. It was a sleeveless tunic, woven from a soft, sandy-colored material. Both Isika and Ivy's tunics reached the middle of their thighs, but Brigid's fell to her knees.

They looked at each other.

"I have no idea what we're getting into," Isika said.

Brigid twirled a hank of her hair, a sign that she was nervous.

"Whatever it is, it will be an experience," Ivy said briskly and led the way out. Isika sometimes wished she had Ivy's courage. At times when Isika hesitated, Ivy just moved, seemingly without an ounce of fear. Isika moved closer to her friend and squeezed her hand quickly.

"I'm glad you're here," she whispered.

Ivy grinned at her. "I wouldn't miss this for all the water in the ocean. I've grown up thinking no one had ceremonies like ours. Now I'm finding that some people have coves just for women. Who knew?"

"Maween was the first place I ever saw anything like what we have," Isika said, somehow not wanting to compare the two places. "I had never seen so much goodness in one place."

"The world keeps opening up to more lovely things," Brigid said.

"And more ugly things," Ivy said.

Images of ships attacking this sacred, calm place flooded Isika's mind against her will. She shuddered.

"Let's put the ugliness away right now," she said. "We need this."

The Hadem women waited near one of the rock pools, but they didn't keep their bodies still. They rose and sank in a line, undulating like a wave as they followed their internal music.

Ivy, Brigid, and Isika walked to meet them and stood facing the women when they arrived.

Vita looked at each of them in turn, her eyes resting on Isika's face the longest.

"Much sorrow," she said. "I see and hear sorrow and heaviness in your hearts, on your shoulders. For this time, you need to let it go. Come this way. We will attend to you in our ceremony of blessing."

"Are there tattoos involved?" Isika asked.

Vita stared at her. "No, child. There are no tattoos involved."

"Okay," Isika said. Beside her, Ivy was choking with the effort of not laughing.

What followed was dream-like. Isika lay next to her friends on the soft sand by the pool, and the women painted their faces and bodies with colored clay. The clay grew warm, covering them from head to foot. Isika could feel tears trickling from the corners of her eyes at the tender care, and she heard soft crying from Brigid beside her. Isika thought of how upset Brigid had been by the desire of her Worker parents to claim her. Her sense of identity had been shaken. Isika understood how she felt.

After all, the man who wanted to claim her—who had claimed Aria—was Maween's most terrible enemy.

As the older woman's strong hands rubbed clay into her face, Isika felt the poison of her father's claim on her identity dissipate, leaving her body free. She felt her muscles relax. At a gesture from the women, she stood up with Ivy and Brigid. Isika smiled at the way they looked, covered in colored stripes and patterns. They looked fierce, like queens themselves.

Isika held her hands out and looked at her arms. The yellow clay was a bright contrast to her dark skin, painted over her in long swathes.

"Your face looks beautiful," Ivy said.

"So does yours," Isika said, looking at the intricate patterns on Ivy's face.

"Time to get into the pool," Vita said.

The water was warm and soft on Isika's skin. As the clay washed away, Isika imagined every other claim to her identity fading. She belonged to Nenyi, she belonged to herself, and she belonged to Maween. She was their queen. It was who she was, all throughout—nothing else.

After the pool, they swam in the sea. The elders went in with them, and as the Hadem danced in the water, Ivy began to sing. Brigid harmonized with her, and Isika joined in as well, lifting her voice as much as she could. The Singers and the Dancers exulted, and for a little while, it seemed that everything would continue in beauty, that everything would be okay.

CHAPTER 14

Most of the company chose to bathe in pools cut into the rocks close to the village, but for Jabari, nothing would satisfy like the sea. He stripped down to his underclothes and ran straight in, diving under the waves as soon as the surf was deep enough, allowing the salty water to tumble him in circles and pull the stress and anger right out of his body. There had been so much to be angry about, lately.

He still occasionally heard Bara, the stable-master, telling him he was arrogant with the smirking cats as witnesses. He had taken her words seriously and had been working on listening to others without interruption. He was trying to remember that he didn't always need to be right. But it frustrated him. Things happened so slowly, with so much unnecessary deliberation. That was one thing.

Another was that Jabari missed Gavi with a fierce sadness that sometimes felt like rage. What had Gavi done to their family by taking himself out of it? Why would he choose the others? Jabari knew Gavi's reasons, but it still wasn't right. Jabari was the one suffering, picking up the pieces that Gavi had dropped.

He dove down to the sand and picked up handfuls, rubbing it along his arms and legs to scrub the grime of his travels away. Ah, the water felt good.

And, it still hadn't rained. Isika was queen of the Maweel, and it hadn't rained. They had a World Whisperer and the seasons were still out of order. How could it be?

Jabari growled in frustration and lay back to float for a while, closing his eyes and willing understanding and peace to flow into him. They were doing all they could. Jabari couldn't control the rain or the betrayal that had tied itself to Isika and blocked her power. He couldn't control the fact that the Desert King wanted to attack the Hadem and the Maweel. All that Jabari could do was support Isika and look for answers to their great question. What would release the present from the sins of the past? How would they heal?

He walked out of the surf, feeling better, his aches soothed, his mind quieter. Rummaging through his pack, he found his dirty clothes and washed them in the stream that fed the bathing pools. He knew he should rinse the salt from his skin, but it felt good to him, sticky, like a day at the beach with his family. Like travel, back before the earth had shifted off its axis, and the World Whisperer had turned out to be powerless to fight Maween's enemies. Jabari knew he was turning loops in his mind again, stuck in the same question. He draped his clothes over the stones near the sea to dry, found a semi-clean piece of cloth in his pack, and tied it around his waist.

The others were sitting around a fire with some of the Hadem elders. Benayeem looked clean and content, his eyes nearly drifting shut as he took long pauses between each bite of his food. And Deto was shoveling food into his mouth, his hair loose. Usually, Deto kept his long black hair braided in the style of his people. He looked different with it down around his shoulders. Jabari had only seen it down a few times before, always when they were traveling together.

One of the elders gestured for Jabari to sit.

"It is good that you are here," the man said. "I have wanted to talk to you and the others. My mother will have a similar conversation with Isika, Ivy, and Brigid."

Jabari nodded and sat on one of the short stools, accepting a bowl of food from another man by the fire. The food was a stew of grains, cactus, and fish. He took a bite and sighed with happiness at the spicy, tart flavors. After a few bites, he turned his attention to the man who had spoken.

"I do not know your name," he said. "And that might be helpful, especially if we are to have a deep conversation."

"I am Radakar," the man said. He had long blonde hair woven with blue ribbon and wore the loose pants of the Hadem, with bells tied around his ankles. "Vita's son and Second Elder. I know who you are, Jabari, son of Andar. And I know your heart is heavy with the loss of your Dancer brother."

"My Dancer brother?" Jabari exclaimed. Beside him, Deto made a similar expression of shock. "My brother doesn't really dance very much."

"Whether he does or not, his origins are with us, from long before Mugunta deceived the Workers. Mugunta spent many years trying to tempt the weak-willed away from here, and finally succeeded by making the people afraid of one another." Radakar paused and rubbed at his face. Jabari noted the gray streaks in his hair and lines on his face and felt a stab of sympathy. The Hadem had been holding their line for a long time.

"This is why I want to talk with you," Radakar went on. "The power of Mugunta is strong now, very strong. We have heard from the Naia that ships approach, full of evil intent. We have been waiting for you, and we dance day and night, forming the protection we hope will save us. But the ships will be too much for us. We need your help."

Jabari stared at the bottom of his bowl. He was still hungry. At that moment, a child slipped over and touched his arm, offering to take the bowl. Jabari watched his bowl go, sadly, but his spirits lifted when he saw one of the men refill it from the large pot on the fire. The child brought it back and offered it to Jabari, a big smile on his face.

Jabari turned his attention back to Radakar.

"We know you need our help, Elder," he said. "This is why we have come."

"Yes, this one heard it and told you, is that true?" The elder gestured at Ben, who nodded.

Jabari wondered what to say. Isika was not with him, and she was the queen. Of course, they would help, that was why they had come, but Jabari couldn't promise anything without Isika beside him. But the elder seemed to be waiting for something. He stared hard at Jabari until he grew uncomfortable and looked away. Suddenly, Radakar slammed his hand on the rock he was sitting on, causing Jabari and Ben to jump.

"You are not paying attention!" Radakar said. "Listen, you come here to help, all of you leaning heavily on Isika's power. But she is weak! She cannot be as strong as she needs to be, with her sister's betrayal magic still infecting her. This whole branch has been weakened by betrayal, young ones. Wake up! Do not come here claiming to want to help, and then sit back and see what will happen! Isika is not the one to save you now."

"You're saying Isika is powerless?" Ben asked, leaning forward with a scowl on his face.

"I do not say that, but you need to step up, Benayeem, Son of Amani. All of you need to step more firmly into your power. If the World Whisperer is to regain what she lost, the Desert King needs to be defeated. You need to restore Gavi and Aria to your families. Only then will Isika have the power to restore Maween and the surrounding lands. Only then will she be able to call the rain out of the sky. But you," he turned to Jabari and pointed a shaking finger in Jabari's direction, "you have been resting for too long. You are very, very powerful, young one. And yet, none of us know it! Because you don't show us. You don't live in your gift. Why do you throw it away?"

"I don't throw it away," Jabari started to say, but the elder held up a hand.

"I don't want to hear your excuses," he said. "You know exactly what I am talking about. You shuffle along, content with the merest sliver of power, following others, playing around, moping about your dancer brother. Meanwhile, your lands are dying!"

"The last time someone lectured me," Jabari said through gritted teeth, "she told me that I am too arrogant. Now you are saying I am not powerful enough. So which is it? How can it be both? How can I be too weak and also too arrogant?"

He looked around the fire for answers, his heart raging against the unfairness of this accusation. Deto looked back at him thoughtfully. The stars had appeared, and Jabari felt both wide awake and sleepy. He wondered where Isika was, and what she would say if she was here. He was thankful, somehow, that she wasn't able to witness this. Ben met Jabari's eyes with something that looked like compassion.

Radakar finally spoke. "It is arrogant not to live from your power, young one. Arrogance and denial of your strength are not in opposition. They are born of the same root. If you believe your birthright is to grow up in a palace and allow your parents to work for you, if you believe your voice should be heard because of your birth, you live in arrogance.

But if you genuinely seek to be what the Uncreated One has made you to be, you will begin to live in strength, asking only for the respect that your actions deserve. It is not arrogant to fulfill potential."

Jabari stared at the elder, his words finally making things clear. They hit him with the strength of a massive ocean wave, and he closed his eyes. The words hurt, and Jabari's mind couldn't take any more. He could feel himself shutting down.

"I need to think about this," he said.

"Radakar," a soft voice said. "We can talk more tomorrow. We need to let the young ones rest. Tomorrow is for dancing and talking, and plans. But they have seen many hard things since they left their homes."

Jabari opened his eyes and saw a woman sitting next to Radakar with her hand on his arm. She smiled at Jabari as the elder nodded.

"This way, guests," she said. "We have caves prepared for you."

Jabari followed Deto, who followed the woman. She walked far back into the winding caves, emerging in a large open space with mats scattered on its floor. Colorful cushions and blankets covered the mats.

Jabari hardly remembered touching the mat before he was asleep.

* * *

THE NEXT MORNING, Jabari woke to music. The others were gone, all but Deto, who groaned and pulled a cushion over his head when Jabari stumbled into him.

Jabari was still shirtless. He realized he had left his clothing out on the rocks near the sea and needed to find it. He could feel the drumming through the stone of the caves. The dancing music of the Hadem was exhilarating, wild, and free. Radakar had said the Hadem danced day and night to build their protection. Well, if they had danced the night before, Jabari had been too deeply asleep to hear it. He needed his clothes.

He tossed another pillow onto Deto's head as he passed, walking through corridors lit by holes carved into the ceiling, letting the sun into the labyrinthine living spaces.

After a while, Jabari walked, blinking, into the sunshine. It took him a few breaths to catch his bearings. When he could see again, he noticed rows of the Hadem dancing in the center of the village. Their dance was done in simultaneous rhythm, in rows and then in circles, a weaving, stomping, shaking mass of people.

Their movement wasn't mere dancing, though. The dancers were weaving a prayer, a call. They were building protection that joined with the magic of the sea creatures. Jabari pulled his gaze away from the mesmerizing dance to see Isika approaching him. She was staring at his torso but pulled her eyes up to his face after a heartbeat or two, eyebrows high.

"Um, where are your clothes?" she asked.

Jabari looked down, grinning. "You don't like this look?"

Isika scowled at him. "Don't be vain."

"I don't know where they are, actually," he said. "I left them out to dry last night."

He looked around, feeling groggy and hungry. His eyes landed on a shelf beside the cave's opening, and he spotted a familiar ser. Someone had folded his clothes and left them on the shelf.

"Hey, here they are," he said, after checking to see whether the whole pile was his. "That was nice. They're so kind to us, here." He pulled his shirt over his head.

"They are. Do you have time to talk?"

"Yes," he said. "I would love to talk to you. I'm famished, though!"

"They have breakfast ready. We can take some to a quiet spot."

There was a large pot cooking over a communal fire, and Isika helped herself to some cooked grains sweetened with fruit, handing Jabari a bowl and taking some for herself. They walked to a hollow in the stones and sat down.

While they ate, Isika told Jabari about the ceremony and the clarity it had given her. Jabari told her what Radakar had said at the fire the night before. Isika looked at his face, thoughtfully, and he reached out to grab her hand.

"I think that's an interesting take," she said. "It's as though you feel that learning skills would be arrogant, but the elder is saying that receiving all the good things that come from your life as a son of the elders is more arrogant than becoming brilliant would be."

"Yeah. I still don't know what to think about it all."

"I don't like being weak when I should be strong," Isika said after a minute.

"There is just one clear thing," Jabari replied. "We have to defeat the Desert King."

"And get Aria back. And you need to figure out how to really use your gifting."

"And I need to figure out how to really use my gifting."

They smiled at each other, and Jabari felt some of the pain of the night before ease. He felt less alone.

CHAPTER 15

Benayeem stood with his hands behind his back and his eyes closed, listening. He knew that if he opened his eyes, he would see the dancing. Now, however, he was listening to what was underneath the music—the peculiar and specific song of the Hadem, the harmonized life song of the Dancers. Ben knew they stayed in their village to protect the song, themselves, and their dance from the Desert King, but he couldn't help wondering what would happen if everyone could hear them.

The song was long and intricate. It unfolded in myriad directions. Ben heard driving beats, inner drummers who mirrored the actual drummers who sat and played for the dancers. He heard long, clear tones and melodies that dipped and rose. Staccato beats. A driving bass line like the depths of the ocean. He stood, immersed in the peace and harmony of these songs. No dissonant sounds, no ill-matched tones or screams. It was restful.

One of the songs separated from the others and became louder. Ben opened his eyes, startled. The elder named Radakar stood very close to him. The man was short and stocky, with long blond and white hair interwoven with ribbons.

"Come," he said. "They are wrapping up the song now, and you and I have much to talk about."

"We do?" Ben asked, clearing his throat.

"You want to hear about our song, don't you?" Radakar asked.

Ben nodded.

"Come to Vita's cave. She has asked to speak with you."

Benayeem looked around for a friend to bring with him. Isika and Jabari weren't there. Brigid was occupied with learning the steps of one of the dances. Ben watched her, struck by the sight of Brigid learning to dance. He didn't see anyone else he knew. Very well. He turned to follow the elder.

They walked through a corridor of white stone to the cave of the elders. Ben had been here last year, and as he ducked into the arch at the opening of the cave, he recognized the cool, weighty feeling of the cave. He hadn't noticed how hot it was outside. Vita sat on a short stool, surrounded by people sitting on square pillows. Ben heard her gravelly song as Radakar bowed. Ben followed his lead. Then they sat on two of the cushions. In the silence, Benayeem took a moment to look around.

There were four people in addition to Vita and Radakar. They wore the patterns of elders—beads and ribbons woven into their hair in the way of the Hadem, but with three black bands on the right sides of their faces. Vita had a sky-blue ribbon in addition to the three black ones. *High elder*, Ben thought.

His skin prickled. There he sat, the single Maweel boy in the room, raised by Workers who had abandoned the dance many generations ago. Ben was used to being surrounded by pale-skinned people, but not by friendly pale-skinned people, and he didn't feel comfortable in this circle. It didn't feel safe. He sighed and closed his eyes. Listening to lifesong was so much more straightforward than looking at faces.

"You have a heavy heart, young one," Vita said. "Your gift shows you the trouble of the world?"

Ben opened his eyes. He nodded slowly. "Yours doesn't?" he asked.

All around, the elders shifted and smiled, or even chuckled at his question. Vita spoke again.

"Our gift is nothing like yours, young one. You are very strong, stronger than any we have seen."

Ben sat and stared at Vita for a moment. He looked around at the other elders and found them looking back at them. Radakar had a faint smile on his face.

"Are you surprised to hear that, young one?" Vita asked. "We told you when you came last that we only hear the song of the dance. We do not know of anyone else who can hear the song of every living thing, the moods, the intent, the connections of every living thing. It is an enormous gift."

Too much of a gift, Ben thought. It could be the end of him. But things had changed a lot for Ben as he went from feeling as though he was on the edge of insanity to understanding what he heard. Then, with Ivram, Ben had learned to control the sounds —at least somewhat. His hearing didn't rule his life as much anymore.

But its strength seemed meaningless, especially when he was with the others. Jabari and Isika's gifts were so much more useful than his. Even Abbas, whose power was only in his training and ability to fight, was mightier than Benayeem.

"But if I am the only one," he finally said, "who will teach me to control it?"

"Ah," Vita exclaimed, sitting forward and slapping her hands on her knees. "That is the right question, young one." She sat back, apparently not bothered to *answer* the question.

Ben looked around. Who could show him? He waited, but apparently, they wanted him to answer the question. Fine, then.

"Ivram and Olumi have taught me about the room," he said. "I have learned to go inside and shut the doors, so I am not overwhelmed by the strength of what I hear. This has kept me from going mad, at times when I thought I would become insane. But lately, people wonder if I hear truly, or if the king is deceiving me. What will happen if the king realizes he can reach me?"

"Your sister, the lost one, communicates with you?" Vita asked.

Ben nodded. "She was the first to realize she could do it." He felt tears prickling behind his eyes. "She has sent me the music of the sea. It's how we knew to come here."

The elders looked at each other. "Yes," Radakar said finally. "I can see why people wonder if you hear correctly. It would be a powerful thing if the king could use the betrayal poison within Aria to send you false images. We can help a little with that. But we cannot ease your burden. You feel more than most people feel. It is a gift with two faces, something that both helps and hurts. It is a good kind of suffering because it is a kind of kinship with the Shaper."

Ben looked up at that. He had been fighting tears, ashamed of the emotions that threatened to pull him under. But the thought that he was similar to the Shaper in this way was a new one. It was true, he realized. Nenyi also saw many things all at once. Infinitely joyful and infinitely brokenhearted, Ben had heard Ivram say, and the songs of the Maweel danced between these twin feelings of joy and grief.

Ben sat a little straighter. Nenyi also cried under the weight of the world—all the tiny rivulets of poison running through the veins of people who should know better, all the ways people betrayed one another, attacked and bit and clawed with smiles on their faces. Ben knew how duplicitous many people in the world were because he couldn't help hearing. He heard the songs. He couldn't block them out. But the Shaper also knew.

"Tell me as much as you can about how to hear only what is true," Ben said.

"We only have a little knowledge that will be useful, but what we have, we will give freely," Vita said. "You will have to learn the rest by trusting in your gift and acknowledging its strength. Even if it can be misused, it is strong. Even if it makes you feel weak, your gift is strong. And it is a gift! The Uncreated One gave it to you when you didn't even ask for it. Maybe that feels like a curse sometimes, but Nenyi is eternal, forever, infinite, and all-knowing."

Her words washed over Ben, healing some of the ache in his soul. He settled back to listen. The discussion went on for a long time. Servants brought food and cold tea, and the elders told Ben what they knew of guarding their song. They hoped that he could translate their knowledge into something that would help in his situation. Ben paid close attention.

The Hadem guarded their song by not reacting to threats to their music. They stayed constant by digging into what the song meant, what Nenyi asked of them, and how she tied herself to them. Vita explained that if they tried to fight the creeping dread that always wanted to come into the song, it was as though the fear expanded. But when they simply listened, Nenyi brought the music back. It was not what Ben had thought. Again, it was surrender rather than force. He didn't really understand, but he tried to absorb it. Perhaps some of it would be useful one day.

A great commotion from outside finally drew the conversation to a close, and Ben realized that no light came through the holes in the cave walls. They had spoken from morning till night, and it was time for the evening meal and dancing. He wondered how much of the dance Brigid had learned and if she would join in that evening. And then he wondered whether the commotion outside had anything to do with people looking for him. They probably hadn't even noticed he was gone, he thought wryly.

When Ben and the elders emerged from the cave, though, he saw that the noise was something else entirely. A dozen Karee warriors stood around a tall man who Ben knew to be the Karee king. What were they doing here? Ben looked around for his friends, and his eyes landed on Ivy and Deto standing side by side. He ran to them, shutting the door of his inner room to the clamor that came from the collective surprise of the meeting.

"What is it?" he asked.

Deto shot him a sideways glance. "Where have you been?" he asked.

Ivy snorted. "He knows perfectly well where you've been," she said. "He's just jealous and wants you to say it. Someone came and told us that the elders wanted to talk with you."

"All day," Deto said.

Ben looked at his friend. Jealousy, that was the sour note he heard in his music. Did Deto want to sit with the elders?

"We talked about my gift, how it burdens me, and how to keep it from deceiving me or making me insane."

Deto's face changed. "I don't envy you that," he said. "It's just that sometimes I feel invisible around you and all the other incredibly gifted people around here." Ivy reached out and squeezed Deto's hand. He shifted from foot to foot. "Do we know what is happening yet?" he asked.

"This makes me nervous."

Abbas overheard and came to stand beside them.

"There is no need to be nervous. The Karee have heard of the threat from the sea and have come to help. Don't be deceived by their looks."

"Wait, are they not warriors?" Deto asked. The men were enormous, with gold in their ears and noses, on their fingers and ankles. The only thing they had more than gold was weaponry. All shapes and sizes of bows and swords draped over them.

Abbas elbowed Deto gently. "Of course, they are warriors. But they are on our side." His mouth twisted to one side. "Although I'm not sure how much it will matter when they board that boat. Karee people are not used to the sea."

"What boat?" Ben asked.

Ivy turned and pointed at the cove behind them. The last colors of the sunset were disappearing, and the stars were coming out over the gently lapping water. Ben smelled food cooking. Then his eyes widened. In the distance was a large ship, armed and ready.

"There are more where that came from," Ivy said, her face gleeful. "But that one is for us. We're pulling the king's attention away from the village. We're going to sea."

CHAPTER 16

Herrith went through the motions of his days in a way that looked like the one that had come before, but nothing was the same.

Since the adoption magic had set into him, he was always keenly aware of Aria. His daughter. The words reverberated through him. He felt the king's power against her. He felt her pain. He felt her joy. It was the first time he had ever been a father. He had never married, never had children. There was no one to continue the line of the golden thread, the Circle warriors. Herrith had no son or daughter to continue after him. Except, now, there was Aria. Hope bloomed at the thought of her, marred only by the fact that she was still desperately impaired by the poison arrow.

Herrith knew Gavi was looking for magic that could fight back against the king's claim on Aria, but they needed to find something before the king decided it was time to attack. The Hadem had strong protective magic of their own, and if King Ikajo attacked at the wrong moment, their power would be flung back toward them.

The king brooded, held long unfruitful meetings, paced, and waited. Herrith continued trying to secretly alleviate the harsh burden of the king's wrath on Aria. It was dangerous work, and the tension of the secret bond combined with the waiting was keeping Herrith up at night. Sometimes he saw the king look at his daughter quizzically. Herrith didn't need to have mind reading magic to knew that Ikajo wondered why Aria wasn't weaker from his poison. Herrith was careful to hide his own magic traces behind shields. It was harrowing. They waited for some sign or word from Isika, and Herrith lay awake in the early hours of the morning, wondering if this was the day the king would ruin all of their lives.

Late one night, Herrith walked upstairs from a lower deck, longing for the kind of deep rest that wasn't available to him anymore. He was about halfway up the stairs when pain flared around his heart. He cried out and stumbled on the steps, falling and hitting his cheek on the railing. The pain could only mean one thing: Aria was in danger.

He pulled himself up and ran, hoisting his robes, knees protesting as his feet pounded against the stairs to the upstairs deck.

There were three guards at the king's chamber door. They moved to block him from entrance, though he vastly outranked them. He tried not to show his reaction, which was pure terror for Aria at their refusal to let him pass. They could not know how invested he was.

"Why are you blocking my way?" he asked.

"The king said no one may enter," one guard replied, his eyes darting to Herrith's and then away.

"If you do not let me in," Herrith said, rage burning a hole in his chest, "I will tell the king about your secret wife. You know the king forbids marriage among his guard."

The man's eyes widened, and to Herrith's dismay, filled with tears. He felt a sharp pang of regret. Herrith didn't want to cause pain or fear, but his survival had depended on his ability to gather information for as long as he could remember. He collected gossip about the people near him like a raven collects bits of string and mirrors. What he gathered kept him safe. He masked his magic and any bits of love or longing with all the power in his line of warriors of the circle. His people had been charged with the job of watching over any who were loyal to Nenyi, who stood against the creeping magic of Mugunta.

The guard stepped out of the way, and Herrith burst into the room. He realized his mistake too late. His urgency would make Ikajo suspicious. Sure enough, when the king turned to him, his eyes glittered with fury and suspicion.

Herrith thought fast, taking in the room, his heart pounding in his throat as he tried to get himself under control.

In his first days on the ship, King Ikajo had spoken words from the Great Waste that pooled into a black marble floor like the one in the king's palace. A few crystals and chains hung overhead. In the center of the room, Aria sat on a chair with her head lolling to one side, and tears running down her dusky cheeks.

The pain was unbearable.

The worst part of Herrith's life work was standing by while someone was in pain. He often needed to wait and watch when the king was cruel, because of his long-reaching cause. Herrith did not have the power to dethrone the king and take the kingdom. All his life, he had been waiting to assist someone to overthrow the kingdom and build something new. If he moved against Ikajo now to stop him from hurting Aria, all this preparation would be in vain. Because of the adoption magic, though, the king's attack on Aria was experienced by Herrith. He felt as though Ikajo was tearing his heart out.

"Do you know what I have discovered?" Ikajo asked Herrith. His eyes were shifting back and forth and he was panting heavily.

Herrith was barely breathing. This was the king's most dangerous mood. Herrith had seen many people die when the king was in a mood like this. But there still might be a way to recover. There might be a way out.

"What? Brightness? What is going on? Is is the child sick?"

"What?" Ikajo's eyes skidded to his daughter. "Her? No, she is not sick. I have increased the strength of my hold on her. I have found her to be strangely non-compliant lately. Her only concern should be to make me happy. It is... disconcerting to find her any other way." He turned away from Aria dismissively.

A strengthened arrow would account for pain, Herrith thought. He wanted to speak, wanted to ask her what was the matter. He bit down on his lip, hard.

"Don't you want to know what I have discovered? the king asked.

"Of course, Brightness."

"The girl has managed to reach her brother with those dreams of hers. I have interfered...but I sense them. She has ruined my plans."

"I am sorry, Brightness," Herrith said. He wished for the gift of communicating without words. He wanted this terrible conversation to be over so the king would leave and he could check on Aria.

"They know where we are," the king mused. "Maybe we can use their knowledge to our advantage?"

Was it safe to ask if Aria could go to her room? Herrith kept his eyes down, trying to send love through the air to his daughter, listening for any indication of the king's mood changing

"Use their knowledge, Brightness? In what way?"

"Sometimes you are so stupid. Which one are you, anyway?"

The king knew perfectly well which red robe Herrith was. Ikajo could sense his magic. Herrith played along and lifted the hood from his head.

"Ah, my less brilliant cousin. If they know we are here, they will come to us to protect the shoreline. We will fight them here, on these dangerous seas, before we attack the Hadem. They will play into our hands, because if we overwhelm the Maweel at sea, the Hadem's protections will be torn down. And we have the advantage here at sea, with the sea people our allies. You know we do. How can you not know that? Why would you ask such a stupid question?" His voice grew into a roar, and out of the corner of his eye, Herrith saw Aria flinch. "I am surrounded by idiots!"

Herrith seethed inwardly. *I'm asking how because I didn't want to display all my knowledge. I'm asking how because I don't want to feed you information and you don't want me to be smart.*

To the king, he said, "You are right, I am stupid, Bright One."

"What can we discern from this information?" the king asked. "We know that somehow they got away from the worker village, though we steeped it in poison." He clenched his fists. "Those stupid children. They go through my traps. I wish I had killed them all!" The king screamed.

Aria flinched again. Her eyes flew open and she pleaded

with him silently. Herrith willed her to see that it wasn't safe to communicate right now.

"Do you really want to say this in front of the child, if she has been noncompliant lately?" Herrith asked suddenly.

The king swung around and glared at him. Herrith stood with his head bowed, willing the king to calm down. He felt prickling at the edges of the adoption magic and realized that Aria—brave Aria—was trying to send him courage.

The king looked at Aria. "You are right, cousin. She is not trustworthy. We will wait and see if she improves any over the next days. Where is that servant of hers?"

"I'll get her," Herrith said, "and then we can plan in peace."

He walked to the door very, very calmly, hearing the tinkling and shaking of the king's anger in the chains that hung from the ceiling, knowing that every single one of them was teetering at the threat of sudden death when the king was like this. He walked to the door and opened it silently.

"Mara," he called softly. She wasn't far away. "Come and take the child to her room."

Mara bustled in after him, seemingly unshaken by the wrath of the king. She seemed to have moved to a place beyond fear. She walked to Aria and took her by the hand.

"Bedtime, young one," she murmured.

"Do not be kind to her!" the king shouted suddenly. "She has been very disobedient and sneaky!"

Mara froze, then continued to pull Aria out of the chair gently. Herrith felt like he was coming out of his skin, he was flushed all over with panic. This was an impossible situation. As a servant, Mara could never be anything but perfectly respectful when touching a member of the royal family, but the king hated to see kindness shown to anyone who was out of favor with him. The only thing Mara could do was get Aria away from the king.

Being out of his sight was the only thing that would save them.

Surely Mara knew this. She had been a servant of Azariyah, a second mother to Amani when she was a teenager. Herrith could barely breathe. She would remember. She *must* remember.

She did. She glanced up only once, to cast a worried look in Herrith's direction, and to his surprise, he saw that her worry was not for Aria, not for herself, but for him. Mara was worried about leaving Herrith in the king's presence.

She didn't need to waste her worry on him.

Herrith was Damek's son, in the line of the gold cord. He was stronger than anyone knew. He gave Mara the tiniest of nods, as she went past, Aria leaning heavily on her arm. The door closed behind them, and Herrith could breathe again.

"You were saying, Bright One?" he asked, clearing his throat.

The king jerked his head up. "We are going to war. As soon as we can."

Suddenly Ikajo marched over to Herrith and backhanded him across the face, hard, once, twice, three times. Unwanted tears sprang to Herrith's eyes at the pain.

"Don't think I don't see. You don't want me to hurt Aria. I worry, Cousin, that you have forgotten who you serve. But because I can see your disloyalty, I will hurt you instead."

Herrith tasted blood, holding his head down, shocked and dismayed by this development. His head was ringing, but even so, he permitted himself the smallest feeling of triumph at the king's words. Ikajo could never know that this was by far what he preferred.

CHAPTER 17

The ship was a masterpiece—tall with carved masts and full sails. Every part of its framework was graceful, like the Hadem and their caves. Isika knew she would have appreciated its beauty more if she wasn't sick with worry. She was afraid for Aria and for all of Maween, and she was worried about her own magic, which seemed cloudy and distant. She couldn't locate the lifesong of the earth, normally so close to her. Her magic felt fuzzy, as though someone had thrown a blanket over it. Jabari had begun to actively try to strengthen his magic, and Isika was glad because she knew they couldn't count on hers. At least not until something changed.

Most of Isika's waking moments were filled with thoughts of Aria. Isika woke up with Aria's name in her heart. She thought about her before she fell asleep. Isika wanted her sister back.

As she boarded the ship with Nat close behind her, she was caught up in memories of Aria when she was younger, before she was given over. Aria was always laughing back then, the easiest little girl to love. Even as a toddler in the desert, she found beautiful things—smooth stones or tiny cactus flowers—to give to their mother to make her smile.

Isika wanted to keep her mind on those memories, but today as always, her thoughts flashed forward to the stunned look on Aria's face when Nirloth announced he was sending her out. She remembered the way Aria sobbed all night, terrified and full of grief.

Isika was wiping tears from her face as she stepped onto the ship deck. She took a shaky breath and looked around at the crew. It was surreal to be on the water, preparing to sail out and draw the king's attack away from the shoreline. In the end, the Karee warriors had decided they could be most helpful if they stayed back to help guard the shore from any breaks in the line of ships. The only warrior coming with them was Abbas, who didn't shrink from anything, even from the ocean.

Maybe, Isika thought, *he'll reconsider. Maybe he won't attack.*

But she knew it was wishful thinking. Ikajo did not have mercy in his nature.

Crew members walked back and forth, stowing goods and fiddling with ropes. Isika caught sight of Jabari, who was staring at her. She looked back at him, waiting for him to say something. In this danger, he had become infinitely more precious to her until he was so radiant that she almost couldn't bear it. His face now was faintly wry.

"What?" she asked out loud.

You need to make a speech, he told her in her head.

Oh. Isika swiped under her eyes again and stood as tall as she could, holding her staff in one hand. She felt the circlet start to glow as she settled into her queen magic and turned to give the crew a speech. As they realized she was about to speak, the

Hadem crew members nudged one another and stilled, turning to face her until every one of the people on the deck was quiet, waiting. What should she say?

"I don't know how to give a speech to a ship crew," she murmured to Nat.

"Just go on," Nat said. "You'll be fine."

Isika decided to begin with the facts.

"We sail today," she said.

They cheered. It wasn't what Isika was expecting, and she blinked, glancing at Nat, who smiled wryly. Isika went on, her voice tentative.

"We go in the name of the Uncreated One. We go to prevent a takeover of your lands. And we go gently if we can. If we cannot be peaceful, though, we will fight to protect our lands from the spreading poison of Mugunta and the Great Waste. Mugunta wants to channel all of this through King Ikajo, the Desert King, who has taken our beloved ones. We answer in power and humility. I will work as much as I can to protect each one of you. I am your friend, your help, and your queen."

The people were mostly quiet until Isika's last words, then cheers erupted and took over the small space on the top deck. At a command from the captain, the sailors ran to take their places, leaving the travelers standing at the railing, watching as they lifted the anchor and set sail.

The captain stood close to Isika, a stocky Hadem man Isika vaguely recognized as a leader in the dance. He had long, braided gray hair, tied with over a dozen ribbons. His beard was braided, too, and wore wide-legged embroidered pants tucked into leather boots, with a vest that wrapped around his waist.

His crew members did their jobs seamlessly, tugging ropes, tying or loosening knots, and cleaning as they went. It made

Isika's head hurt to think of everything that went into sailing a ship. She appreciated not knowing the details. Her mind felt full enough as it was.

"When do you think the king will attack?" the captain asked her.

She looked at him, surprised.

"It's not even a sure thing that he will," she said. "He could have another plan, after all."

Wishful thinking, not queenly, she heard, and looked up to see Keethior flying above her.

Either come down here or stay out of my conversation, she told him, and he gave a wheezy Othra laugh and flew away.

The captain shifted from foot to foot. "I've been captaining ships for many years, young one," he said. "And I know the king. I haven't been attacked by him, but I've spoken to plenty who have. He's ruthless. He'll attack as soon as he has the chance. He won't hold back."

She stared at him, then at the rapidly receding shore. She looked around at the people who had accompanied her on the journey.

"Then I hope we find some ease at sea first," she said.

But they didn't have any time to rest. They were eating dinner later that night when it started. Isika was staring at her plate, wondering why she felt such deep unease, when a boom shuddered through the little galley. Jabari was on his feet in an instant, Abbas right behind them. They ran out of the room, leaving Isika staring at Benayeem and Nat, eyes wide.

"What was that?" she asked, willing it not to be an attack. They weren't ready. It was too soon.

Ben's face looked gray. "Let's go see," he replied.

They walked out to the deck. Isika felt increasing dread in

her stomach as she walked. Even after hearing the explosion, she wasn't prepared for the sight of a row of ships facing them in the water.

"They weren't there just a minute ago!" she heard a crew member exclaiming. "Where did they come from?"

In the distance, Isika recognized the ships of the sea people; weathered, with red and green flags, beautiful in a stark kind of way. Isika's heart seemed to be beating very fast as though it wanted to escape through her throat, and her eyes opened wide with alarm as she sensed the malevolent force reaching to her from the front ship. She shivered in her loose clothing, despite the heat on the windless night.

"It's him," she said. "We don't get any time after all."

"No," Nat said, her voice grim. "It appears that we don't."

The Desert King sent waves of malice toward Isika, attempting to lock her in a ray of power as he had in the past. She resisted, and the Palipa swarmed around her feet, pressing up against her, keeping her close, keeping her here. Othra flew overhead. Isika had grown and was resilient against the power of the king, but she could sense Aria on that ship, and the need to keep her sister safe nearly pulled Isika off her feet.

Beside her, she felt Benayeem shudder.

Another boom sounded, and this time she saw the cannon send a giant arc of fire straight into the sea, directly in front of one of the ships. Were they simply showing their power to scare Isika and the Hadem? Or were they trying to hit the ships? Isika looked around and saw the sailors swaying as they hauled ropes and took up weapons. They were singing as they did it, weaving protective power. The Hadem's defensive magic was blocking the bolts of energy.

This was so wrong. Surely Ikajo would not command their

ships to be sunk. Whatever his intention, Isika needed to put a stop to it.

She reached deep into the sea, clutching her staff, which glowed brightly in her peripheral vision. Her circlet blazed with heat on her forehead. Isika didn't know what she was about to do—she only needed to respond to this strong feeling, like a magnet drawn deep into the heart of the earth.

She closed her eyes and felt everything—her link to the land, her gift, and power. But then, without warning, the link fizzled and burned away. Isika opened her eyes, panicked, and reached out again. But there was nothing, no matter how hard she searched. She was dry of magic; she felt only the barest scrapings.

Another boom. This time, it hit close to the protective barrier in front of them. Isika saw the marks where it burned some of the web away. Panic erupted. Jabari came close to Isika and put an arm around her. The captain approached. Isika's ears were ringing from the noise of the last blast.

"The barrier won't hold out against much more," the captain said, standing next to Isika. "We're not as strong here as we are on land. And the sea people have the power of the Great Waste with them."

"What's going on?" Ben asked from beside Jabari. Jabari was silent, but his eyes were deeply concerned. Nat's jaw was clenched and she was gripping her spear so hard it looked as though it might snap in half.

"You mean with me?" Isika asked. Her voice cracked.

"Yes, with you. You have the strangest music."

Another boom. All around, the light of tiny fires burned. This bolt hit directly in front of Isika, and she saw a spiderweb of cracks hit every part of the barrier. Like

Azariyah, she thought, when the king had tried to burn down the city.

"I can't reach my magic," she said. "I can't connect with the earth or find my gift."

Jabari stared at her, then turned to look out at the sea. He pulled his arm away and gripped the railing, hard.

Ben nodded. "I can hear her," he murmured.

"Aria?" Isika whispered.

Ben leaned forward over the railing, straining to hear, and Isika fell silent so her brother could listen to their sister's music. She felt her heart beating rapidly. She was the queen, and she needed to command the sailors of these ships. But her magic was gone. She reached out again. Nothing.

"Isika," Ben said, his voiced hushed with awe. "Call the Naia. I can hear them."

Isika leaned forward. She hadn't even thought of calling the Naia. Another boom sounded, and the spider cracks around the protective barrier stretched until they touched overhead. Isika heard Ivy's voice from somewhere nearby. She saw Jabari shouting into the wind, using his gift to make tall waves rise up. Directly before her, a giant wave rose.

Isika called the Naia.

Friends, she called. *We need your help. Come if you can, come and help us.*

And she waited. She sang lightly under her breath, songs to Nenyi. *Help us, help us, help us,* she called.

It felt like forever as she stood there waiting, feeling energy pouring off Jabari as he and Ivy caused the waves to roll against the hulls of the ships. She watched Ben as he leaned over the railing, listening.

And then they came. Naia after Naia swam to the surface of

the water, leaping out into the night air, arcing diamonds of water in their wakes. They leapt and tumbled, almost laughing, before joining as one in knocking against a small ship. They had far more might than seemed possible. They were ancient ones, friends of Nenyi, and held large pools of magic in their compact bodies.

But what was that? Nat clutched Isika's arm as another creature surfaced. Isika stared as it emerged, rubbing at her eyes. Finally, she realized that the huge thing she was looking at was a creature's tail. She gasped as the rest of it surfaced. It was a whale, five times as long as any of their ships, swimming around them until Isika felt dizzy. The tail came up and flipped water onto the deck of one of the sea people's ships, causing its magical cannons to sputter and cease shooting.

Isika started to cheer, but just then, another boom sounded. The spiderweb of fire reached throughout the barrier, all the way around it, and broke through, pushing Isika back, breaking the railing. Nat grabbed Isika and yanked her off her feet, reaching for Ben as well. She wasn't fast enough. Ben was over the edge. Ben was gone. Isika shrieked and ran to the side of the boat, grabbing the broken rail and staring at the sea. She had the barest impression of the whale swimming away with Ben curling on its body, and then he was gone from her sight.

CHAPTER 18

Aria did everything she could to fight off her father's influence, but it was no good. She had been barely lucid ever since he sent the arrow burrowing deeper into her heart. Everything had shrunk down to this moment, to her breath wheezing in and out of her lungs, her arms like dead sticks at her sides, her hair sticking to her face.

Don't. Fight. Isika. Aria told herself. But again and again, the Desert King used her power to send bolts of energy across the sea.

"That's right!" he told her now. "We'll blow them up. Then use the power of the Whisperer to take back the land across the seas."

Herrith dabbed at her forehead with a cloth. Sweat poured down Aria's face, soaking her clothing. Her eyes were closed, but Isika knew it was Herrith because he was humming.

"You can fight this," he whispered, and if she could have spoken she would have told him that she was trying to fight with every molecule inside of her.

Aria, called a voice. *Aria, don't give up.*

I thought you only spoke to her, she answered in her head.

I'm speaking to you, aren't I? The Othra's voice was wry.

Okay, okay, a little late, but okay. What?

I can help you, he said.

Come and help then, she answered.

I can't come there. Here is what you must do. Look at your hands. Find yourself in the maelstrom.

That's your help?

That's the beginning.

What comes next?

First look at your hands.

She peeled her eyes open, surprised, in a way, to find that she still had a body, that she wasn't just a mass of magic and will, struggling like a worm under the pin of her father's power. She sobbed under her breath. How she longed to be away from him, away from this place. If she could go back, she would change everything, she would never have listened to his call, she would have resisted the arrow while she still had the chance, and not locked herself and everyone else into this intense battle of betrayal magic. Her hands. She was supposed to be looking at her hands.

She looked down to see them lying in her lap like two stunned animals. They didn't feel connected to her.

I'm looking at my hands, she said.

Good. Now move them.

She would have rolled her eyes, but her face wasn't listening to her commands. She looked as far as she could, trying to understand what was happening to her. It seemed that her father was using her as a conduit for his own magic, piling their magic together, or putting it into the same stream. She didn't know the rules. And because he was using her this way, she was lost to herself. But she could see, and she slowly began to realize where she was. She was sitting on a chair on the top deck of the ship, looking out over the ocean. The sky grew dark and there was a line of ships in front of her. She noticed their beauty, even from her stuck place. They looked like intricately carved birds. As Aria watched, another energy bolt arced at the lead ship, and she stared in horror as a few black shadows plunged into the sea.

Move your hands, the command came again.

I... can't, she told the Othra.

Try. You are still there, in your body. You have to take it back.

She tried to wiggle just one of her fingers, but everything felt so far away. Herrith was hovering over her now, speaking to someone in sharp whispers.

"If we can wake her," he said. "We can get her out of here. But it's like she's not even there. I feel he will use her all up, and she will be gone forever."

Another person came close. The person smelled of spring time, despite the salty air. Smelled of walks in the garden in the rain.

Aria closed her eyes and thought of her mother with equal parts love and despair. Her mother combing the knots out of her hair with oil, braiding or twisting it. Humming over her when she was little with knobby knees, stroking her head so she would go to sleep. Calling her outside to play. Her mother in the garden, in the rain.

This was not the same smell, but it was as close to it as she got these days.

She moved her hand, just her thumb, just the tiniest bit, but as she did so, it was as though air rushed back into her lungs and she was back with herself, promising her poor tired body that she would never leave again.

Mama loved you, she told herself. *That makes it worth it to stay.* The noise came back all in a rush, and she heard the sounds of the cannons, heard the screams and the crackling of fire, heard the breath in her ear, turned.

"I'm here," she whispered.

"I'm so glad," Gavi said. "Come on, I have to keep you with us, and I think I know how to do that, but we need to move quickly."

It was a respite. Her father must know that she was untethered now, but he was too busy with the attack to come and capture her again. In the meantime, she felt strange, but strong, with strong arms and legs, and she walked along in Gavi's wake, clinging to his hand.

They climbed down stairs, climbed down and down, into the belly of the ship.

"Where are we going?" she asked.

"You'll see," he told her. "No time or energy wasted on talking, okay?"

"Okay," she murmured.

The went down and down, until they were as far down as they could go, and Aria smelled the stink in the air and cringed away from it. But there was something else, something besides too many sweaty bodies. She felt magic, a whole system of it, a tower of strength.

"Are they magicians?" she asked.

"No," Gavi said. "Although, yes, in a way. Remember, I was telling you? They have been enslaved."

She stumbled on the step. What did he mean? Her head felt fuzzy again, and she fought it off. Aria followed Gavi into a large room, sectioned down the middle, with row after row of people rowing giant, heavy oars. Sweat poured off their faces, and the only air came from the holes that the oars emerged from. She felt surrounded by deep and ancient magic, and for a moment, it shielded her from the tainted magic of her father. But what was it?

"There is only one supervisor," Gavi murmured beside her. The supervisor was peering out a hole in the back of the slave galley and hadn't seen them yet. The people with the oars had, though. Every eye was trained on Aria's face. They watched her closely, impassively. They were of many races. Maweel, like her, which clamored at her, their dark skin shiny with the sheen of sweat, their backs bent by the labor of sitting and rowing, sitting and rowing. Northern people like Deto, pale-skinned Workers, of course, and people who looked like they were either Karee or Gariah.

"Come," Gavi said. "He must not see us."

Aria glanced at the supervisor, who was backing away from the hole in the ship. Gavi pulled her out of the large room and through a narrow corridor, into a quiet room at the back of the ship. Inside, several children were huddled together, clinging tight to an old woman who sang over them. The boat was rocking with the battle, the sounds of booms and faint cries drifting down to these quarters. If the ship sank, Aria realized, there would be no help for the enslaved people here. They wouldn't be able to get out. The children were frightened, and Aria wanted to try to comfort them, but Gavi was pulling her to the other side of the room, where a handful of old men and women sat.

One old man, a northerner with a graying braid, smiled at her as she sat down, his face creased with long lines.

"You managed to bring her, young one," he said to Gavi. "You are more powerful than I first thought."

"Thanks, I think," Gavi said.

He must already know this man, Aria thought.

She looked at her hands and breathed deeply, realizing that down here, despite the heat and stench, she could breathe well and easily.

"Why do I feel better?" she asked boldly, surprising herself.

The man smiled again. "Do you come to us for answers?" he asked. "We are not sages; we are merely people who have been bound by an evil man's chains, far from our homes."

Aria bit her lip, ashamed. But wasn't she a slave also, here against her will?

You are here because he wants you to rule with him. It is different, Nirral said in her mind.

Why are you still talking to me? she asked. *And are you listening to my thoughts?*

These are not ordinary times, daughter, the bird answered.

Gavi spoke, and Aria pulled her attention back to the room she sat in.

"Elder Rema," he said. "Will you help us?" he asked. "I believe that this magic you speak of, for those who have been hurt, pushed down, or enslaved, might be our only hope. We must break Aria free of her father's curse."

"What will you do for us if we help you?" Rema asked. "We are not bent with the desire to help those who have enforced their wills upon us."

"I have not enforced my will upon you," Gavi replied, looking hurt.

"No? Do you row this ship you travel upon? Or do you sit and glide on the network of rowers beneath you, working when you sleep, when you eat better food than we ever will. You walk in the open air, and we are bruised and kept in the shadows."

Outside, another boom sounded. The sky outside, visible through one small hole on each side of the boat, flared with the lights of many fires.

"We are running out of time," Gavi said, his voice subdued. "It does no good to your people if the ship sinks."

"I will not help you out of the goodness of my heart," said Rema. "But I am always willing to bargain."

"What do you want?" Aria asked.

The elder turned his eyes to hers, and she nearly gasped as he held her gaze. His deep magic swirled around her, and she saw a vision for the first time in her life. She saw a small child, black as night, her skin full of stars, weeping.

Nenyi, Nirral said to her.

The child raised her head.

"Freedom," she said, looking at Aria. "When one person cuts another person off from space and time, they are lost in the world without a place to breathe, a space to move, to have the life of the Uncreated One wash over them like water. Every enslaved being is mine. Give them back to me."

The child disappeared and Aria was once again looking into the old man's eyes.

"If you help me defeat my father," Aria said. "I promise you that you will be free."

A whirling, rushing sound filled the little chamber, like a sigh, and Aria felt power enter her bones and muscles. Then in her mind's eye, she was above the boats, seeing through Nirral's eyes. She saw what she must do. Already, three of the other ships were on fire. She must stop this. She must push the boats to shore with her magic, run them to ground. Scatter them. She flew higher. This power was heavy with grief, and Aria found that she was sobbing with the aches in the child Nenyi's skin.

She breathed out, hard, and the boats began to push away from one another, moving faster and faster. She blew harder. Many ships ran aground on an island, scattered far from one another, hitting beach and stone, but Aria's magic kept them from exploding. She must protect the enslaved and other people aboard. More boats ran aground. Now all the ships were distant from one another. Safe. Ashore, far from explosions or fire. She came back to herself like a leaf drifting to the earth. When she woke, her head was cushioned on Gavi's leg. He was stroking her hair.

"Very good, little one," Rema said. "But we are not done."

CHAPTER 19

When Aria fell, it hit Gavi like lightning. He could feel something big happening as she dug deep into the gift of the Shaper for the oppressed. She fell, and the falling reverberated through him. He scooped her close to protect her, even as she left, as her awareness spun far away, into the night. The other elders came close to watch over Aria, and Gavi could feel the peace coming from them. He knew he didn't need to fear their intentions toward Aria.

"What is happening?" Gavi asked Rema, his voice cracking.

"She is finding her way," Rema replied, the creases around his eyes deepening. "But it means that we need to be ready to flee. The king will not like this."

As he spoke, the boat began to move. The children yelped, looking around to see what was happening. One curious boy jumped up and pressed his face to the hole in the side of the ship.

"We're going to the shore," he proclaimed. "Really, really fast!"

Gavi felt a stirring of unease. He couldn't tell if the feeling was from the boat moving so quickly or from what Aria was doing.

"She is very powerful," Rema murmured. "I sense movement from all the ships." He closed his eyes for a moment, and when he opened them, they were full of intent. "Lize," he called to the boy. "Go tell the others to be ready to fight and run. We must get off this ship if she runs it aground."

"If she runs it aground, won't we break apart on the rocks?" Gavi asked.

"That depends on you," Rema replied.

Gavi stared at him. "How does it depend on me?"

"You must help me cushion her magic so it doesn't harm us."

Gavi blinked. In the other room, he heard a commotion—shouts and loud noises. The rowers must be fighting against the supervisors. Near to Gavi, a woman cradled two infants, one in each arm, while another bundled blankets and pieces of clothing together, finding two long strips of fabric and tying one baby to the other woman's back, then turning so the same could be done for her. Both women were Maweel, with the dark brown skin and long limbs of Gavi's adoptive people. One woman turned and looked at him as though she noticed his attention. Gavi could sense the cords of magic that bound her, kept her enslaved. She bowed her head slightly. The Unlike Twins, Rema had called Gavi and Jabari. What rumors had traveled about them, what had been said about them? Whatever it was, Gavi knew they were just brothers, only people who wanted to help. His gifts weren't up to this challenge.

Gavi was alone here. Aria was still far away, leaning against him with her eyes closed, her magic wreaking destruction on the boats. Gavi's "twin" was somewhere on another boat, and maybe still angry with Gavi. Their parents were far. There was no way that Gavi was prepared for the task at hand, but the enslaved woman's eyes still held his, and his heart rose up hot against the injustice for these enslaved people and the girl near to him, so fragile under the king's thrall.

Gavi closed his eyes.

Immediately, he found Aria's powerful net, and the way she blew the ships to shore with her breath. All would crash on the rocks, would splinter to pieces, if Gavi didn't do something. But Gavi was a gatherer! What could he do? *Gatherer*. Gatherer. An idea came to him and he acted immediately, calling forth jungle vines to cover the rocks on the shore. The vines were reluctant to move at first, but eventually, they listened to him, springing up into large untidy nests that formed cushions for the ships, with tentacles that gripped and held the hulls away from the sharp rocks. At the same time, he sensed Rema forming a net to blow back against the boats, to slow their approach.

He rushed back into his body. Then Aria opened her eyes, and Gavi stroked her hair, willing her to be okay after such an immense amount of spent magic.

"Well done, young one," Rema said, "but we are not done yet."

As soon as the words left his mouth, there was an intense explosion. A deafening creak clapped against Gavi's ears, a sound like a ship breaking apart.

"It's him," Aria whispered. "He is very angry. He is looking for me."

Screams came from the rowing room.

"What do we do?" a young man cried, running into the room and looking at Rema, who was standing now, holding onto the wall as the ship threatened to break apart.

"We build a raft for our people," the elder said. "This is what we have been saving our magic for, all these days, all these songs."

The man calmed immediately. He was a northerner like the old man, his long hair still black, braided in one long braid that fell behind him.

"You lead them," Rema went on. "Have courage, son. We are ready for this."

"Come with me, please, Elder."

Rema looked at Gavi. "Help me, young one, my legs don't work so well these days."

"Why did the Gariah even bring you aboard?" Gavi asked as he went to help the older man. "Why would they make someone of your years work like this?"

Rema looked at Gavi with dancing eyes. "What makes you think they know I am aboard?" he asked.

"Oh," Gavi said. "Okay, then."

Things moved quickly after that. Gavi had a weak Aria on one arm, and the elder on the other. In the main room where just a few minutes ago all the people had been endlessly rowing, an entirely different scene played out. A giant hole had been torn in the side of the ship, water flowing in each time the boat tipped, which it did often. No one was sitting anymore, and people shrieked, clinging to one another as the water threatened to overwhelm them. Rema began to sing, and as he did, the people calmed. Many voices joined with his, and a protective shield formed between the ship and the water, preventing any more from flowing into the hull. The young man began to call out instructions, and the people brought their oars to the hole, throwing them through the shield into the sea, all the while, singing. As Gavi watched, breathless with fear and wonder, the oars joined together, golden threads weaving them into a mass.

The ship shuddered without pause, and new cracks split the hull. The people sang faster and worked harder. Suddenly, the raft was still and ready, tossing lightly in the rolling sea, its edge flush with the ship.

Gavi couldn't see how the raft could survive with the ocean stirred up as it was, but it seemed that the same magic that had woven the raft together and protected the ship also had the power to calm the sea around it. There was a circle of calm water around the raft's edges. People began to board the raft, women and children first, climbing out of the tear in the ship's hull. Rema climbed aboard the raft as well, holding a hand out to Aria to follow him, and as they walked onto the strangely stable vessel, it stretched and stretched, forming a barrier against the roiling sea.

Gavi held back, waiting for the others to board. He could still hear screams and explosions from the upper levels. The king's anger was raging. A few crew members ran down the stairs, but enslaved men who remained at the entrance fought them quickly and efficiently. Gavi began to help, using his skills to disarm and incapacitate the men without killing them. Finally, everyone was aboard the raft, over fifty people, and Gavi followed the men who had been protecting the door as they ran to join the others.

Just then, there was a thunder of footsteps down the stairs, and when Gavi turned to block this last intruder, he found himself face to face with the king.

No, thought Gavi, in a panic. They had to get away. He couldn't allow the king to stop the raft.

"Go!" he screamed, turning to catch Rema's eyes. They had to go. The man nodded once, and the raft began to move. Aria screamed Gavi's name, holding out her hands. Gavi's heart pounded, but he knew they needed to get away before the king could break the raft.

He turned and ran straight at the king, calling out every bit of gifting and power in him as he collided with the man. He felt the rolling power of the king immediately. It was enough to crush him instantly. Gavi did not have the power of Isika, Aria, or even Jabari. He was only Gavi, a gatherer, a rescued one. But the king was distracted by his anger over Aria and his slaves escaping. His anger shook the whole ship until the wood gave one last shriek and broke apart. Seething water filled the hull as the ship splintered. Gavi and the king disappeared into the inky waters, still locked in one another's arms.

GAVI WOKE SLOWLY AND PAINFULLY. It hurt to breathe. He opened his eyes and saw a dark sky with smudges of light at the horizon. Dawn was approaching. Gavi was wet, and hurt, but he was alive. He tried to get his bearings, to figure out where he was. After a few long, painful blinks, he realized he was lying on a sandy beach, half in the water, waves washing over him. He was shaking with cold. He groaned and sat up. Bits of wood were everywhere, but he didn't see the king, or anyone else, for that matter. The beach was different from the harbor at the worker village. It was lush and green with vines, scattered with tall trees that had feathery fronds coming from their tops. He had never seen this place before. An island, then.

Gavi hoisted himself to standing, his legs wobbly. He checked himself for wounds but didn't find any, though he was freezing, with cramped muscles and joints that didn't want to move.

Where was Aria?

Panic nearly choked him, and he fell onto his knees. Where was the raft, and the enslaved? Where was the friend he had spent his life trying to protect for the last years? He pressed his face to the sand. Slowly, calm returned to him. Aria had left on the raft, with the enslaved, who had successfully escaped. Surely they would protect her. He sat up. Actually, with them, Aria was safer than she had been since she went to her father in the Desert City. But Gavi knew she would die if she left Ikajo's circle of power.

Gavi needed to find her and make sure Rema and the others didn't try to leave with her. Had all the ships washed up on this island? Where was Herrith? Where was Mara? Had anyone else survived?

Gavi pushed himself to his feet and started walking, hardly knowing where he was going, only knowing he was weak with hunger and thirst.

He walked parallel to the shore, eyeing the thick jungle, scanning the water and the beach for signs of others people. He and the king had washed out of the ship together, but Gavi didn't see a sign of the older man. He saw detritus from the crash— rags and sticks. He had tried to keep the ship together, but the king's anger had destroyed. Gavi examined every pile of debris, searching for human life. Food would be equally welcome. He was dizzy and his head hurt. His lungs hurt. He must have choked on water and coughed it up before he woke.

The light grew on the wrecked beach. Piles of rags and wood were everywhere. As he approached one heap of rags, it moved, startling him so much that he jumped and nearly fell. He stared at the pile. A hand popped out of the mess, startling him further. It was not the light brown, ringed hand of the king.

This was a long arm and long hand, dark brown, and bare. Gavi walked closer.

"Hello?" he called. "Are you okay?"

There was more rustling, and then a Maweel boy with short curly hair sat up, blinking.

"Gavi? Is that you?"

Benayeem. Gavi hollered and ran toward his friend, stooping and pulling him into a hug. Ben groaned.

"Sorry," Gavi said, releasing him. "Are you hurt?"

Ben looked down at himself.

"I don't think so," he said. "At least, not badly. Just achy and bruised. Where are we? How did you get here? How did I get here?"

Gavi grinned, thankful to be with another human being, but especially a friend. "I washed up when the Desert King broke our ship to bits. I don't know how you got here."

Ben stared at him. "The last thing I remember is looking out at the ships firing at us." His eyes grew unfocused. "No, I remember a song, a long deep song." He inhaled, his eyes growing wide and filling with tears. "The whale. The whale was with me. Its song was so beautiful. I think it brought me here."

Gavi reached out and gripped Ben's shoulder. "I'm glad you're safe, and so thankful you're here. Ben, I'm worried about Aria. She's with a group of escaped captives, and though they mean her well, they might not know that she can't be taken far from the king. She may not be in any condition to tell them, either. We have to find her." He stood up and took a deep breath. "We have to find food and water, also. Can you stand?"

Ben smiled. "I'm glad you found me, Gavi. You're so practical."

They continued to walk along the shore, and as they went,

Gavi realized that though he was hungry and thirsty, his headache and pain and started to ebb. He felt energy returning to him, almost disturbing because it was so unfamiliar. The king's poison, he realized, or rather, being away from the king's poison. Ikajo's proximity had been sucking the hope out of him. It must be so much worse for Aria, with the arrow. Enough was enough. They needed to get her away from the Desert King. Forever.

"Is that a path?" Benayeem's voice startled Gavi out of his thoughts.

Gavi looked. The beach had widened, rippled sand leading up to a break in the jungle that looked wide enough to be a path into the island's interior. "Maybe," he said. "Let's go see."

CHAPTER 20

Ben stood looking at the path he had pointed out, half wishing he hadn't. It looked...well, they couldn't stay here on the beach. He nodded, half to himself, but then his stomach growled with hunger, so loudly they both heard it.

Gavi grinned. "Maybe we should find food first," he said.

Ben looked back at the thick jungle. "Will there be food in there?" he asked.

"I have no idea. But out here I can catch fish."

"With what?" Ben asked.

Gavi was already striding toward the beach. "You've never seen me do this?" he called.

Ben didn't answer. He squatted down on the sand, his arms around his knees, and watched as Gavi waded into the water, thigh-deep. The older boy stood there, still as a mountain. Suddenly, he moved, clamping his hands together in the water. Ben held his breath, but Gavi shook his head and waited again.

After some time, Ben got off his heels and sat all the way down on the sand. The song that Ben heard from his old friend had changed, and he looked thin and tired. There wasn't poison in Gavi's song, like Aria's. And Ben didn't hear the alien song of another person. But Gavi's music was heartbreaking. It belied the grin Gavi shot Ben as he stepped out of the water, a huge fish in his hand.

Gavi very gently laid the fish on the beach and whispered over it, then lifted a rock and clubbed it on the head. Ben stood and dusted himself off, looking for wood to build a fire. The wood from the boats was too wet to burn. He found large hunks of driftwood, as well branches that had fallen at the edge of the jungle. When he had enough, he dug a hole in the sand and used his Seeker training to coax a fire into life. By that time, Gavi had cleaned the fish and now he lay pieces of it on flat stones over the fire.

"How do you still have your knife?" Ben asked.

Gavi glanced up at him. "I tie it onto my waist-belt, always," he said. "I'm not taking chances." He smiled.

"No," Ben answered, as they watched the flesh of the fish begin to steam and then sizzle. "I've never seen you do that. I mean, I've seen you do it with a rod or a net."

Gavi blinked, his face blank. After a breath, he laughed. "That was the longest pause in a conversation I've ever heard."

"You don't live with Isika," Ben said, smiling himself. "Sometimes she continues a conversation a full day after it started, and I have to sort through a thousand moments to find the right connection."

Gavi smiled and turned the fish over with a stick. "The fish catching is part Ranger training, part gathering magic," he said. "I can catch almost anything, if I stay still long enough. But I can only catch what I need. It's Nenyi's way of protecting her world." He sat back on his heels, gazing up at some of the tall trees above them. "Have you ever had a globe-nut?" he asked.

"I've never even heard of a globenut," Ben answered.

"I'm going to try to get us one. Watch the fish."

Gavi put his knife between his teeth and leapt up the tree, planting a foot on each side of the long, straight trunk, and climbing by hopping, then pulling his body up, then hopping and planting his feet, then pulling again. Soon, he was so high that Ben felt dizzy. When Gavi reached the base of the large fronds of the tree, he pulled the knife out from between his teeth and used it to hack at something Ben couldn't quite see. A bundle of large roundish seeds, it looked like.

Two of the seeds plummeted to the earth, thudding onto the beach, and Ben finally turned his attention back to the fire and the fish, flipping them just in time, before they blackened. They were nearly ready. Ben's mouth watered.

Gavi returned, swinging a large pod in each hand. His music sounded triumphant.

"Globenut," he said. Then he took the large pod and chopped around the top of it, handing it to Ben when there was a small hole. Ben looked inside and was surprised to see water.

"Drink it," Gavi said, already at work on the other globenut. Ben lifted the globenut to his face and drank, discovering he was thirstier than he was hungry. He drank the sweet water until it was gone. Gavi held his hand out and cracked the globenut in half with a few chops of his knife.

"I miss the fruit of Maween so much it nearly kills me," he said. "The restorative fruit. But this is excellent."

They used stones to coax the globenut meat out of the shells, eating bites of fish and scoops of globenut together. Ben's head started to clear as his hunger eased. All the while, Gavi kept glancing at the path they had found earlier. Ben could hear eagerness in his music, and knew he wanted to find Aria. Ben found that he was reluctant to leave the peace of this beach.

"This reminds me of better times," he told Gavi. "When you cooked for us on the road."

Gavi looked at him thoughtfully. "Each time we went on a journey, we thought we were in peril. We couldn't imagine it would get worse. What will become of us, Ben? Will Nenyi turn and listen to us? Will he bend down to save us?"

Ben blinked, startled. He still felt like the new one, new to worship and understanding of the ways of Nenyi and the Maweel. Why was Gavi asking him? But Gavi stood, not waiting for an answer.

"Enough time sitting around," he said. "We need to go find that sister of yours."

They walked into the jungle. It was dark under the thick leaves of vines and trees that grew so close they hid the sky. The path merged with a stream, running alongside its bank. They drank from the stream, cautiously at first, and then voraciously when they found the water to be sweet and pure. Ben's stomach was warm and heavy with food. He grew sleepy as they walked in the day's heat, swatting at biting insects. They talked occasionally, but mostly walked in silence, and though they saw no sign, for a long while, of other people, this was certainly a path formed by humans. So they were not surprised when they saw the first signs of a village.

Ben stopped when he saw the smoke rising above the trees again. He listened. The music was soft, muted. It didn't impinge on him, the way music so often did, pressing against his brain until he thought he would go mad. It drifted over him, light, sweet notes. And better, it was untouched by the king's music.

"I think this village is safe," he said to Gavi. "At least as far as I can tell."

Gavi nodded, turning to look in the direction of the village, a pensive look on his face.

"We don't have much choice other than to find out," he said. "I can't think how we are going to find Aria if we don't ask people for help. Do you hear her?"

Ben considered. "I hear something that sounds like her, but it is muffled, far away. As though someone is hiding her from me."

Gavi looked at him thoughtfully. "Hmm," he said. "I wonder what that is. Well, let's meet the inhabitants of this island."

They approached cautiously, with their hands showing, but it seemed unnecessary, because no one ran toward them, weapons drawn. Instead, people spilled out of huts that were on stilts to squat by the side of the road and watch Ben and Gavi. The people looked different from the Maweel or the Workers. Neither did they look like people from the Desert City. They more closely resembled the northern people of the mountains, Deto's people, but they were short, with softer cheekbones, and wore their hair short, cut straight over the eyebrows, men and women alike. The women wore loose cotton dresses and had long beads around their necks. The men were shirtless, with straight cotton cloths wrapped around their waists, and wore their hair plain. They watched, silently, as Ben and Gavi walked along the path.

"What does their song sound like?" Gavi asked. Ben heard the nervousness under Gavi's words. "Are they getting ready to attack?"

"No," Ben murmured. "Their song reminds me of Keerza song. Gentle and curious. Ancient."

"Should I ask who is in charge?"

"You could try. Do you think they speak the language of our continent?"

Gavi shrugged. "I'm as lost as you are," he said. He took a breath. "Uncle," he said to a nearby man. "Do you know where we can find the leader of this village?"

The man Gavi had addressed had smile lines that spread from his eyes down to his cheeks, joining the lines from his mouth. The deep creases deepened as he grinned at Gavi.

"Do you mean the mother?" he asked, his voice lightly accented but clear.

Gavi blinked at the man.

"Is the mother the person I should speak to? We desire a place to sleep."

"And you desire to find someone?"

Ben was taken aback. "How can you tell?" he asked.

"Why else would you be here?" asked a young girl who stood near the old man. The old man grinned again.

"We don't get many visitors," he said. "We have nothing of value for people to take. And you both have a searching look."

"Yes, we are looking for many people, in fact."

"Does it have something to do with the big smash?" the girl asked.

The man looked at her. "Hush child, not now. Take these young ones to the mother."

The girl did as he said, running ahead in bare feet. Her hair was cut in the same straight-across-the-forehead cut as the others, and she had lost some of her baby teeth, giving her a ragged, lopsided look that reminded Ben of Ibba when she was younger. They followed as quickly as they could as the girl ran ahead, stopping every once in a while to wait for them to catch up. The village was larger than Ben had thought at first, a network of huts that stretched a long way in all directions. The huts were sometimes connected to trees, and had walkways between them, high up, so that people could get from one to another without touching the ground. Many people still watched, but now that Ben and Gavi had a guide, many went back to whatever they had been doing before the interruption of strangers in their village. The sounds of their conversation and laughter were like dancing wisps of cloud over the ground notes of their mild song.

Ben realized that he found it strange to meet people who were curious but not defensive.

Eventually, they reached a wider space between the hut. A tall stilted hut that was built into a tall jungle tree, with many layers and floors, sat in the middle of the clearing. There were flowering vines climbing its floors, spilling out of windows. The girl pointed.

"That's the mother's house," she said. "You can go. She's probably expecting you."

A few other children had joined them on the journey through the village, and now they all scattered, laughing and talking.

"Are we supposed to go on our own?" Gavi said.

"Looks like it," Ben answered.

Gavi squared his shoulders. "Alright then. Let's go."

They walked to the house, hearing a voice as they approached.

"Come in, young ones. Just climb the ladder."

Ben followed Gavi, climbing to the upper part of the house. As he climbed, a strange feeling settled around him. The steps of the ladder seemed to move under his hands, vibrating with sound. Or buzzing. He remembered how Isika always described the feeling of the trees as a buzz, the life song of living things. That was when he saw that the ladder was woven from branches of a living vine. He called to Gavi, showing him.

Gavi gave a low whistle. "How is that done? That's strong building magic."

He kept climbing, disappearing into a hole in the roof above his head. Ben followed, but as he did, his sense of being held by this living tree only increased, until he was sure he could feel hands around him, holding him securely. When he clambered through the hole in the roof, he found himself somewhere far away.

He was in a desert, under a night sky filled with stars. He looked around wildly, disoriented. Where had the hut gone? Where was Gavi, or the mother? He looked down at his hands, hoping he hadn't disappeared. No, he was still here, still wearing his ragged clothing. His long brown hands looked exactly the same.

There was one tree in this desert. And a man under the tree, singing. Ben walked toward him.

And then he fell on his face, because he knew who the man was.

"Are you the mother of this village?" he asked.

"No," he answered, and his voice held a laugh and a snort and love all at once. "I just saw an opportunity to talk with you."

"You've never come to me before, Shaper," Ben said.

"All things in their time," he said. His face seemed made of the night sky, dark, rich, and brilliant with stars. His eyes were deep with kindness. "What do you want?" he asked.

Ben felt, then, that he could put his face to the sand and cry for a thousand years, as the weight of all the things he wanted rolled over him. Hardly anyone ever asked him what he wanted.

"For things to be right again," he finally said, and a small globe of light left his chest, floating to Nenyi. He caught it and held it to his own heart, turning to Ben with a stricken look on his face.

"Oh little one," he said, and then Ben was weeping, because the Shaper was too. Aria, Isika, Auntie. All the songs of loss and abuse and fear Ben had heard over all the years. He crumbled under them. He thought he would splinter into a million pieces. But he opened his eyes to find that the Shaper had grown very, very big, and he was cradling Ben next to his heart, and now he had the song of a mountain.

"Now you know my voice," he said. "And you cannot forget it."

When Ben blinked his eyes open, he was on the ladder. Gavi held out a hand, and pulled him up to meet an older woman who gazed at him with wise, human eyes. They sat and began to tell her what they needed, but Ben could still feel the sound of Nenyi's voice under his skin, hear it in the motion of the tree beneath them, hear it in Gavi's words, and in the sound of the earth that surrounded them.

CHAPTER 21

J abari had washed up not far from Abbaseet, and after they regained their senses and checked that their limbs were intact, the two of them set off to find the others. Jabari was dazed, but had enough wits to be thankful for Abbas by his side. The Karee warrior prince was the exact person he would have chosen as a companion in a disaster. Jabari also had a raging worry for Isika, though, hampered by her lack of magic the way she was. He reached out for her with his mind, but heard nothing in response. Where was Ben? The last time Jabari saw him, he'd been pulled away by sea creatures. Had everyone survived? And, now that he thought of it, what had happened?

They stopped to forage and eat.

"Abbas?" Jabari asked, while they were gathering wood for a fire, "What did you feel when the ship crashed?"

"Not much of anything," Abbas said. "Just a big wave and then I was flying through the air. I had time to tuck in my arms and legs before I hit the surface, and that was about it. I'm glad I know how to swim."

"Does everyone, though?" Jabari asked. His stomach hurt. This had grown so much more serious, now that they were separated. Could the others survive on their own?

"What did you feel?" Abbas asked.

"A huge surge of magic," Jabari said, "and then everything started rushing by until we hit the rocks and splintered apart. And now there is nothing left of the boats." He looked around. "Where are all the Sea People? How are we by ourselves? Where is everyone?"

Abbas looked thoughtful. He stirred up some coals and buried the roots he had found in the hot sand next to the red coals. He stood when he was done, walking over to a patch of wet sand and picking up a stick.

"I think I know where we are," Abbas said, drawing something in the sand. Jabari went to see what it was. The sea washed up on the shore in little, gentle lapping motions. The sky was completely clear, the heat from the sun beginning to grow stronger. Soon they would need to find shade. The picture was a map.

"What do you Maweel know about the continents?" Abbas asked, pointing at the two large pieces of land he had drawn.

Jabari thought about that. "I think we know a lot about the continents, but I am a terrible student. Ivram got most of his gray hair from trying to teach me. I know that we are on the western edge of our land, and that across the sea is the next continent, that the emperor from across the sea tried to absorb us and join all the languages."

"He succeeded," Abbas said in his deep, accented voice. "It is why we all speak one language. But that was hundreds of years ago, and now his great, great grandson rules. There was a great war of separation, and the Maweel, Gariah, Karee and

Hadem fought for their independence. The language of the emperor's people has shifted and changed, though I met one man from across the sea and his phrasing was similar. I couldn't understand him exactly, but I could catch the meaning of what he was saying. And then Ikajo pays tributes to the emperor still, which makes it seem that the independence is not as thorough as we have believed.

But, we are not only two continents. There is a whole string of islands in between the two shores. Many of the people of these islands are still independent, still fierce about their freedom." He drew a long, wide island, surrounded by smaller islands.

"I think we have landed on the largest of these islands. That would explain the large mountains...that way," he pointed away from the shore, "and the way we can't find one another."

Jabari nodded. It seemed right. Faintly, he remembered Ivram telling him about these independent islands.

"Better that we landed here than that we ended up on the far continent," Abbas remarked, brushing sand off of his hands and striding back to the fire to check on the roots. They were done. "There are dangerous creatures that guard those shores."

"Really?" Jabari asked. "I thought those were just stories to scare kids out of wandering tendencies."

"The flying guardians? That is the truest scary story your parents ever told you. The man I met, the one from the continent. He verified it. Their magical people can ride them. They are evil beasts, I hear."

"No beast is evil," Jabari said.

"Well, these ones are," Abbas insisted.

They lapsed into silence as they ate. "We need to look for the others," Jabari said, finally, "and get off this island."

"If all the ships washed up here," Abbas said, "the Desert King is on the island somewhere, too."

"All the more reason to find our friends and get away."

They finished the tasteless food, and then set off. Jabari laughed at Abbas's torn-up clothing, and Abbas in turn made fun of Jabari's legs sticking out of his torn pants. Deep down, though, Jabari felt a fierce urgency. They didn't know what had happened their friends, or the Hadem, or the more vulnerable people in their company.

As they walked, they went over theories, discussing who had caused the ships to suddenly throw themselves against the rocks. Jabari went back in his mind, over and over, to that great surge of magic, how it had overtaken all of them without warning, halting the fighting and explosions immediately.

Jabari squinted as they rounded a sharp rock and arrived at another cove. There were two figures walking on the sand in the distance.

"Abbas," he said. He would have broken into a run if Abbas hadn't thrown out an arm to stop him.

"Remember that anyone could be on this island," Abbas said. "Not only friends."

It could be Isika, Jabari's heart protested. His whole body ached from being separated from her. Where were the Othra, or the great cats? And why couldn't he reach her in his mind?

The people in the distance seemed wounded, walking toward them, but strangely, with a shuffling gait. Jabari and Abbas approached cautiously, and as they drew closer, Jabari saw that their strange pattern of walking was due to the shorter person leaning heavily on the other, much taller person. Both of their heads were bent as they watched their footing, so that they did not notice Jabari and Abbas until they were quite close. But then the taller of the two people looked up, and Jabari realized that it was Herrith.

His face was Herrith's face, but he looked so different. His red robes were gone, and he wore torn pants and a short tunic, his long hair braided behind him, strands of gray hair tossed by an occasional breeze. He looked oddly vulnerable, and older than Jabari remembered. The woman leaning on his arm was Mara, eldest member of the Circle, the resistance to the Desert King. Jabari had not imagined that Mara would ever leave her home in the Desert City. Jabari held his hands in the air in a show of peaceful intent in case Herrith did not recognize him. After a moment, though, Herrith slumped with visible relief.

"Son of Andar," he said, his voice wry. "Fancy meeting you here."

"Can't get away from me, I guess," Jabari said, smiling. Abbas hurried to Mara.

"Is she hurt?" he asked, taking the grandmothers's arm so Herrith could rest.

"I'm not hurt," Mara said, indignation in her voice, "and I can speak for myself. It is only that I am an old lady, unaccustomed to being tossed off of ships."

Jabari grinned widely this time. "Shall we rest for a moment? Compare stories?"

"Yes," Herrith said. "I also am not so young. And do you two have any food? I believe you are more accustomed to scavenging for edibles than we are."

Abbas went to retrieve more of the jungle roots while Jabari built another fire. *Keep going,* his mind screamed at him. *Find Isika.* But he could see the two older peopler were shaking with fatigue. He needed to care for them before anything else.

Abbas emerged from the jungle, excited because he had also

found fruit to go with the roots, and while he sliced it open with the tool he always had on him, Jabari peeled the roots and laid them over the fire.

"I take it that you haven't found anyone else," Herrith said.

"No," Jabari said. "Only you."

"I am worried about Aria," Herrith said.

"And I about Isika," Jabari said.

"Worry is not a competition," Abbas said mildly, handing a piece of juicy fruit first to Mara, then to Herrith.

"I worry that the king will kill her if he finds her," Herrith said. "For foundering the ships."

Jabari was stunned into silence. Abbas spoke the thought that Jabari had no voice to speak.

"Aria foundered the ships? Was she under the king's influence?"

"No," Mara said, "We don't believe so. She was far from the king, and I believe she was far less influenced by him than usual. Gavi was with her—they were both down in the belly of the ship with the enslaved."

Abbas drew in a breath. "Do you think she learned from them? The magic of the enslaved?"

"Perhaps," Herrith said. "We will need to ask her. But first we need to find her, and for that, we need a plan. Son of Andar," he went on, taking the charred piece of root that Jabari handed him. "Can you hear the Othra?"

"I haven't been able to," Jabari answered, finally finding his voice again. "But I will keep trying." He turned the conversation back to Aria. "I'm confused though, why do you think she would have sent the ships to the rocks? Wasn't that playing right into the King's hands?"

Mara scowled at him over her charred root. "Does this one

use his brain?" she asked. Her deep brown skin was a map of lines, but she could still deliver an insult as well as any of the women in Jabari's life. He grinned at her, his spirits lifting just with her presence.

"Help a stupid boy understand," he said.

"The king was well on his way to destroying your ships with cannon fire," Mara replied. "Aria sent them to the rocks to save them from the explosions."

Jabari nodded. He wasn't sure that they could trust Aria's intentions, but they didn't have another explanation.

"Why does everything feel sort of...muffled...here?" he asked. "I think that's part of the reason I can't hear Isika or the Othra."

"I think it's part of the magic of the island people," Abbas said. Herrith was already nodding.

"The warrior prince is right," he said. "The people hide themselves from the poison of the king, which always stretches as far as it can go to take as much as it can. There is a sort of hiding magic over the whole island. We will have to learn to work with it."

"So we search blindly."

"Like regular people," Mara corrected. "Without magic."

"Isika's magic is blocked by her sister's betrayal and the king's teeth in Aria," Jabari said. "So I have been learning how to use my own. And now you say it is muffled, and that I will have to adjust again."

"I don't think the magic is muffled, actually," Herrith said. "It may be that our senses are muffled. Try something you can normally do."

Jabari stared at the fire for a few breaths. It burst up, the flames growing three times higher.

"Whoa, Yab," Abbas said. "I've never seen you do that before." Jabari shot his friend a wry smile.

Herrith was right. His magic wasn't affected. It was his magical senses and listening ability that felt muddy and blocked. Helpful, because the king wouldn't be able to sense them. Unhelpful because they couldn't sense each other or call out to each other.

"Like regular people it is," he said, standing and holding an arm out to Mara. "We'll search on foot."

"You'll search on foot, you mean," she said, taking his arm and hauling herself up. "As soon as we find a safe space with some friendly island people, you can leave me to sit and recover from my little swim."

They walked, then, and to Jabari, it felt that they moved at a snails pace.

Keethior, he called. *Where are you? Help me to find Isika. Do you hear me, you dumb bird?* He called at intervals while they walked, but he heard nothing in response. All he could do was keep walking.

CHAPTER 22

Following behind the others on this long walk, Herrith felt as shaken as a tree leaf in a strong wind. Separated from Aria and King Ikajo, he was adrift.

He had always been connected to the king's wellbeing, one of the paradoxes of his lifelong resistance work. Herrith had been nearly tied to the king for his whole life. He didn't know a different way of being.

He missed his father, Damek with a strength that made him feel like a young child, running after his father to say goodbye, or into his arms after he returned from a long journey. It had been so many years since Herrith had been able to sit down and speak to his abbi. He wanted to talk to someone about the odd relationship between service and resistance that was the inheritance from their ancestors.

Jabari spoke, and Herrith pulled himself out of the past, to the very real needs of his shipwrecked companions.

"We won't find them tonight," Jabari said. "We should make camp, eat, and rest. Grandmother, you look as though you need some sleep."

Mara looked completely spent. Her normally warm brown skin was gray with exhaustion, and one side of her short curly hair was mashed against her head. She listed to one side as she walked. The elderly woman was used to being home, running the headquarters of the Circle, and feeding hungry people. She hadn't left in year, and yet here she was, wandering a beach in tattered clothes, like a castaway.

"Come, mother," Herrith said, holding out a hand to her. "Sit with me while these able-bodied warriors care for us."

Mara gave him a look filled with gratitude. He took her arm, guiding her to a large piece of driftwood. They sat on the sand and leaned against the wood. Mara leaned against his shoulder. He patted her hand. She was like an auntie to him. His mother, hers, and Azariyah had all been close, in the palace, when he was a child with Amani.

Amani. You should see your children. They have become so brave.

Herrith wished Amani was here to see them, and yet he couldn't help feeling that her grief would overwhelm her if she knew what had happened to Aria.

Jabari caught fish while Abbas foraged for greens and roots. Finding these two had been a stroke of luck, or Nenyi watching over them even now. He found that he hoped for the second option, but that hope was almost painful. Mara was heavy on his shoulder, and he could tell that she had dozed off. He must have fallen asleep as well, because the next he knew, a fire flickered before him. The sky was dark, and Herrith smelled the delicious fragrance of blackened fish.

He sat up and Mara stirred from her place on his shoulder. Abbas leaned down, holding two pieces of bark with servings of fish, greens, roots, and globenut.

"We don't have spices," he said. "But it will fill you."

Herrith handed one bark plate to Mara, then took one for himself. The fish was flaky and hot, the globenut perfectly roasted. The roots were nutty and crunchy. Herrith was shaking with hunger, and nearly burned his mouth from eating too quickly.

"Thank you," he said, when he could speak again. "How could we have washed up in a better place, right Auntie?"

The old woman nodded vigorously. "You are such lovely boys. Your mothers must be very proud of you."

Jabari and Abbas grinned.

"Uncle?" Jabari said, once they had all finished eating. He leaned on one elbow in the sand. Abbas remained upright and alert.

"Yes?" Herrith answered.

"Will you tell us more about the resistance?" the boy asked.

Not a boy, really, Herrith corrected himself. The young man was strong and stupidly handsome. Herrith knew that he was likely to become Maween's next king once he married Isika, and tonight, feeling weakened by the food and company and this strange unmoored feeling, Herrith couldn't help wishing he could go and live in their palace. He could let a little of their warmth surround him, play with their babies, be happy. The thought was dangerous. He shivered it off.

"What would you like to know?"

"How long have you been in the Desert City?"

"There was a splintering, did you know that? Many hundreds of years ago, a king of the Desert City turned his face from Nenyi, severing the cord that connected them. That was the point when my ancestors held onto their own cord. From that moment, the resistance has always been there."

"I never really thought about it before," Jabari said, tossing a stone from the beach in one hand. "But the circle existed when Queen Azariyah was in the Desert City."

Herrith stared at the boy. Beside him, Mara sat forward. "Of course it did, young one. It was me, and Damek, Herrith's father, and Ina, his mother, who took care of Azariyah. We helped her when she needed help. That's not news to you is it?"

He looked sheepish. "I'm a little slow I guess, but I never thought about it in those terms. We've been so used to thinking of her as lost."

"She did good things when she was with us," Mara murmured.

"We never saw her again," Jabari said, and his voice carried not only his own emotion but the heartbreak of an entire land that had lost its queen. "I'm terrified that the same thing will happen to Isika. Where is she, and why can't I hear her?"

"It's this betrayal magic which is overcoming her," Abbas said suddenly. "That's why the key to healing Isika is finding healing for Aria."

Herrith felt a strong pain near his heart at the sound of Aria's name. The stars were very bright overhead. Where was she? She must be safe, Herrith knew. He felt no crisis or warning. But, still, he desperately wanted to find his daughter. He picked up a handful of sand, letting it run through his fingers. The feeling brought back a memory he had nearly lost.

He was sitting in the palace courtyard in the sand garden, listening to the low tones of his parents talking with Azariyah. Amani had come out to sit beside him. She was still very small, and when she saw that he was trying to pile sand up, she joined in, scooping large handfuls of sand and heaping them on top of his pile. After a few moments, though, she fell into the pile and it spilled into a flattish heap, destroying what he had made.

Herrith glared at the smaller girl, angry at her. But she cowered, holding a hand up in front of her face. Who had hit her? It was the first moment Herrith remembered thinking that the king was not a good man, really realizing it in his own heart rather than only being told, and it changed him forever. He changed the glare to a soft look, and patted Amani on the shoulder.

"Let's begin again," he said, and a smile broke over her face like the sun rising.

Now Mara stirred beside him.

"Have you told them?" she asked.

He turned to look at her. She had shifted to lie on the ground, her head pillowed on her arm, eyes drooping and tired.

"Maybe now is not the time," he said. "You look like you need sleep, Auntie."

"You can tell them. I'll fall asleep to the soothing sound of your voice," she joked. But she closed her eyes, and it did seem that she had fallen asleep.

"What does Mara mean?" Jabari asked, sitting up.

Herrith hesitation. He supposed they needed to know. "I did an... adoption ceremony with Aria," he said. "It is very powerful magic. It happened very quickly—I did not plan it. She is my daughter now, and she is stronger," he picked up another handful of sand. "For the first time in a long while, I have real hope."

"What do you mean, adoption ceremony?" Jabari asked. His face was a bewildered as he leaned forward, legs crossed tailor-style in front of him. Abbas was silent, but equally captivated. "Aria was already adopted," Jabari added.

Herrith considered the two young men sitting before him. Both were princes, in a way, loved and cherished by their strong families. How hard it would be for them to understand. It would have been hard for Herrith to understand also, if he hadn't grown up beside Amani.

"The arrow that is lodged within Aria is full of poison. This poison is formed from years of betrayal, centuries, even. It is strong, so strong. She feels it in her body, hurting and weakening her. I understand that you have a system of adopting the sent over children of the Worker village, like you did with Aria. And I've heard that her family has cared for her generously. But she has gone through so much in her life. She has held large quantities of fear in her body. The sweet magic of her adopted family cannot combat this poison."

"So what did you do?"

Herrith looked at his handful of sand. Tears sprang to his eyes as he remembered that moment with Amani, the way she had flinched away from him, readying herself for a slap or heavy blow. He knew he had carried that memory inside him, just as he had carried love for Amani with him all these years.

"He tied his well being to hers," Mara said, her eyes closed, her voice sleepy.

"I thought you said you would sleep, Auntie," he chided her lightly.

"Well you're not telling them properly."

"Herrith took some of his strength and gave it to Aria. He took some of her pain into his own soul. He feels what she feels, and shares it with her. This is the true magic of this kind of adoption. It is a type of magic that every mother gives to her own child, but those who live without the love of parents have lost this magic. Herrith has taken this part in Aria's life. In ordinary circumstances it is not dangerous, but now, with the poison of the Great Waste in her, the battles that she is waging, and her own strength dwindling, Herrith is in great danger."

"That is not the point, Auntie," Herrith said quietly, glancing at Abbaseet and Jabari, seeing the stricken looks on their faces, then looking down at his pile of sand again. "The point is that with this strong magic, Aria has a fighting chance. And because Aria has a fighting chance, so does Isika."

There was a long silence. Herrith finally looked up.

Jabari and Abbas were both staring at him. Mara seemed to have finally dropped off to sleep, and was snoring slightly, having delivered her bombshell.

"Will you die?" Jabari asked.

"I hope not," Herrith said, with a slight smile. "But if I do, it's part of my life work." He shook his head, chasing away the visions of his death he'd had since the adoption ritual. "Let's talk about you, Son of Andar. Isika is weak in magic. Aria will not die immediately, but she is struggling."

"She blew up the ships," Abbas inserted.

"That is true. And the feel of it was something new. If I was going to compare it to anything, I would say it was like the kind of wild magic Queen Azariyah began using after she was captured. Healing and making things right, but with a wild power. But that is not what I want to speak about.

Jabari, the strongest forces, the strongest gifts, are quiet. When will you stop holding back? When will you give us what you have? When will you burst out of this container you have made for yourself?"

Jabari looked a bit stunned by this question, coming as forcefully as it did from Herrith, whom Jabari hardly knew. Herrith was glad that it had shocked him. He knew there was an ocean of magic sleeping under the boy's skin, an ocean he had never deigned to touch.

"All I really want is for things to go back to the way they were," Jabari said. "Not before Isika came, but before we were all separated. I want to run down paths with my brother. To drink ... fruit and eat spicy food in my parent's hall."

Mara stirred. Once again it seemed that she was awake and had been listening.

"It is not Nenyi's way," she said, "to go backward. The Shaper is ever traveling forward and leaning upward, ushering us along with gentle arms. He never stops creating things from the substance of his own essence. He never stops discovering. You may find new joy, young beautiful boy, but you can't go back."

Herrith looked at his pile of sand again, wishing for Nenyi to stop the pain in his heart as he pretended not to see Jabari's tears. But pain seemed to be Nenyi's way of making his heart bigger.

CHAPTER 23

The first thing Isika had experienced, coming back to consciousness, was a tongue bath from a persistent cat. She groaned and put out a hand to shield her face.

Get up, she heard.

Isika opened her eyes. Hera's face was inches from hers. She yelped with a scratchy, creaky voice.

Hera! What under Nenyi's skies are you doing? she asked.

Then she realized she was lying in shallow, warm water.

From there it was a jumble of explanations. All three Palipa were with her. The cats told her in their own way about the boats coming apart. When she asked how they had found her, they answered with half-lidded stares and their signature slow blinks. Isika sighed. She was wet, hungry, and uncomfortable.

After she had crawled out of the surf and sat in the sunshine for a while, she asked Hera if she knew where the others were. Hera told her that a couple of her two-legged friends were around the bend of the beach, in the next cove.

"What?" she asked aloud, stunned. "You are so strange, Hera. Why did you take so long to tell me?"

Hera rolled over and licked her flank. *You didn't ask.*

Isika stood up on shaky legs. The sky was blue and clear of even a single cloud. The sand beneath her was soft, a kind golden color, and the trees back from the beach were brilliant green, edged in light. She felt restored just looking around. She looked down at herself. She was remarkably unharmed except for a long scratch along her upper arm that would probably leave a scar. Her tunic had torn along one arm in the same spot. She ripped the rest of the sleeve off, and ripped the other side off for good measure. Then she ripped her pants just above the knees. Better for wading. She soaked the pant legs in water, then tied them into a kind of *ser* to protect her head from the sun, which would be blazing when it got higher in the sky.

"Ready," she said. "Show me where they are."

As she followed the cats, she thought about her current situation. She had washed up on a shore she didn't recognize, without an Othra in sight, separated from her friends and the elders with the king who knew where, possibly lying in wait for her. It was all rather dangerous. Not that anything in her life had been safe for a very long time.

Or ever.

And then, the sea looked like a thousand jewels glittering in the sunlight. Despite her situation, Isika felt her heart lift. She could hear the buzzing of the earth, the life song of everything. It wasn't effected by a shipwreck, and there were new trees on these shores, trees she had never seen before.

The cats padded ahead or alongside of her, tall and dignified. Isika turned her head to look behind, and saw the line of her footprints crossed and surrounded by the large paw prints of

Palipa. Proof that Queen Isika and her strange companions had been here.

To round a curve of the beach where a large rock jutted into the water, they had to wade into the surf. Isika paused for a moment to listen to the song of the Naia. She wanted to call them, if only to feel their strength and be reassured that not all was lost. But it might be more important to have them close later. She decided to wait.

She put a hand out to the cliff. When she closed her eyes, she could feel the barest shudder of magic. The life song of this island was quiet and deep. Different from the land she had just left. Different from the lifesong of the sea. It was peaceful, reassuring. She pressed her face to the warm stone, then sighed deeply and continued walking. On the other side of the giant rock, the Palipa sat licking their paws or lay sprawled in the sand. It was another beach, identical to the last one, curving softly into the distance. Isika could see two figures sitting on the sand a long way away. She couldn't tell who they were.

You said they are friends of mine? she asked the Palipa. *Which ones?*

We don't remember names, Hera told her. Isika waited. Hera gazed back at her. *You need to know who they are?* she asked.

It would be helpful, Isika said.

They feel like this, one of the younger Palipa said, and after a moment, a series of images and recollections slid into her mind. She heard a laugh, saw long hair like a waterfall, and a stork-legged amble. Isika gasped. She felt them as the cats would. She knew them instantly, and broke into a run.

When she drew close, she saw Ivy staring in her direction, and after a moment or two, she grasped Brigid by the arm and pointed. The girls jumped up and ran. All three crashed into a giant hug. It hadn't been that long since they had seen each other, but then had never washed up on a beach after a ship-wreck before. They held on tight. Isika wiped tears away from Brigid's eyes.

"Where is everyone?" Ivy asked finally, when they had let go of one another. "I don't understand. Shouldn't we have washed up together? We were together before we fell."

"I don't know how Aria did it, what the magic was or what it meant for where we ended up..." Isika began.

"Aria?"

"Yes," Isika said, nodding. She paused. "Didn't you feel her?"

"I think you're the only one who can do that," Ivy said.

"I bet Ben knows too," Isika said. "Wherever he is. I hope he's safe. Yes, Aria did this, but I didn't feel any malice in it. I think she was trying to prevent Ikajo from blowing up the ships. But she has scattered us"

"Well," Brigid said. "This island must be big, then."

"Huge," Isika agreed, thinking about the size of the beach she had washed up on, alone. "I'm worried about Nat. Not worried about her safety, but worried about her worrying about me."

"That's a legitimate concern," Ivy said. "Can you ask Keethior to help you find the others?"

"I haven't been able to find him yet, but I'll keep trying. Can we forage enough food to eat?"

"We are three seeker women," Ivy said, jumping up to start a search for food. "We can do anything."

Later, when their bellies were full of fruit and roasted roots and a small lizard Ivy had caught with her bare hands, and they were drinking a hot infusion of gana leaves (for strength, Brigid told them) Isika reached out for Keethior again.

Her ability to sense was muted, somehow, by the magic of the island, but she could hear little echoes.

Keethior! she called.

Faintly, she heard his voice. *There you are. Can you sing something? I'll be able to hear it more clearly and I can come and find you.*

Not so fast, Isika said. *I've fallen for nonsense like this before. Not this time.*

No, it's real this time, Keethior said. *There is a double strand of awareness, the singing and the magic underneath the singing. Looking for you, I feel as though I've been trying to listen through cotton. I need extra help.*

Do you promise? she asked.

By my mother's wingfeathers, he responded.

Isika rolled her eyes."I found Keethior," she said aloud. "We need to help him locate us. He said singing would help."

I didn't say they *needed to sing,* Keethior interrupted.

I'm not singing by myself! she shot back.

Ivy nodded from her seat on the beach. She began to sing a familiar Maweel song of the breaking day. Brigid joined in with her deep voice, and after a moment, Isika joined in, too. The three women harmonized, smiling at each other and watching the globenut fronds dancing in a slight breeze.

deep calls to deep,
your soul is close to mine
today the sun
today the sun
today together.

Their voices blended in the traditional Maweel harmonies, and Isika felt tears sting her eyes. Her mother had sung to her all her life, and until she had come to Maween, Isika had never known how many songs were from her people. She was queen of these people now, stranded on a beach with very little magic and a father who wanted to destroy her. But Isika's people sang, and no one could take their singing from them. Isika felt pride igniting inside her, somewhere near her heart. She loved her people and wanted to protect them, to get them past the war with the Desert King. To learn about life out of his reach.

With a flap of wings, and a gust of hope, Keethior landed on the beach in front of them. The cats sat up and eyed him.

Nothing to eat, Hera said after a few heartbeats. *Just another Ancient One.*

Isika nearly choked on her laughter as Keethior ruffled his feathers until he was twice his normal size.

Just try, he said.

Then he spoke so they all could hear. "I asked you to sing, not to bellow like cattle," he said. "You nearly deafened me."

"Hello to you too, Keethior," Isika said. "I'm sure you'll be fine."

"Why did you call? What do you need?"

Ivy spluttered. "Keethior, of all the... listen, we're washed up on what we assume is some island, separated from everyone we know and love. What do you think we need?"

"I can think of any number of things, but many of them are things I can't help with," he said.

"Well let's start with what you can help with," Isika said. "Can you take a look and see what's around? I need to borrow your eyes."

"You should have said that earlier," Keethior replied. With a long singing call, he launched himself into the air.

Tell your friend not to let the bird upset her, Hera said.

Isika turned to look at Ivy, who was scowling.

"You know he just enjoys annoying us, right?" Isika asked Ivy.

"I'm just glad I don't have a "faithful servant" like Keethior," Ivy replied, crossing her arms over her chest.

Are you coming or what? Keethior asked Isika.

Coming, she said. She lay back on the sand and looked up at the sky, then closed her eyes and fell into the bird's sight.

It was always such a jolt, seeing as a bird. The whole world opened up and the expanse took her breath away. She could see the island as it was; a huge emerald jewel in the expanse of ocean. Keethior flew up and up until Isika could see the whole long length of it. She saw places where boats had foundered. Many had split completely apart, but there were a few also which were almost completely whole. most of the island was forested thickly with jungle, with a rim of beaches around the edge, and a tall mountain range in the center. The broken up boats stretched along the entire eastern edge of the island. They were spread out over an incredible distance.

Show me where we are, Isika told Keethior.

He flew lower, through wisps of clouds. Flying felt like freedom and belonging. Isika had goosebumps from the beauty of the day and the swooping, diving feeling. She saw Ivy and Brigid at once. Ivy stood shading her eyes, looking at Keethior in the sky, while Brigid sat beside Isika's prone body, stroking her hair from her face. It was a very strange thing to see.

Touching, the bird said wryly.

It is, Isika replied. You know it is. Can you follow the jungle for a while, to see if there is anyone close enough for us to reach today?

Keethior flew inland from the beach, close to the trees. Isika felt the ripples and buzz of their lifesong as they flew over the canopy. It thrilled her. Soon they found a little clearing and smoke drifting above the trees. As Keethior swooped down to investigate, Isika saw huts on stilts. People gathered under a large tree, eating and talking, and suddenly Isika spotted two figures she knew well. The shock jolted her out of Keethior's vision. She found herself back on the beach, coughing and spluttering as though she'd been doused in water.

"I saw Ben and Gavi," she said. "They're not far away."

They drank water from a nearby stream, and then they ran in the direction of the village, not wanting to wait any longer to be reunited with the others. They ran along paths in the jungle, directed by Keethior, who was flying overhead.

As they drew close and heard the noises of a village, they slowed, not wishing to startle the villagers, especially since the cats were still running alongside them. Isika, Ivy, and Brigid clutched each others hands before they stepped into the square Isika had seen from Keethior's eyes. Isika led. Her circlet grew hot on her forehead and she knew it was casting light. The people of the village saw her and stared, but then Isika was hugging her brother, and Ivy was tackling Gavi. Everything seemed perfect and real and good.

Later, sitting by the fire beside a hut the villagers had loaned them for the night, Gavi spoke with a serious voice. He looked different, Isika thought, weathered and thin, with haunted eyes. Ivy sat close to him and leaned on his arm. They had grown up as close as siblings in the palace, and she kept surreptitiously wiping tears away.

"We have to find Aria," Gavi said. "Maybe she is separated from the king. Maybe his hold on her is weakened. Maybe this is our only chance."

Isika knew he was right. They all looked at her expectantly.

They wanted her to lead them. She shrugged. She was a queen, after all. "Yes," she said. "Let's start looking tomorrow."

There was a scuffle at the edge of the firelight, and suddenly, Nat broke through. Isika jumped to her feet. The older woman looked exhausted, her short locs standing on end with a few twigs caught in them. She caught sight of Isika and the relief that slid over her face was so palpable that Isika could feel her own face mirroring it. Nat staggered, then bowed in half with her hand on her heart.

"Forgive me, my queen," she said.

Isika went to her quickly and pulled her into a hug. "Hey, hey," she said. "It's all level now. You can keep trying to guard me if you feel like it, but I'd say we're pretty far from normal."

Nat straightened and looked her in the eye. Then she gave Isika a bone-crushing hug and the others, sitting around the fire cheered.

Later, as she lay sleepless in the hot air of the hut, Isika reached out again to Jabari, as she had been, like a reflex, all day.

Yab? Can you hear me?

And unlike the other times, this time Isika heard what might have been the faintest sigh of a yes. She went to sleep smiling.

CHAPTER 24

Aria spent two days with the slaves on the island before she realized that no one was coming for her. She didn't know how she had done what she had done, but she and all the slaves from her ship had reached the island together, safely.

Even the children were okay.

Aria spent a lot of time lying in the sand, staring at her hands. She didn't recognize them anymore, and didn't know whether she ever would again. Was she even more damaged now that she had used magic for destruction? She wanted Gavi and Herrith. But every day, the kids came over to play with her, and she allowed them to draw her out of her sadness.

One child, in particular, wouldn't leave Aria alone. A little girl, around five or six, who reminded Aria of Isika, back when they were little. The others called her Zozee.

Zozee wanted Aria to see something. She pulled her by the hand to a section of the beach where three or four of the children had dug a wide hole in the sand. Inside the hole they had sculpted little chairs and beds. Two kids were in the process of decorating the sandy home with stones, sticks, leaves, and feathers. Zozee ushered Aria to one of the sand chairs, and Aria sat down, tears stinging her eyes. The care these children showed for her and each other was a soft place after everything that had happened in the last year. It threatened to reopen parts of her heart that Aria didn't know whether she was ready for. She let them pretend that she was their pet, though. Their make believe was complicated. She was some kind of person in charge, but fuzzy around the edges. She told them what to do, softly. They had made her this house. She wasn't a queen, but these kids wouldn't have the best impressions of royalty. Still, they wanted her to be special in their game. She closed her eyes and let them pull her braids up on top of her head.

Later, Aria went to the fire to see if she could help with anything. The night was bright with stars. Aria could barely look at them because of the sharp longing in her heart. The stars were far off and impossibly beautiful and free. Their only existence was beauty, unlike her own, which had become a life made to serve her father's whims. The thought brought back the memory of him using her magic to shoot cannons at the ships. She turned her eyes away from the stars and walked to the cooking fire. Several women and one man sat chopping foraged roots, opening globenuts, or cleaning fish. They glanced up when she arrived, but didn't say anything.

"Can I help?" she finally asked

One woman looked up and regarded Aria for a few minutes. "You look strong for a princess," she said.

"I'm not a princess," Aria answered.

"That's not what we were told," the woman said. "We were told that you were a princess and if we put an oar out of place or put your life in danger in any way, we would be killed immediately."

Another woman snorted. "Isn't it telling that she's the one who put *us* in danger?"

A protest was in Aria's throat, but a third woman glanced up from smashing a root on a stone.

"Come now," she said. "The elder said this one protected us in the sea. We barely got wet and not one lost."

The other women didn't say anything in response, though their eyes were still hot on Aria's face. The woman who had spoken last looked a lot like Aria's memory of her mother. Not her foster mother in Azariyah, but her real mother, Amani. Aria didn't know whether she could trust her memory, though. She hadn't seen her mother since she was eight years old.

"Can you clean a fish?" the woman asked.

Aria nodded. Of course she could clean a fish. She had trained as a seeker, after all.

The woman looked faintly surprised, and the man opening globenuts chuckled. One of the other women tossed a knife and a fish at Aria and she caught them easily. For the first time she realized that her soul felt lighter than it had even after Herrith had done the adoption ritual and taken some of the pain of her arrow. Why was that?

She lay the fish down on a log and began cleaning it, smiling to herself. She remembered her training leader scolding her over the way she cleaned fish, screwing up her face against the work. She had never liked this job. The scales stuck to her hands.

"One day you'll be out seeking," the leader had told her, "and fish will be the most delicious thing you can imagine. You won't make that face then."

The smile left Aria's mouth. The training leader would

never have foreseen this. But he was right, it had turned out that she needed the skill. She looked up and saw the women watching. All right, then, she would clean this fish better than she ever had cleaned a fish in life. Guts, scales, and all.

Later, her belly was pleasantly full, and she sat hugging a fizzy sense of pride to herself. It was nice to once again eat a meal that she had helped prepare.

After eating, like the other evenings, the little group of refugees sat around the fire, having conversations in low tones. Aria felt sleepy and contented. A fish stew with nutty roots from the forest wasn't half bad, she thought. It was much better than the oily food her father ate.

Even the children were quiet, playing and talking in whispers. The littlest ones were already sleeping, curled around each other puppies. Some of them had mothers here. Others had been separated from their mothers during their enslavement, and a little gang of older girls had become the mothers to those without parents.

Aria stared into the red embers of the fire. She could make out shapes in the embers and was pleasantly daydreaming, especially about one shape with hair in ropes, piled on her head. She pulled herself back with a start when some people arrived and the talking grew more excited. No one invited her into the conversation, and Aria was just beginning to feel very lonely when the woman next to her turned and said, "These two have just come back from a scouting trip. They found a ship that is mostly intact."

"Oh?" Aria said. She smiled, but she didn't really understand.

"We will repair it," the woman said. Her eyes reflected the light of the fire. "And then leave this place. It's our way out."

Aria frowned. "But what about me?"

Whatever desire for connection there had been in the woman's eyes faded immediately.

"What about you, princess?" she asked. "Our story is not about you."

"I didn't mean that. I'm sorry. I just meant...will I come with you?"

"That I don't know."

"Who should I ask?"

The woman tilted her chin to indicate the man directly across the fire from Aria. It was the elder Gavi had introduced her to. The highest elder, Aria guessed now, watching the way people brought him tidbits of food and information. His long hair was braided away from his face, and his eyes danced with emotion in the firelight.

She stood. The woman grabbed her arm and hissed at her. "Not now, princess, he has a lot to do. Wait and ask in the morning."

But Aria couldn't wait. She didn't think anyone here understood how desperate she was to get away from her father. She was the only one who knew the hold he had on her. She was the only one who could speak for herself. So she would speak for herself. She went to him.

"Ah," said the man as she approached. "It's the little daughter of Azariyah."

Aria looked down at herself. She saw her ragged skirt, hacked off today so it wouldn't keep tripping her up in the jungle. Her bare arms and legs, still far too thin, even after all the oily food her father had insisted she eat. Was she the little daughter of Azariyah? She supposed she was. It was the kindest term anyone had used for her in a while. Azariyah was the most beautiful place she had ever lived.

"How do you know who I am?" she asked.

He chuckled. "I can hear it. I've heard that you have a brother with a gifting like mine."

Her eyes rounded. "You can hear? You can hear the songs of people?"

"I can. I had rather hoped to meet your brother. There are not many of us in the world."

Aria looked over at the jungle. "Sometimes I can call him," she said. "But now I wouldn't want to, in case my father heard me."

The old man shook his head. "No, you're right, little daughter," he said. "We will not draw Ikajo's notice. If I am meant to meet your brother, I will meet him."

"Why hasn't the king found me?" Aria asked, but just then a man came close and began whispering urgently, close to the elder's ear.

"Excuse me," the elder said to Aria. "Have a seat, we will talk soon. With interruptions, I am sure."

Aria looked down and found a clear, dry patch of sand. She sat, crossing her long legs and smoothing the scraps of skirt over them. After the man left, the elder turned back to Aria. He opened his mouth to speak, then turned as if listening.

"Ah," he said. "We have company."

Aria steeled herself for whatever it was that she couldn't see, but after a moment she felt it as well. Othra presence. People around the fire laughed, or leaned in to hug one another, as the strongest surge of hope overwhelmed Aria. She turned to grin at the old man. He was smiling as well.

"It's not often we are visited by Ancient Ones," he said. "They must be here for you."

"Oh, no," she said. "They're never here for me. It's always for my sister."

But they were here for her. It was Nirral and Eemia. They flew into the little camp on wings that shone with blue and red tints in the firelight, making a stir in the air and waking a baby, who sighed, smiled, and went back to sleep.

"Aria," Nirral said. "At last we have found you. Your sister has been very worried. Not to mention Gavi, the fretter." Aria grinned despite herself, wondering if Gavi knew about the nickname the Othra had given him.

The old man spoke. "Ancient One, Aria just asked me a question. Maybe you can answer it. Why is it that her father cannot find her with us here?"

Both Nirral and Eemia cocked their heads to the side. Aria hid a smile. Though they were Ancient Ones, they were just so *bird-like*.

"Because of the magic of the enslaved, of course," Nirral said. "It masks Aria because it is so similar to her own magic. In the past, the king has been able to track you because of his arrow and because of the flavor of your magic. But you have the magic of your ancestor in you, and this magic has been gifted by Nenyi to everyone who has ever been enslaved. He can't see you in this large group."

"I'm confused," Aria said. "I haven't been enslaved."

"You may have walked to him," Eemia said, "but that arrow...what the king has done to you is a strong enslavement."

"So will they lose they magic if they become free?" Aria asked.

The birds fluttered their wings. "That would be a poor gift

from your namesake—the first one who had this magic. No, it becomes stronger, finished, complete. But only if it is allowed to grow. This man has cultivated the gift in all those who have been in his presence, warming them with the knowledge of its existence. So it is very strong here. And Ikajo cannot see you."

"Will you help me defeat him?" Aria asked the elder, turning to look at the old man with wide eyes. She wanted to be free so badly that it felt like hunger, like she was starving.

The elder chuckled. "Very direct, little daughter," he said. "We do not do anything without trade anymore. You will need to help us as well. You will need to vow that in as much as it is in your power, you will fight to make sure we stay free."

"I will do that."

Nirral gave a long, low cry, and Eemia stretched her wings out to their full span. "That is no small thing," Eemia said. "You should think it over tonight."

Aria turned to the bird. "Who is my namesake?" she asked.

"The woman you have seen in your dreams and in the coals of this fire," the elder said. "The woman whose voice you sometimes hear. Azariyah, of course. Queen of the Maweel. Stolen and enslaved by the Desert King's father. Her magic was more powerful than any the Desert City had ever seen. This is your namesake, little daughter of Azariyah. Aria, from Azariyah. Your grandmother. It is her magic that you reflected when you foundered the ships. But not the magic from before she was captured. You were like her in her captivity, strong and wild and fierce in the desire for freedom."

CHAPTER 25

Everything was different now that Nenyi had spoken to Ben. Ben himself was different. Tree leaves looked sharper, edged in gold. Water was filled with jeweled light. The huts didn't look like mere structures but like places of rest and friendship. But the most significant difference was in how Ben saw and heard people. People looked luminous; their songs moved him to tears. It had never been easy for Ben to be himself, to hear everything from everybody, but he was starting to feel thankful for this gift. The Shaper was showing Benayeem a piece of her heart each time she revealed a person's life song to him. *This is what I know*, she was whispering. *This is what I hear.*

He often woke earlier than the others. The days since Isika, Ivy, and Brigid had arrived had been filled with hope and purpose. They talked and worked with the villagers during the day. In the nights, they sprawled around a fire pit and discussed what they needed to do the next day. But there didn't seem to be any rush. Not yet, anyway. Their bruises were still healing.

Gavi had a cut on the side of his face that was looking bad until the head woman of the village smeared a sticky orange goop on it. It was healing well, now.

Inside, Ben knew they needed to act soon. But for now, he savored the way they could sit close together and laugh over Isika's attempts to eat the way the villagers did. She used her thumb to flick the food into her mouth when she ate with her hands, which was the way the Maweel did it. But in the village, they used more of an upside-down scoop, and the laughter of the villagers, ringing into the night air, was like a song.

People told Ben and the others about their lives, and they started to understand the island a little more. At Isika's advice, the people of the village were fortifying their perimeters. It made Neeva, the village mother, irritable because they were a people who refrained from fighting. She didn't want defenses or fortifications to be in their vicinity at all.

"It may be true that you have lived in peace," Ivy told Neeva, "but war has come to you."

So, with Nat's coaching, the villagers used the tall, hollow, wood-like grasses that grew all around the village. They cut them and bound them into fences that would deter the magic of the king. At first, Ben couldn't understand how something so flimsy was support to do any good at all, but when he realized they were fortifying it with song, he stopped doubting and began asking questions. He needed to learn, and Neeva was willing to teach him.

"We have many secrets," she said. "Many things that Ikajo doesn't know about us. Our arrows can follow our song. Our trees bend to protect us. Our sand will rise up and muffle unfriendly magic. Our land works with us."

Ben started to understand the quietness of the island. This piece of land calmed magic by holding it. When the magic got too wild, the earth would sing over it. The trees swayed over a family to keep them safe when a child was born or when a grandfather died.

After coming out of the desert and then growing up in the worker village, the city of Azariyah had always seemed like the most connected place in the world to Benayeem, with its gatherers and weavers, builders, protectors, and discerners. But this place was beyond anything he had seen. Because the people and the land were so connected, they had a different kind of life and love.

One evening, as the stars came out and people were eating the last of the evening meal, Ben looked at Gavi and knew for certain that it was time to go. Gavi's face was nearly healed, though he would always have a scar. Ben felt a pang of sorrow, thinking of how scarred Gavi had become during this long fight. When Ben had met the older boy, it seemed that he had never known a moment of hardship. But after the sword wound, years of living in the Desert City, and the months of seeing Aria suffer, Gavi had changed.

And he was losing patience. Just that day, Gavi had told Ben it was past time to find Aria. Ben had agreed to bring it up with the others.

He looked at the circle of people around the fire. The villagers on the island had magical fire similar to the red rocks of the Maweel but made from a sea mineral. It burned in a more contained way than wood, but it was still hot enough that they needed to sit at a distance from its heat in the humid night. In the island's heat, Ben had grown used to having a sheen of moisture on his upper lip or the back of his neck.

Gavi lay with his head on Ivy's leg, and Isika leaned against Ivy. Brigid lay on her back near Ben, gazing up at the stars. Three of the villagers who had become good friends were arranged on the simple mats that were the village's main furniture. Nat sat on the ground, cross-legged, as relaxed as Ben had ever seen her. For one moment, Ben considered just...staying. What would it be like to forget about everything, to stay in a place where the magic was muted, and the people were friendly and relaxed? It would be wonderful.

He took a deep breath.

"We have needed this rest," he began. "But now we need to act. What should we do, friends? Where do we start?"

Isika sat up. "Ben's right."

"We've only ever had one task," Ivy said. "Defeat Ikajo and rescue Aria. And Gavi. But Gavi has been rescued."

"Rescued?" Gavi snorted, swatting at Ivy's arm. She grinned at him.

"So. We need to find Aria." Ben said. "What else?"

"We need to find Jabari," Isika said softly. There were a few smiles exchanged, but they all wanted to find Jabari, so no one poked too much fun at Isika.

"Okay, so we need to find everyone we have been separated from," Ben said. "And defeat the Desert King. Easy enough." The others laughed.

"Can you hear Aria?" Isika asked finally. "You usually can, right, little brother?"

It was true. Benayeem had been training his gift to listen for Aria for a long time. "I can hear...something," he said. "But it's crowded out by all this other...something, and I'm not sure what it is. What I'm hearing is like a jungle full of birds that all sound the same. Hard to pick out one of them, you know? But I will keep trying."

"What about Keethior?" Ivy asked.

"He disappeared and hasn't been responding," Isika said. "I'll try again to get his attention. It would be really helpful." Her voice was dry.

"What about the king?" Brigid asked. "Can anyone sense or feel him? Isika? Ben?"

Ben considered this. He had been trying to hear Aria, not the king, but when he had listened for Aria, the king's horrible music had been absent. He listened for the king now but couldn't hear much past the excited, nervous, and pensive music of his companions. The villagers had quiet music, almost like the sound of the sea.

"I think I'm going to need to go somewhere far from people and really try to hear him," Ben said. "But I don't think he's with Aria."

"What happens if we find him and don't find Aria?" Ivy asked.

"Defeating him will help us save Aria," Isika said, after a moment. "So defeating him is maybe the most important thing. But getting to Aria before he does is also essential."

Gavi stirred. He had been unusually quiet, but he sat up now. "Finding Aria before the king does is the most important thing in the world. He will be very angry with her for what she has done, and she will be in immense danger. It might be our last chance to extricate her from his poison."

"Do you have any ideas about how to find her?" Isika asked.

"Remember, I think she is still with the enslaved people from the ship," Gavi answered. Ben nodded. "That's why I haven't worried about her, but it's still important that we find her. They may be your flock of birds, Ben. They have a very certain kind of magic, and Aria's could be hidden in theirs."

"We could follow that music," Ben said. He frowned, trying to listen. "It is strange, though. I can hear them but can't tell where the music is coming from. They're shielded from me."

"Which means they are likely shielded from the king," Isika said. "Which is good." Beside her, Nat nodded.

Gavi looked up again. "If we found Herrith, he might know where she is."

"Why would he know?" Ben asked.

Gavi hesitated, rubbing at his face. "Herrith did some sort of adoption ceremony with Aria. Stronger than the adoption we have in Maween. It allowed him to share the arrow's poison with her. He got weaker, and she grew stronger. He may be able to sense her location because of that link."

Isika shook her head. "This is insanity. To find Aria, we have to find a shielded group of enslaved people or find an old man who could be anywhere in the jungle on this huge island."

"Call your bird," Gavi said. His music sounded riled up. "In the meantime, I'm going to see whether the islanders know of a cove big enough to shelter a hundred people."

"And I will travel far away, alone, and listen for Aria," Ben said. "To see whether I can hear through the shield."

"And I will call my bird," Isika said grimly.

THE NEXT DAY, Neeva gave Benayeem a few small packets of cooked grain, wrapped in triangles of fruit leaves, as well as a knife, a skin of water, and a piece of cloth to tie the knife around his waist and hold the food supplies.

"I'm not going to be gone all that long," Ben told her.

"We travel prepared for predator, thirst, or hunger," the mother of the village said. "You can tie this large cloth between two trees and sleep in it if you like. It is something we do when we cannot sleep in our huts on stilts. At night the snakes come, and it is good to be off the ground."

Ben's eyes widened, but he simply nodded and started walking, following the path back out to the sea. The jungle growth made the walk long and slightly treacherous, as Ben learned when he was slapped in the eyes by a vine. After the third time it happened, Ben blinked tears out of his eyes, pulled his knife out, and started slashing as he walked.

Eventually, he reached the sea. At first, he just stood and listened to its music. There was the physical music, the sounds of the waves against the sand or rocks, the cries of birds. And then there was the inner music that only Ben could hear—the song of the millions of living things within the home of water that supported them, lifted them, fed them. It was beautiful music, but it wasn't why he was here.

Ben tied the large piece of cloth between two globenut trees, then climbed into the hammock. He leaned his head back and listened. He had seen Nenyi, and now everything was changed. Her voice called to him from behind every rock, every tree.

"Shhhh," he said, not sure if he should be shushing the Uncreated One. "I need to hear Aria."

He was sleeping then, he realized, because he heard a clear response.

Let me take you to her, sang the Shaper, and her voice was the deep song of the whale who had carried him here.

Ben's dreams took him away from the hammocks then, floating along the beach until he found a cluster of lights and dropped down among them. There was Aria, his little sister, sitting in the center of a ring of children, singing one of the songs their mother had sung to them when they were small. Ben felt his heart reach out to her, yearning to let her know he was there, but swiftly, softly, Nenyi carried him away and back to his hammock.

I have her, Nenyi said. *It's all you need to know for now. Trust.*

CHAPTER 26

Gavi squatted in the dirt at the center of the village square, drawing a map in the dust. Neeva, two of the more curious children, and a young man named Makree hovered nearby. Gavi used a stick to draw, first dipping it in water that had been mixed with the fruit of a long gourd called moon.

"Why is it called moon?" Gavi asked Makree.

"After you are finished drawing, and it sets, it stays for one moon cycle," Makree answered. "When you draw your map, it will remain. Even if all the children of the village run over it. We use it to make the markings on our houses."

Gavi looked up at the huts of the village. Most of them were covered with swirls, all different. It looked like a lot of work to do if it only lasted one month.

As though Makree knew what Gavi was thinking, he added, "It lasts longer on the walls than on the ground."

Gavi nodded and looked down at what he had drawn. He had sketched what Isika had described from flying with Keethior: an oblong island curved like a seed pod. They were

218

close to the long curve, where they had washed up. In the center of the island were the mountains. As Gavi drew, Makree and Neeva offered suggestions or told him where to make changes. Gavi used the heel of his hand to wipe away the mistakes. When he had a sketch that both Neeva and Makree could agree on, Gavi called Isika to come over and check it.

"Looks good. There's more of a hook at this top part, though."

Gavi fixed the place she pointed out and looked up at her as she stood back and nodded, squinting against the bright morning light. Across the square, Nat and a group of boys played with a ball constructed of the tall grass the people used to make their houses and fortify the village.

"Where are the boats that you saw?" he asked. "I'm especially looking for the larger ones. We may find the king somewhere near them."

Isika screwed up her face while she thought. "I remember them being here." She pointed to the hook, all the way at the top of the island, far from where they were. "And there was one here." She pointed to a cove on the western side of the island.

She continued to show him where she had seen broken boats and other landmarks. The sun beat down heavily, just beyond the shaded spot where they sat. As Isika spoke, Gavi began to sense something happening in the ground around the map. The earth grew warm under his hands. He leaned back to get a better look. The lines of the map were moving on their own, tightening and shifting.

"Makree," he said. "Is this something that moon does as well?"

Makree hugged his knees. "No," he said. "I've never seen anything like that before."

As they watched, the lines rearranged themselves into more precise shapes. Dots appeared. Gavi's heart pounded, and he heard Isika inhale sharply. Gavi could see each dot and sense its identity, as though each shimmered with the person's essence. There was Aria, surrounded by a large group of dots. There was Jabari. Who was with him? Abbas, certainly, and oh, Herrith! Mara. And all the way up at the tip of the island was the king.

Gavi leaned forward and put his hands on the map so he could feel what was happening underneath. He exhaled a long breath, feeling his skin react to magic that he knew. It was beautiful and broken, from the person who had become his closest friend over the last years.

"I know what this is," he said in a low voice.

"I think I'm starting to see as well," Isika said, drawing near. "But, tell me more."

"It's Aria. Whatever she did when she moved the ships determined where we ended up. Don't you think it's strange that none of the king's people or the sea people washed up on the same shores that we did? That was Aria's magic."

Isika was nodding, a look of awe on her face.

"I see," she said. "The king is far north, and we are all down here in the middle. Aria is on the south end of the island. It's too much to be a coincidence."

"Beyond that, I can feel her in it. I feel her magic wrapped around this map."

Isika put her hands down and gasped. "You're right. Oh, my. She is so much more powerful than I knew," she said.

"She has gained strength from Herrith and the magic of enslaved people."

They sat like that for a long time. Gavi kept his hands on the map, just to feel the sense of Aria's magic, but slowly it faded and became only a map once more. The dots disappeared as well. Isika made a small sound of protest. Gavi leaned over quickly to sketch the places they had seen Aria, Jabari, Herrith, and the king.

"How do we make it do that again?" Isika asked, poking at the map with one long finger.

"I don't know if we can," Gavi said. He felt quiet and tired. Instinctively, he knew that what had just happened was powerful magic, formed because of the connection between him and Aria. It would not be easily replicated. "But now that we have a general idea, I'm going to find Yab."

"I'm coming with you," Isika declared.

Gavi felt pain bloom in his chest. He gazed at the map for a few breaths, trying to sort his thoughts.

"Isika?" he said. "Can I ask you for a favor?" He laughed humorlessly. "I mean, it's a little odd that I'm asking since you are now my queen and can do as you wish."

Isika's face went through several emotions: tired, sad, overwhelmed, attentive. "That feels like you asked for a favor and then shoved me away, but okay," she said.

Gavi made a face. "Sorry. It's just that I haven't seen Jabari for a long time, and the last time we were together, he was angry with me. To be honest, I was angry with him. I know that he will want to find you. I just..."

"You need some time with him," Isika said gently.

"Yes."

"I can wait here," Isika said.

Gavi looked up. "Really?"

"Of course." She smiled at him. "If there's anything I understand, Gavi, it's sibling worry."

Gavi smiled at her, then felt the smile fade as he realized

that he was going to see his brother, and for the first time in his memory, he wasn't sure what his reception would be. *The unlike twins.* Gavi's Worker mother had called him by his birth name—a name he didn't recognize. Gavi felt as though being away from his family—Andar, Laylit, and Jabari—was loosening their connection. He was afraid. He didn't want to lose them. Were Gavi and Jabari still brothers? Could Jabari accept that they had such different experiences in the world and be okay with it? Gavi couldn't do anything but go and find out. He stood, brushing off his pant legs.

"Thank you," he said. "That means a lot. You have no idea."

Isika stood as well, wiping the dust off her hands. She shrugged. "No big deal, I'll—uh, I'll go help in the kitchens!"

Makree gave a snort of laughter, and Gavi jumped. He had forgotten that Makree was still nearby.

"They won't let you help in the kitchens," he said. "Come with me. We can hunt."

Isika looked at Gavi. "I can hunt!" she said. "Come back soon with him, okay? And Gavi?"

Gavi had already turned to go, but he looked back at her. "Yeah?"

"He may seem arrogant, but he has been heartbroken, away from you."

Gavi tried to smile. "Thanks," he said.

He began to jog down the path in the direction he had seen his brother on the map. If Gavi wasn't mistaken, he had seen Herrith there too. Gavi would really like to talk to Herrith as well. Finding Jabari was one more step toward finding Aria, but he knew it wasn't only that. Gavi needed his brother. He needed to be with someone who knew him well, who had known him since he was small.

The jungle was thick, and soon the path grew too narrow for running. Gavi walked, using his knife to clear the way. The jungle seethed with life. At every step, there were thorns to avoid, bugs that bit him, or insects crossing the path. At one point, he saw a long trail of ants and stooped to watch them. They poured over sticks and rocks, intent on their destination, ignoring Gavi completely. Their shells looked armored and thick. He shuddered. Then he went on. Insects bit his legs where his pants were torn or swarmed around his exposed neck. When a branch caught at his *ser*, pulling it off his head, Gavi stopped to unwrap and rewrap it. He used the opportunity to take a long swig of water from his flask.

And then he heard it—the sound of gentle waves at the shore. He started walking again, eager to get out of the close, damp jungle and into the open air of the beach. It only took a few more steps for the plants to thin, and then a stand of globenut trees opened up to a welcome sight. The sea stretched to the horizon beyond a length of white beach, an endless wash of blue.

Gavi stumbled onto the sand and ran down to the water to wade into the surf. The coolness of the water eased the sting of his bites, and he washed his face and neck, too, unwinding his ser and rinsing it. He turned to look back at the beach and saw, for the first time, the people sitting around a fire a little way away. Tired and hot, Gavi's first thought was pride that his sense of direction had been so accurate, and then one of the people was standing and running toward him, and then he and Jabari were down in the waves, laughing and trying not to swallow the water.

After some hugging and shoving, they stood and staggered, out of the water, soaking wet.

"Thanks, brother," Gavi said. "I was a little overheated from my walk."

Jabari grinned at him. But his look was concerned. "You're welcome," he said, his eyes searching Gavi's. "Where were you going on your walk?"

"I was coming to find you," Gavi said.

Jabari's face shifted, maybe ten times, as Gavi watched him. *Brother*, Gavi thought, gazing at the face he had seen next to his own for as long as he could remember. What did brother mean? What did it mean that they were the unlike twins?

"How did you know I was here?" Jabari asked, and Gavi realized that his brother was close to tears. He understood then what Isika had said. His brother felt unloved, rejected, by Gavi's refusal to come home.

Sorrow begets sorrow, he thought, his heart heavy. It was something that Herrith had told him. But this was something he could soothe, at least. He pulled his brother into a real hug. In the past, they hardly ever hugged. It was enough to run down the road together. Their unity wasn't spoken; it was assumed. They had no need to reassure one another because they lived in the warm tide of assurance. But the sorrow of the world had caught up to them, and now there was a chasm, a place they needed to reach across to find one another. A gap that called them to remind one another that they were loved.

"It was a map," he told Jabari after he had hugged his brother for a long moment. " A map showed me the way to you. I have a lot to tell you."

CHAPTER 27

Jabari heard someone making his or her way through the jungle toward the beach and grew quietly alert, gesturing at the others to stop talking. He grabbed a large stick, ready for anything, he hoped. When the person broke through the last vine and stumbled across the sand toward the sea, when Jabari saw that it was Gavi with his sheaf of sun-whitened hair and long limbs, he felt genuine shock. The blood left his face. He fought through the buzzing in his ears to run across the beach, into the water, to his brother.

When Jabari and Gavi were two years old, they shared a baby bed with short walls to keep them from falling out. As the stories went, Jabari climbed out each morning to find Andar, Laylit, or one of the palace nannies, while Gavi sucked his thumb, waiting quietly for someone to pull him out of the baby bed.

Gavi had been so quiet when he first came to them, not wanting to call attention to himself, and Jabari's first memories were of feeling worried about his sad brother. He tried to make Gavi laugh at any opportunity like it was his job. And Gavi did laugh, a low deep chuckle that seemed out of place from his scrawny body. There was nothing that could keep Jabari from Gavi, except, perhaps, Gavi's own decision to stay away.

It took forever to run through the sand, but finally, Jabari reached his brother and tackled him. They fell in the surf, laughing, and something missing clicked into place. Jabari was close to tears.

Their brotherhood was the soil that Jabari's life had grown from. What *was* Jabari without his brother? Gavi's absence felt like a missing limb.

As they walked to meet the others, thoughts crashed over Jabari, thoughts he didn't even want, like anger at the Hadem leaders and their insistence that Jabari should master his power. How could he comprehend his magic without his brother nearby? He was a tree in the desert with no one to bring him water.

They walked back toward the others while Jabari composed himself. Too many thoughts, too many feelings.

"Have you been alone since the ships crashed?" Jabari asked.

Gavi jerked his chin up, surprise all over his face. "Alone? No. I'm with many of the others."

Jabari felt his heart pounding again. "Isika?" he whispered.

Gavi nodded, his eyes on Jabari's.

Jabari swallowed and rubbed a hand down his face. "She's okay?"

Gavi nodded again, smiling. "She's okay. She even has several of her guardians with her."

Jabari took a deep breath and told himself to get it together. They reached the little group that sat around a small fire. Jabari took the opportunity to hide his face while Gavi greeted Herrith, Mara, and Abbas. By the time the hugs were done,

Jabari had a grip on his emotions again. He could meet their eyes freely. He didn't understand why he seemed to be growing more vulnerable over the years rather than stronger. It felt as though he grew weaker with each person that he loved.

He busied himself with turning the fish on the fire.

"Tell us," Abbas said. "Where did you come from? Who are you with?"

Jabari listened as Gavi told them about the village he and Ben had found and about Ivy, Brigid, and Isika joining them. He was deep in thought about the frustration of not mastering his magic, drifting in and out of the conversation. He paid more attention when he heard Gavi explaining the map.

"You think it is Aria's magic that did this?" he asked, astounded. "She formed a map and sent us each to these places?"

"It is certainly her magic," Herrith said. "I can sense it. There is even a whiff of it on the boy because he has found us through her magic."

"How can she be so powerful?" Jabari asked. "We're talking about Aria, right? Is she more powerful than Isika?"

"She is neither more powerful than you or Isika," Herrith said, "though she is close behind you, Jabari, son of Andar. But she is drawing from the magic of the enslaved, and it is powerful now. They have escaped. This is Nenyi's liberation power. When rescue is necessary, the Shaper's power strengthens the arms and legs of his people.

When will the Shaper become strong for me? Jabari thought. As soon as he had the thought, he felt something like a mental slap.

Ah, he said. *Hello, Keethior. How I have missed you.*

Son of Andar, you are foolish and stupid, Keethior told him.

Thanks.

Do you not understand? Why do you not have power?

Why? Jabari asked, clenching his fists. *Would someone, for once in my life, just explain it to me rather than making me guess?*

I will make it simple because you are still a child: You orient yourself to others, Son of Andar. I just heard you thinking about this. You made your life all about cheering Gavi up. You don't know how to go on without him. You made your life about finding the World Whisperer. You are afraid of spending any time in your own soul. You would rather make people feel better, make people laugh. But the truth is, if you become an entertainer for long enough, you lose the ability to dig deep.

Jabari shifted irritably. *Ugh, you are honestly the worst, Keethior. Go away. Why are you eavesdropping anyway?*

You are sending your thoughts out so hard I would be surprised if Isika couldn't hear them.

Okay, wise bird, Jabari shot back. *Tell me what I am to do if I want to find my magic. Isn't it a good thing to orient on others?*

To give to others is good. To not even know anything of yourself, to form every response, every course of action based on others is foolish. It is the reason for your blocked power, your stunted magic. You do it again and again and again, Son of Andar. You continue to do it now, in your love for Isika. The bird's tone shifted from scolding to slightly more compassionate. *It is not entirely your fault. I do not blame you altogether. But if everyone in your life wants to help you with this and you do nothing with the information you receive, it will be your fault.*

"Yab! Yab, where are you?"

Jabari blinked. The others were all staring at him. He felt intense irritation at the looks on their faces and knew that he was not being fair. Everything felt stupid. Jabari was irritated, itchy with loss, untethered in this unfamiliar wet air. He longed for a journey, a day of running and pulling down walls. But these days, even this probably wouldn't be enough to make him feel better.

"Isika's bird was talking to me," he muttered.

Herrith drew in a breath, nearly a gasp. "It is strange to me how you take the attention of the Ancient Ones so lightly. I would love a conversation with an Ancient One."

"You think that," Jabari muttered. "But then what they say is so annoying, you would prefer for them to shut up."

"Tell us," Gavi said.

"Shouldn't we talk about the plan? Finding us was only stage one, isn't that what you said?"

"Yes, we should talk about it," Abbas said. "But you have evaded the question, Jabari."

"Fine, the bird wanted to let me know that I don't have full power because I orient my life around the lives of others. Because I'm afraid to 'be in my own soul.'"

Jabari expected them to laugh. He was notorious for being arrogant. He thought people considered him selfish. But they didn't laugh. Instead, the four of them looked at him with serious faces. They seemed to be considering his words.

Gavi nodded, measuring.

"Yes," he said. "I could see that."

"What?" Jabari sputtered.

"I see it too," said Mara. "A lot hides behind a sense of humor. I think you are afraid to look inside."

Jabari stood. "Okay, that's good enough for now. Auntie, can you walk? Let's go meet the others in this village. That's the next step, isn't it?"

The looks and shaking heads around the circle let Jabari know that he wasn't fooling anyone. He was too annoyed to care. They were terrible people.

It took some time before the little group was ready to journey on. Jabari wanted to storm ahead, but he knew it was petty, so he slowed and offered Mara his arm. She smiled and took it, leaning on him for support.

"One last hike," she told him, "and then I'm finding a nice tree to lean against and not going another step."

Gavi walked with Herrith. Herrith didn't need to lean on Gavi, but he was clearly feeling weak. Jabari was glad that Gavi was sticking close to the older man.

As they went, Jabari felt his anger receding. It was Mara, he realized, as he looked down at the top of the old woman's head. Walking arm in arm with Mara made it hard to stay upset. He lost his irritation slowly until there was just bleak confusion in its place. Lost in his thoughts, he jumped when Mara patted his hand.

"It will be okay," she told him. "You'll see. Everything becomes a little less urgent, the more days and years you spend on this earth."

He smiled at her, struck by the thought that she had spent her whole life in resistance to the shadow of the Desert King. She had never experienced the freedom or lack of worries that he was missing now.

"We're close," Gavi said. "The village is just up ahead." He reached over Jabari's shoulder, pointing, and Jabari saw how the foliage thinned in the spot his brother indicated. After a few more steps, they walked into a clearing. He could see shapes that looked like huts farther along the path.

His heart started beating fast.

Isika?

Jabari? Her voice in his mind sounded breathless, as though she had leapt to her feet.

Vaguely Jabari noticed that they entered a village square and that people were around. Some of them scrambled to pull out stools and cups of water for Mara and Herrith.

But Jabari's attention was caught, focused on the other end of the village. Isika was somewhere over... there. He walked in the direction he could feel her, and then she appeared in an opening between a hut and some tall trees, and she was running across the square to him, and he couldn't even move, but she was there, and his arms were around her, and she fit in them perfectly. She reached up and kissed both his cheeks and his chin, and then he kissed her mouth, and she was laughing.

After a while, he just gazed down at her. She looked rough, scratched up, and her clothes were torn, but she was utterly perfect, down to the wide flare of her nostrils and the jut of her cheekbones, her dark brown skin, and her lovely strong jaw.

"I wish I was an artist," he murmured. "I would paint you a thousand times."

She laughed and pushed his face away. "You're the work of art," she said. "Look at you. Shipwreck suits you."

"I was worried about you."

She stopped laughing and hiccuped something that could have been a small sob. "You're not entirely wrong to be worried," she said. "My magic is like the barest scrapings of leftover soup."

Her voice was light, but Jabari could sense anguish beneath the words.

"And the birds are telling me that I'm hopeless because I don't know how to access my own magic," he said.

She gazed at him. "We're a terrible pair of gifted ones," she said. "What's going to happen to us?"

"I'm tempted to get in a boat with only you, nobody else, and row away," he told her. "We could find another continent entirely." It sounded amazing when he said it. She smiled sadly at him. "And I know, I know, we could never do that," he said before she could say anything.

"Not before we fix the world," she agreed. "Come. Let's find a quiet place—we have an audience—I want to talk with you, my love. Tell me about accessing your magic. Help me know how to find my own again. Between the two of us, we must be able to come up with something."

He looked behind him to see a group of children giggling and whispering behind their hands.

"Mm, you're right. That's a cute audience."

"Cute or not, I know a place we can sit and be away from everyone."

She slipped her hand into his and led him toward a hut on the edge of the village. As he walked with his hand in hers, he was overwhelmed by her. Being next to her washed away his annoyance and anger, leaving nothing but a deep sense of rightness. It was the same kind of rightness he felt when he traveled with other Seekers, and Gavi made them the morning drink over a fire, or Isika pulled down walls with only a few motions. He was glad to find that this feeling could still exist, far from everything he knew or loved in the world.

The hut was on stilts, and under the stilts was a large hammock, sheltered from the surroundings by some of the tall, thick grasses he had seen growing around the village square. Isika climbed into the hammock, and Jabari climbed in after her.

After they were settled, her head under his chin, their hands entwined, Jabari told her what Keethior had said.

She laughed at his blistering description of the bird but grew quiet as he told her more. She was silent for a long while after he finished talking.

"We need to find a way for you to become acquainted with yourself," she said finally.

"It seems like the worst possible timing for soul searching," he said.

"It does," she agreed. "But we need you, Jabari. If your magic is blocked, we are in real trouble."

He knew she was right, but he found it hard to think of bad things when her head was so close to his, and he could smell her sun-warmed hair. For this tiniest of moments, it seemed as though maybe they had already fixed the world.

CHAPTER 28

At night, when the sky was dark, Herrith felt his
sorrow ease a little. It was the best time of day for his
weary soul. Around the fire, the faces of the young
ones softened and glowed, and their wounds faded. Herrith
hated seeing the marks on their bodies. They had received these
scrapes and cuts because of the actions of the king. Herrith had
served that king his whole life, even if it was for the resistance.

Abbas handed him a bowl of grilled fish, flaky, tender, and
steaming, with sour leaves cooked in the style of the villagers. If
Herrith was honest, he knew he felt unworthy to be here. It had
become hard to identify himself by the gold cord tied in his hair,
by the knowledge of who he truly was. Herrith would have
imagined that he would find it easier to know himself away from
the king. He was away from the Desert City, from the oppres-
sive silence of his quarters in the palace. But it was as though
the beauty of the jungle was unpeeling him, leaving him raw
and full of sorrow.

Father, he thought. His father, Damek, would have understood this feeling. Damek had lived in the Desert City his whole

life, had known fear and pain and overwhelming loss every day. Herrith was more like his father than these Maweel children with their joyous laughter that both soothed and hurt him. He had seen too much, stood by while the king's cruelty affected too many people. He put a hand over his eyes. After a moment, he felt someone sitting down beside him.

He looked up to see Amani's son, the one with her face, looking at him.

"Are you feeling okay, uncle?" the boy asked. *Benayeem*. Another one Herrith hadn't been able to help. Herrith saw Amani's desperate face in front of him, felt again the longing to change the world, to change her circumstances. Then he felt a flash of irritation that came from outside his mind.

Stop, Herrith, he heard. His jaw dropped, and he looked all around him, but no one was there.

Ben leaned closer and touched his elbow. "Your music is so sad," he said.

Herrith was overwhelmed. "You look so much like your mother," he murmured. Ben sat back, his eyes large in the light of the fire.

"I sometimes forget that you knew her," he said, his voice full of wonder.

Remember, Herrith, the irritated voice said again.

Herrith flinched and looked around again, craning his neck to look behind me.

"Herrith, Uncle, is something the matter? Are you looking for someone?"

Herrith sighed. "I'm sorry. This has been a lot. I think that perhaps an Othra is speaking to me, but I don't have animal speech."

Ben nodded. "Yes, they can make themselves understood if they choose. What is this one telling you? Do you know who it is?"

Images and memories seemed to flood his eyes. It was hard to keep himself in the present. *Which one?* he thought. *Which one?* A gust of air brought him back to his senses, and a large bird dropped down in front of him, stirring up a cloud of dust. Across the fire, there was a burst of laughter. Herrith wondered if they were laughing at him. But the bird brought strength, and Herrith sat a little straighter.

"It was me," the bird said. "Do you know me?"

"Keethior," Herrith managed to say.

"Very good. And now, old man, you need to pull yourself together. We need you. Aria needs you."

"Aria, my daughter. She is far away."

"Aria is pulling on your strength," said the bird, "because she is doing powerful work, and that is why you are struggling. If you want your gift to her to matter, you must eat and be strong while you can. And stop the self-loathing. Do you remember who sent Amani and her children to safety? Who took care of young Benayeem when he was desperately afraid? Who held Amani's hand when she felt she could never escape?"

"Who?" Ben asked, leaning toward the bird.

"Herrith," Keethior said, and this time his voice was soft. "Herrith, wearer of the gold cord, Nenyi honors you. Keep your strength, for he is coming to you."

The bird flew off in a swirl of happy memories, and Herrith tried to catch his breath.

He stared at his hands. Wearer of the gold cord. The gold cord. *Not all jobs in the service of the Shaper are equally honorable*, his father had told him, while teaching Herrith about staying, about being in proximity to wrong in pursuit of the long goal of justice. And he saw it then, clearly, as though it was a flag that had been thrust into the ground before him. The people around the fire had gone silent. Beside him, Mara squeezed his arm. The Palipa were on their feet.

He spoke as though it was forced out of him.

"I have spent my life," he said, "in what looked like service to the king, waiting for you children to appear. My father, and his father before him, also spent their lives this way. I have no children because I could not bear to bring them into the world, and because my true love was forcibly married to another."

His eyes drifted from Ben to Isika for a moment, then he stood.

"So this...*need* for the gold cord must end with me," he said. "This is the finish, these days of fighting, this shipwreck. The Desert King and his line of terror must end. He must not be allowed to continue it with Aria or any other of his children or relatives or slaves. He must be stopped, stopped forever."

He stood, shaky, but determined. "The cord, the line, stops with me. The next ruler will be a just ruler, a warrior with an open heart."

And then his strength left him, and he staggered. Benayeem was immediately there.

"Come, Uncle," the boy said. Herrith remembered how hard it had been to watch the little one struggle, back in the palace, when he was just a small boy, cowering from his father. He wasn't small anymore. He took Herrith's elbow. "Rest," he said.

Herrith allowed himself to be guided to his sleeping mat, and he lay there, eyes drifting shut, as Benayeem covered him with a sheet and tiptoed away.

He fell asleep like a long dive underwater. When was the

last time, before this wild flight to the ocean, that he had seen any large body of water? He had grown up in the desert. It was the will of the Shaper. He dove down deep and knew that he was dreaming. The water was dark, and he looked for light, any light at all.

Then he was on the open sand, and a line of figures walked toward him, wavering in the bright light of the desert heat. Amani, first. She kissed him on the cheek, and he tried to grasp her hands to keep her, but she slipped away from him and kept walking.

"Soon, beloved," she said.

Then there was his father, and Herrith choked up, feeling love like desperation. Herrith's father wrapped him in a hug, and he was a child again, loved, cared for. Then his father was gone, and there were two more figures. The first was Azariyah. He gasped and started to bow to the queen, but she wouldn't let him.

"Come, friend, you know me," she said. "Isn't this all so beautiful after so many years?"

"They washed up on the shore," he said. "I couldn't help them."

"You didn't have to. And yes, they are wounded, but they have more strength than you dreamed. They are full of life as the whole earth is full. You have done well."

When Azariyah left Herrith, he fell and pressed his face to the earth. He couldn't bear anymore, and somehow he knew what was coming, knew he could never prepare himself for this, and Herrith felt as though he needed to run away, far, fast, but he was an old man now and couldn't run.

Nenyi picked him up from the sand gently, holding him in

strong, giant arms. His voice was like the rumblings of an earthquake.

You are nearly through the hardest part, the rumbling said. *Don't stop now. Aria needs to be free.*

But how? he wailed. *I am not strong enough.*

Ah, but I am, the voice rumbled. And then it was as though Herrith was standing on the peak of a mountain looking down an unfathomable distance, and he could feel the depths of every living thing, every bit of creativity and goodness that stretched out before him in a long wave. And the Shaper came to the mountain, and the Shaper was taller than the mountain.

Here, the Shaper said. He swept a hand over the mountain, and everything changed. There was the island at night, and the constellation of fires that Herrith knew was their own village. His sight zoomed out, and he saw another constellation, close to the water's edge, and one fire that winked at him, and he knew it was Aria. He drew in a breath. Then he zoomed out again, and there was the wave of malice that was the King, surrounded by sea people and desert people, and they all seemed as tired and oily as old pieces of cloth, trodden by an ancient evil. *Mugunta,* they all breathed. *Mugunta, we want your power. We want the Great Waste.*

Herrith flinched, but Nenyi took him by the shoulders and made him watch. Slaves packed like oranges in a crate, tired people without enough food, the king feeding himself, gorging himself with their labor. Women at the king's feet, trying to get out of the reach of his vicious kicks. Herrith felt tears on his face.

You know I have seen all this, he pleaded. *You know I have lived it.*

What needs to happen? Nenyi asked. *How will we heal this?*

I don't know.

Gather your strength, the Shaper said. *I have come to you. Do not lose hope.* And the Shaper kissed Herrith on the forehead. The kiss felt like the touch of fire, but one that healed, and the heat of it spread through Herrith. He felt the moment it reached the part of his heart where Aria lived. He felt her wake up and begin to move, and then he saw what he knew was the future- where she would go and when the king would meet her, the place they needed to travel to— the point where they would all converge.

He opened his eyes. Morning had come. Herrith felt as though a thousand mornings must have passed, and also as though he had been asleep only a short while. He stood, stiff at first, and shook out his brown robe, so torn and dirty now. *Perhaps,* he thought, *I will never have to put on the red robe again.* He pulled the gold cord from his hair and unbraided the plait he always wore. He pulled his fingers through his long black hair that was now streaked with gray, then rebraided it and wound the cord around it again.

He straightened his spine and held his face to the sunshine, still gentle at this early hour.

Some of the young ones were already beside the fire. Isika sat staring sleepily into the flames, waiting for the water to boil and the morning tea to be ready. Jabari was beside her, holding her hand. Herrith sat. He would wait for the tea before he spoke. Gavi poked at the coals. Neeva added the leaves from the jungle to the water. She poured fragrant, steaming cups of the hot drink and handed them to Herrith and his sleepy companions. Ivy and Ben joined then, then Mara and Abbas, Brigid.

People spoke in murmurs, glancing at him occasionally. Slowly Herrith realized that they knew something had happened and were waiting for him to speak. He straightened his spine.

"I know what comes next," he told them. "I know where we have to go."

Isika sat forward, her eyes intent on his face. "Tell us," she said.

"The Shaper has shown me the way." He felt a nudging in his chest and prickling over his arms and legs. He had instructions for them. "Isika," he said. "You are more than strong enough for this. Your power at this moment will not come from your own magic."

She nodded, her eyes serious.

Herrith took a breath and looked up at the perfectly blue sky, exulting in its beauty. *Carry beauty with you,* his father had told him when he explained how hard his life would be, how hard it was to wear the gold cord.

There was beauty enough. It would have to be enough.

Herrith turned to Jabari, the lanky black-skinned son of Andar and Laylit. This one would be a king someday.

"Jabari, you need to ask yourself what you have always loved, what you have always been good at. And Gavi, you will know what to do. Ben, you are the same as you have always been, the beloved of Nenyi. And all the rest of us, we will know."

Around the fire, people shifted, and murmured. He looked at them, these beloved children, as well as his old friend Mara. He took Mara's hand, hoping to tell her with his touch that everything would be okay. "There will be no need for the gold cord anymore," he said. "But this fight will break us in some way. We will need great strength. We must go quickly, and we must be prepared for violence before peace."

CHAPTER 29

Aria was thankful that the others had agreed to her plan, but she also hated that it was necessary to convince the escaped slaves to help her fight the Desert King. *Wouldn't it be better to just slip away?*

But Aria knew that until she defeated the Desert King, he would follow her. He would track the arrow he had placed in her heart, and he would find her. And if he captured her, if she was with him, she wouldn't evade him again.

Then, he would turn his attention to the slaves who had dared to escape him, and he would use Aria's power to punish them. No, they had to defeat him, or none of them would remain free. Thinking any other way was wishful thinking.

So, Rema, Aria, and a few of the others had devised a plan to defeat the king. They hoped that the web of magic they had been weaving was strong enough to resist the king's foul powers. The plan was simply to find, attack, and disempower the king. And then they would leave him behind forever. Aria hoped the group of fighters could force Ikajo to release her from the arrow's poison. But what could they do to move him? What would make him give? That was the part of the plan that was like a blank space in Aria's mind.

She was lost and unsure. Nothing seemed to make sense anymore, nothing at all. She fell into periods of despair frequently, and then she believed she would never be free. For some reason, Aria thought—she had been born to suffer. It was the only door open to her.

No, no, Aria, she reminded herself. *One step at a time, deep breath. First, find him.*

She had fallen into a rhythm of helping the women and men in the kitchen each day, then sitting with the elders and warriors after dinner, talking through the plan. She knew they needed to turn their talk to action at some point, but they were still injured, and the elders didn't want to rush anything.

"And besides, little daughter of Azariyah," the elder would tell her when she grew impatient, "our ship needs to be ready."

Aria closed her eyes whenever they talked about the ship. She would imagine it carrying her far, far away. The wind on her face, body and soul free from the king's poison, away from the heavy burden she had been carrying for so long. What would it feel like to be free of the tension she held, wondering if he would hurt her or someone else at any moment?

There was a time, Aria knew, when she had felt free. But she could hardly remember.

She missed Herrith and the peace that he brought her. She missed Mara and Gavi. But she found kindness in the eyes of these companions who had begun to trust her, not think of her only as a princess. Aria knew she didn't deserve their kindness. But they offered it anyway. And she had promised to make sure they stayed free.

For that, they needed to defeat the Desert King. And Aria

didn't have any idea about how to do that. Her thoughts went round and round.

One evening, after the ship was done and the last injuries were healing, Eemia flew into the camp and told Aria and the others that the king was north of them, about a two-day journey away. They all looked at each other, silently agreeing that it was time.

So the next day, after the early morning chores were done, the whole camp finished the packing they had started the night before and began walking. North and inland, Eemia had said. They would walk along the shore for one whole day, then slant inland sometime in the middle of the next day. They would find a way to fortify themselves and hide the children, and then Aria would walk a little way away from the others and try to lift their protection. The king would be able to sense her, away from the others, sure that she was unprotected and alone, and that was when the runaways would attack.

This was the plan. Aria could sense massive flaws in it. Often she was certain that she would die following this plan, but then glimmers of the hope of her companions got through to her, and she began to feel brave again.

Maybe, just maybe, she would live.

The first day, she walked, holding two things in her mind. She tried to build a burning, long-lived hope that she would live. That she would live to feel the breeze on her face at sea, and be free, be free, and someday find Isika and her brothers and Ibba again. She would hug them and be with them as a girl who had escaped, who was no longer tied down. And the other thing she held in her mind felt like one long goodbye to the world, a farewell to everything she hadn't yet been able to explore or understand. And she wondered why she had been chosen for the arrow, for this long, drawn-out weakness that might lead to her death.

Why had Nenyi turned her back on Aria?

She couldn't stay too deep in her despair, though, not with the pack of kids who had adopted her as a sort of half child, half adult. They skipped around Aria and found stones or flowers to offer her until her hands were full, and she needed to make a little pouch with her shirt.

This was the way she passed the day. They paused at noon for food and sleep, then continued until the sun was gone beneath the horizon. There was a hush in the camp that evening. No one said anything sharp or called Aria 'princess.' They knew what she was risking. She helped with the food, as usual, improved tonight by an unfamiliar root one of the scavengers had found, as well as some rich, ripe fruit that the children had foraged.

When Aria's belly was full, she went to her place beside the old elder, curling her legs under her. She felt a weight in her heart like tears ready to spill. It was a sad feeling, contemplating her own death, but not a poisonous feeling. It wasn't like being enmeshed in the twistedness of her father's mind.

"How are you, child?" the elder asked. "I'm sensing many things from you. There is still time to turn back, you know."

"I don't want to turn back," Aria said.

"You could die in this fight," the old man said.

"I know," Aria said, entranced by the firelight and the quiet faces of the men and women sitting around the fire, listening to their conversation. "I've been thinking about that all day. But I think I feel content with it. I could die. I could live. I'm so tired, too tired to keep running. The only terrifying thing to me is that I could be captured. I don't want to be captured. I want freedom, of one sort or another. You know, when I was eight years old, my family put me in a boat and sent me to the sea, for sacrifice. I have been living with poison in my body ever since. It makes me so tired."

"What voice does this poison have?" the elder asked.

"Voice?"

"What words does it whisper to you? How did the Desert King's arrow find you? How did it convince you to walk to the Desert City?"

She stared at his lined face, feeling her eyes sting, though they remained dry. She looked around the circle, wondering about this question. What voice did poison use for her? It was betrayal, the strongest poison, but what was its voice?

She looked into her empty hands. Her wrists were still far too thin. There was a jab of pain somewhere near her ribs, and she gasped. She could hear the voice, and she felt impaled by the sound of it.

"It tells me that I am invisible, unwanted, and sent away from human love," she said. "That Nenyi does not see me because there is always someone stronger, better, or more beautiful. That I will never be seen. That I will only ever be *used*. Used to get to someone better, the way Ikajo uses me to get to Isika."

She had to bite out the words. They felt hot and horrible, falling out of her mouth, and she imagined that the others recoiled, but when she looked up, she saw compassion in their eyes. The elder patted her hand, shaking his head.

"That is too much poison for such a young one," he said. "Too much poison."

Aria lay down to sleep a little way away from the others, but even that was too close. She couldn't breathe properly. Speaking

246

the words that had hurt her for her whole life had used up her strength. She felt that she could barely lift her head, but at the same time, she couldn't sleep. Her heart ached and ached.

"I'm going for a little walk," she told the woman who lay closest to her. "I'll be back."

The woman nodded but seemed too sleepy to care.

Aria walked away from everyone, her bare feet silent on the sand. She walked until she couldn't hear anyone's breathing, then sat on the sand on a dune that raised her above the water. *Alone, I am always alone,* she thought.

The sky was dark, without a moon, and brilliant with stars. Again, Aria felt despair and longing when she looked at them. They were so beautiful, so perfect, removed from betrayal, the fear of death, or the knowledge of the world's sorrow. She couldn't bear their beauty.

That is too much poison, the elder had said.

Nenyi, why? Aria called to the stars. *Why did you leave me and stay with everyone else?*

She stared into the sky, looking for hope that anything would ever be different for her. And she blinked. It looked as though the sky had a face. She rubbed her eyes. No, she wasn't imagining it. Above Aria was an enormous, beautiful face, made of night, with stars in its skin. And the face gazed at Aria. For a moment, she recoiled, turning her face away. It was too much to be seen by eyes filled with stars, but after a few breaths, she couldn't help it— she opened her eyes again to see if the face was still there, looking at her. It was, smiling tenderly, looking more and more like a person with every moment, a person who loved her. The whole sky seemed to fold in on itself then, bending down to kiss her. The far-off thing she had longed for— the beauty and goodness that seemed so distant—leaned all the way down to her and kissed her. As it came near, or as she was lifted—she had no idea what was happening—a giant hand seemed to close around the arrow in her heart and pull it out in one sharp tug. She gasped, and light poured into the wound.

She saw herself in the boat.

She saw herself with her new family.

Finding Isika in the market place, seeing her again for the first time. World Whisperer. Better, special.

But for the first time, she saw herself without the poison of betrayal. Without comparison. She saw herself.

Everywhere she went, stars trailed after her. She left them in her wake.

She saw herself walking through the desert, half-mad with poison, stars trailing her just as Gavi did, led straight to Herrith and Mara, who loved her.

She curled herself up against the knowledge of this love, sure that it would kill her.

But she couldn't stop seeing. She saw her sister's longing for her, how despair for Aria had killed her mother. It was grief for Aria, for her dear sweet face and little hands. Then she saw Isika at the boat, throwing herself at the men who held her back, desperate to rescue Aria. Screaming at them to let her go. Aria gasped a shuddering breath.

She stood and looked down at her hands and arms and legs. The sky had gone back to being a sky, but she shimmered as though the stars had entered her skin. Love poured and poured and poured into her, and she heard Nenyi's voice.

You hold your eyes tight shut when you sleep. You don't like the smell of the Hoona tree. You look under every rock before you sit on it, checking to make sure you aren't going to squash a living thing. You long for your mother. You love the feeling of running.

You've never been happier than when you are running along the road with the others.

"Shaper," Aria breathed. "You see me."

Of course, I do. I can't look away. You are so beautiful.

And then it was like an explosion inside Aria's heart, where the arrow had been. She felt strength fill all the veins and muscles of her body, and she nearly flew back to the camp. She had never felt so strong. It was like nothing she had ever felt or known.

When she got back, the elder was sitting up in his bedroll, smiling at her.

"Well, now we might stand a chance," he said. "Sleep, child, the day will be long tomorrow."

Aria would have sworn that she could not sleep, but as soon as her head reached the sand, she was gone. She dreamed of skies filled with stars all night long.

CHAPTER 30

I sika jolted awake and opened her eyes to see that the sky outside the hut was still dark. Her heart pounded wildly, and she blinked, trying to figure out what had woken her and why she felt so strange.

She sensed no danger. Actually, she felt excellent, almost as though she was in Azariyah... she sat bolt upright, reaching deep into herself. Her gift, her magic. It was all there. She was filled to the brim.

The Palipa sat up and lifted heavy eyelids to peer at her. In the distance, Keethior gave a long, exultant call. Herrith stirred in his sleep, letting out a sigh.

Power hummed in Isika's body, singing the lifesong of the Shaper, calling her to come and float along the veins of the earth, swim in the seas, rest on the sand.

She held her hands out and looked at them, turning them, so they were cupped. She felt such a powerful connection to her gift that it seemed as though she should be able to see it, as though her palms should be full of light.

She laughed softly, but tears were flowing down her cheeks.

The poverty of magic that had pinched and injured her was gone. The ease in its absence was almost too beautiful.

She lay back down, and Hera padded closer, flopping down and resting her head on Isika's stomach. In the distance, Isika heard a Naia calf call to her, but his mother shushed him.

Shhh, little friend, the mother said. *We all need to sleep. We have work to do tomorrow.*

As Isika lay there, drifting to sleep with the soft breaths of her friends around her, she reached into the earth to hear its song. It sang to her softly with welcome, and she went back to sleep with its music in her heart.

She woke to Jabari's teasing voice beside her.

"Wake up, sleepyhead," he sang. "Lazybones."

She opened her eyes to find him hovering near her in the hut, looking at her with smiling eyes. She smiled back at him, and his eyes widened. He watched her for a moment, then leaned down and pressed a light kiss to her lips. A spark arced between them, and they both got a shock.

"Aarrghh!" Jabari yelped. "What was that? What on earth, Isika?"

Isika was helpless with laughter. She turned on her side and held her ribs, laughing until she couldn't breathe.

When she finally felt normal again, she sat up to find Jabari staring at her with wide eyes.

"It's back, isn't it?" he asked, his voice rough.

She nodded, and she saw something in him, the slightest shift toward sadness before he smiled and pulled her into a hug. She pressed her face into his neck and sighed, happy with the closeness but also puzzling over the sadness she had seen. *Of course*, she thought. *He can't access his full power. He felt closer*

251

to me when I couldn't either. So he is happy and sad. People are so intricate.

She felt determination stiffening her jaw. She would help Jabari figure out how to access his power. What was it Herrith had said? Jabari had to stop shaping himself around others. He had to learn about himself. Well, Isika could help with that.

There was a thundering sound on the ladder, and then Ivy popped her head above the hole in the floor. Her face shifted to exasperation.

"Oh gross, you guys, okay, okay, we get it, you love each other. Come quickly, all of our seer friends have sensed something major, and I think we need to move soon."

The others were gathered around the morning fire, and there was a new tension in the air. While Abbas and Nat prepared the morning meal, Gavi, Herrith, and Ben were deep in conversation. Ben jerked his head up sharply as Isika approached.

"What happened?" he demanded. "Isika, your song..."

"My power has come back," Isika said, squeezing Jabari's hand as she said it. He squeezed her hand in response but then pulled away and went to squat by Abbas, not meeting her eyes.

Gavi spoke. "Does this mean...?" he trailed off.

"I don't know what it means, but something significant has happened," Isika said. "And it must involve Aria."

Herrith was nodding. "I don't feel the arrow anymore," he said simply.

Gavi looked back and forth between them, his jaw hanging open. He stood suddenly and grasped his hair in both hands.

"But this is amazing," he said. "This is such good news."

"It could be..." Jabari cautioned. "Unless the king has decided to reward her for something by taking the arrow away."

The way Gavi's face changed would have been comical if it wasn't so sad.

"There are any number of things that could have happened, Son of Andar," Herrith said, and Jabari looked up, but Herrith was speaking to Gavi. "And we won't know which one is true until we see Aria." He sank into himself a little, his chin nearly touching his chest. "But it doesn't seem malicious, whatever it is."

"No," Isika murmured. "It doesn't."

"We have big problems that need a quick solution," Ivy said. "Or did everyone forget?"

"What is happening?" Isika asked. "What is this about?"

Brigid looked up from her cup of tea. "I had a vision. There will be a battle very soon. Today maybe, or tomorrow."

"And I hear it," Ben added. "Drums of doom."

"And I saw a picture of the map again," Gavi said. "And saw the paths of Aria and the Desert King converging, but not in the right place."

"So, you think they are not together yet?" Isika asked, holding her breath.

"No," Gavi, Ben, and Herrith said together. "They are not together yet," Gavi finished, looking relieved. "You are right, Isika. If I saw their paths converging in the future, they must not be together yet."

Abbas stood and carried a plate of food to Isika. She took it, feeling her stomach rumble. She smelled the roasted fish and roots, and every part of her seemed to buzz. Tears sprang into her eyes. How had she ever lived without her magic? She glanced over at Jabari, who was bent over his own food. How did Jabari bear it?

"The thing is," Ivy said urgently, "that Gavi says the place where we three parties converge will be at this village. We can't let that happen."

Isika stared at Ivy for a heartbeat or two before the meaning of her words broke through. Here. She gasped, looking at the quiet village where they had found shelter, the children scampering in the square like Palipa kittens, the flimsy grass fortifications. Neeva walked over with more pots of tea, setting them down with wooden cups by the fire.

"No, we can't let that happen," Isika agreed. "What do we do?"

Gavi explained that if they left, heading north, they could draw the other two groups away, possibly even to the shore, heading them off before they got close to the village.

"But we will have to run," he said. "They are only a day's journey away. To draw them away, we have to come to the center of their path before they meet, and trust that the signs or senses of our own journey will be enough to guide them toward us instead of back toward this village."

"So it's time," Brigid said. "We're going to do this."

"Again," Ivy said, her voice glum.

"But this time, we will get Aria back. We have to," Isika said.

"We have to," Ben agreed.

"Things certainly look hopeful if you have your magic back," Herrith said.

"And you don't feel the arrow anymore," Isika replied, and her eyes filled with tears.

They made plans swiftly after that. They had come with almost nothing, so they would leave with almost nothing. They only took the spears Abbas, Jabari, and Nat had made, some gourds filled with water, and, to Isika's surprise, packets of food that the villagers had prepared. The villagers had also sensed that something big was shifting and had spent the morning making traveling food for Isika and the others. They also send some of their young, strong people along to fight. Isika tried to protest but eventually realized their sense of hospitality and honor was involved.

"Thank you," she said to the village mother, Neeva, and bowed her head.

"Thank me later," Neeva said. "We've never been very good at fighting." She elbowed Makree when he protested.

Mara stayed behind, with Neeva. She was still weak from being in the sea and didn't think she was up for the journey.

Herrith insisted on coming, though, after a short, explosive argument with Jabari.

"You don't have to wait for me," Herrith said. "But I'm not staying behind. This is my fight. That's my daughter now."

And love and pain were marked so clearly on his face that Isika put a hand on Jabari's arm, and he subsided.

So they ran. It was not like running on Maween's open roads, Isika thought, after a branch had hit her in the face for the eleventh time. Jabari was in front of her, Nat behind her. The air was heavy with humidity, and the jungle grew close over the path. Their arms and legs were striped with scratches. There was the beautiful fragrance of flowers, which helped but didn't change how sweaty Isika was.

"We're going to run for half a day?" she complained when they took their first break.

"Getting soft, Queen?" Jabari teased.

Isika swiped at him, but he danced away. He grinned at her, and her eyes narrowed. She suddenly knew exactly how she could make the time go faster. When they set out again, she took care to run close to Jabari.

"I think it's time to get to know each other," she said to him when Abbas said they could walk for a while.

Jabari whipped his head around, a suspicious look on his face. "You don't think we know each other?"

"I missed out on a lot of your life," she said. "I want to know more."

He shrugged. "Okay," he said.

"What is your first memory?"

"Meeting Gavi," he said.

"Really?"

"Yes, I don't think I had ever seen someone so pale, and I remember touching him to see if he was real."

"But you were almost three years old when that happened, right? You don't remember anything before that?"

Jabari was silent so long that Isika thought he had perhaps forgotten the question.

"I do remember," he said. "I remember realizing I could speak to animals."

Isika looked up. "Really? Do you remember what it felt like?"

Jabari seemed far away, remembering, and Isika waited.

"This is so strange," he said, "because this memory is just now coming back to me, but I remember how I used to have these long conversations with the birds that nested outside my mother's window, and how they told me about faraway journeys they took every year." He shivered. "I remember how it felt...their words, the feeling of faraway places. I felt almost as though I could experience them through the sound of the birds, as though I could taste them." He looked at Isika then, and his eyes came back into focus.

"It was when I could barely speak the human language. I

was maybe younger than two when I learned I could understand the birds. No, that's not right. I always knew I could understand the birds. But I learned that not everyone else could."

"What else?" Isika asked, squeezing his hand, which had somehow found its way into hers.

He gazed at her, then looked along the path again, taking a breath. But then Abbas gave the order to start running.

Jabari looked ruefully at Isika and said, "I'll think about it and tell you in the next walking break."

Isika tried to concentrate on placing her feet and moderating her breath, but her mind was racing. When Jabari had told her about his animal speech, something had sparked behind his eyes. He had changed into someone else entirely, as though his self had been hidden behind a shell. Isika had glimpsed his true magic, something he had been hiding for all this time, and it took her breath away.

She thought of that little boy learning his powers. And then that little boy beginning to believe that he was made to bend to the shape of others. To be the comforter, the brave one, the elders' son, the brother. And later, to seek the stolen queen. It wasn't that these weren't good things, Isika knew, but she was beginning to see that every time he had slipped those clothes on, it made it a little harder for Jabari to find himself.

She ran and waited until she could talk with him again. She wanted to hear more of the wonder in Jabari's voice as he remembered who he first was.

CHAPTER 31

J abari was relieved that Abbas let the company run for a long time before he called a break. He missed this on the island. Jabari was from a running people, and he associated running with understanding and with belonging. He missed the breath hitching in his chest, muscles burning, finally relaxing into the stride.

And he needed to think.

"What else?" Isika had asked.

Jabari felt like his insides were being rearranged. The memories of talking with the birds were new and brilliant, soft-edged, and yet powerful. He wanted to linger with them and feel those feelings. For so long, he had believed he remembered nothing before Gavi came. After Gavi, Jabari knew that part of his work as a human being was to hold Gavi's hand everywhere they went until the little boy began to adjust to his new life. Jabari had always had one eye on his brother.

It was no wonder that Jabari had been lost lately. He didn't know who he was without Gavi. In Gavi's absence, he had begun to transfer all his attention to Isika, focusing on keeping her safe rather than allowing her to be what she was called to be.

It was hard to face what he had felt when Isika's magic was restored to her. Jabari saw that he would rather that Isika continue being powerless than leave him here by himself. And he realized he really would leave everything, that he would abandon Maween if it meant he didn't have to be alone in the absence of magic anymore. The thought nearly choked him. What kind of terrible person would do that?

You would not do that, Keethior told him.

Jabari stumbled into a thorn-covered vine at the sharp reprimand in his head. *Stop reading my thoughts, bird,* he said inside his head, annoyed.

You're sending them to me. You would not leave Maween. Stop this line of thinking; it does nothing. If you feel alone in powerlessness, find your power.

How?

You had a good start already. Go back to the days when you were a small one. Rebuild.

How can I abandon Gavi in my memories? Jabari asked. His breath came faster, and he tried to regulate it, to run the way he had been taught.

Stop being dramatic. You are not abandoning Gavi. You are letting go of the idea that your only purpose is to take care of him. What came before? What was other? What is with Gavi but also you?

Not only taking care of him. Jabari ran, sweat stinging his eyes. Isika ran in front of him, glancing back at him over her shoulder occasionally. He knew that she had seen how he felt. He saw the moment she noticed that he wasn't happy about her power coming back. Or wasn't *only* happy. He was ashamed that she knew it about him.

Stop wallowing and find the memories.

Jabari scowled but did as the Othra said.

He went back to the memory of sitting with the nesting birds outside the palace window. How small would he have been? He started to have images of other talks with animals, like the palace cats or the puppies in the stables. Their warmth and way of seeing the world, the shapes and smells they showed him. He remembered feeling like he belonged there.

Then a clear memory came. Jabari was sitting in the play-room, Gavi nearby, and his mother entered the room to find Jabari sitting with small birds lined up on his outstretched arms and legs. There must have been twenty or thirty birds on him, and she looked at him with a horrified face. Jabari felt afraid—it seemed that something beautiful had turned out to be wrong. Now, running in the humid jungle, Jabari realized his mother had probably just been shocked to find her toddler covered in birds.

Those days with the animals on the palace grounds had been the warmth of his childhood. Even after Gavi came and Jabari shifted into the role of the protective brother of a trauma-tized kid, he had the stables and the fields. He could lie for hours in the shade, watching the birds in the canopy overhead or listening to the clicking thoughts of beetles.

When he and Gavi ran through the Maween landscape as seekers, it had always been easy for Jabari to find water and the best shelters. He realized now that it was because of an uncon-scious reflex. He knew what the animals thought about their landscape. He shared their memories and knew which creeks had dried up or shifted course. Even now, if Jabari stopped to listen, he could sense where they were in relation to the sea because of the conversation of the birds, the way their talk of food shifted to fish rather than grubs.

Abbas called for a break when they reached a deep part of a stream.

"Refill your drinking skins," he told them. "We're all sweating buckets and don't need to collapse. We'll walk for some time and then run again."

"Where's Herrith?" Isika asked. "I don't see him."

"He's behind us," Abbas said. "But he told us not to wait, remember?"

"Is that safe for him?" she asked.

"None of this is safe," he responded, cocking an eyebrow. "But he has been doing dangerous work since before you were born, so we owe him the honor of trusting his judgment."

Isika stared at Abbas for several breaths, obviously wrestling with her opinion. She seemed to decide not to argue with him, crossing her arms and biting her lip. Jabari watched her, fascinated by the way emotions played on her face.

She looked up and saw him watching her. She gave him a look and came to sit beside him next to the stream.

"So?" she asked.

He couldn't help smiling. "You're as persistent as the Palipa."

She grinned, looking over at the cats sprawled on the ground nearby. "They do tend to follow me everywhere."

"Everywhere," Jabari agreed.

She looked at him again, her face open and expectant. He raised his water container over his head, pouring some cool water onto his hair, closing his eyes. Then he moved it over Isika's head, dousing her. She spluttered and shrieked, grabbing his hands and pushing them away. Nat grunted and moved farther away from them both. The Palipa stalked away. Jabari laughed, refilling the container while she wiped water from her face.

"You remember that I can call springs from the ground, right?" she asked.

He gasped. "You wouldn't abuse your magic like that!"

"If you push me, I might."

"All right, lovebirds, time to walk," Abbas called.

Isika and Jabari fell in behind the rest, Nat trailing them as usual. Isika glared at Abbas's back, glancing behind them with a worried look on her face.

"I really wish Abbas would let us wait for Herrith," she murmured. "Do you think he remembers that he's been adopted into the Maweel family, and that means I'm his queen?"

Jabari snorted. "Abbas is a nomadic prince whose father is a king. I don't think he has much fear of your royal status." He looked at her, reaching out to grab her hand.

"Herrith will be okay," he said. He wanted to distract her from her worry. "I remembered more," he told her.

It worked. Isika's face lit up with a smile. "Go on," she said.

"I remembered a time when I was very small, and I ran away. I could barely run with my short little legs, but I had heard creatures talking from somewhere nearby, and I wanted to meet them because they sounded so nice. They spoke to me in pictures of meadows and warm grass, and I didn't even know what any of it was, but it was all so enticing."

Isika was wide-eyed, apparently holding her breath.

"Horses?" she asked.

He nodded. "My parents found me curled up under a horse in the stables, and they nearly exploded from fright. I was watched more closely after that. But I think my early years were completely full of living creatures. I was connected to every one of them. It got distracting, so I learned to turn it off, but..." he trailed off, not knowing how to continue.

"But you think your animal speech might not be just a side effect of your power."

"Right. I think I have less of the life gift, the gift that contains all giftings, and more of something different. I don't know what it is, but I've been looking in the wrong direction to find my magic."

"Are you a Whisperer?" she asked, her eyes wide. "What if the whisperer gift is larger than we know?"

As soon as she said it, something clicked into place inside of Jabari's heart, and he felt instant relief, almost as though some terrible thing that had troubled him was eased.

That was when it came to him; he wasn't jealous of Isika's status, he never had been. But he knew what it was to have the ease and connection with the earth that she did. Not with elements like water and air, the way she did, but with living creatures. And Jabari had put so much aside, he had abandoned his gift and himself to contort into another shape. He yearned for the connection he had lost, and he felt resentful, deep inside, because he wanted what Isika had. He wanted himself back.

That's it, son, Keethior called.

A burst of inner light. The world rocked and stilled. Jabari could suddenly hear again. He heard birds, thousands of them, for miles and miles. He heard small furry creatures in the branches of the trees above him. He heard them noticing him, calling out to him, marveling over him. Friend, they had called him, back when he was a toddler. Friend, they called him now.

But before Jabari could even really understand what had happened, there was a terrible noise.

A grinding, wailing sound went on and on. Isika cried out and covered her ears. Farther along the path, Ben slumped against a tree. Jabari gritted his teeth against the pain and looked around for the source, trying to understand what was happening.

Ivy was clutching her head. Brigid looked as pale as a white sea bird.

Then there were words layered over the wailing. "You have had more chances than you deserve," came the voice that they all knew and wished they didn't, smooth but terrible, frightening in a way that none of them could avoid. It seemed to leach courage out of their bones. Jabari felt his muscles trying to collapse into a puddle. He grasped a tree and hauled himself upright.

"I will find you, wretches. You will wish, both for your sakes and for the sake of this island, that you had listened to me. There will be nothing left of this place when I am through with it."

Isika screamed something that pierced through the wailing and the talking, and both ceased abruptly. She panted, looking around, her eyes as wild as Jabari's mind felt.

"Well," she said. "That was about enough of that."

"He's coming," Brigid said.

"We can't fight him here," Abbas said. "Not enough space to see or be seen."

"We need to get to the sea," Ivy said. "It's the only open space."

Jabari closed his eyes. He felt connected to his magic in a way that he hadn't since he was toddling toward those horses. He could see where they were because the squirrels and birds told him. He could feel the fear of the birds behind them, where the Desert King was. And he could hear the curiosity of the jungle animals who watched Aria's determined progress toward them. He knew everything because the animals told him everything.

Yes, young one, Keethior said, and his voice was filled with warmth like sunshine.

Jabari snapped his eyes open.

"If we run that way," he said, pointing to the faintest of paths, a different direction than the one they were currently taking, "we will get to a wide, spacious beach. The king will arrive after us, and Aria after him. So he will be caught between our force and hers. She has a lot of people with her. We will have the sea behind us, for safety. But the king will be trapped." He looked at them with surprise. "We have a chance," he said. "Aria's force is strong. And the king will be stuck."

Abbas nodded once, curiosity all over his face. He didn't question how Jabari knew, though. He simply gave the command to run and started off. Jabari was glad for it. There wasn't much time.

"I don't like this," Isika said after some time running on the smaller path, which was worse than the first, with vines and branches scratching them constantly. "I mean, I like what you saw, I like this new power. But where is Herrith?"

Jabari felt a flash of impatience. "Herrith is fine," he said. "He knows how to do this better than us. At this point, I don't see how we could lose. We have every advantage and far more magic. This is a good thing, Isika. Try not to worry."

Isika fell silent, but when Jabari turned to look at her, her face was full of misery.

When they broke out of the jungle, the sea stretched before them, and before the sea, a vast expanse of sand. Jabari breathed a long sigh. The jungle had been stifling. They all ran to the sea to bathe their hands and heads, then listened to Abbas explaining the formation he wanted them to make. They spread out, spears in hand, waiting.

"It won't be long," Jabari said. He could feel the alarm of the animals building, and despite the danger, he couldn't stop smiling. This was amazing. His power seemed to build the longer he was aware of it until he felt he could hear even the clams under the sand. But then the smile slid off his face as the jungle waved and stretched in a long, drawn-out screech. Three trees fell, and fish threw themselves out of the water, gasping on the shore, as King Ikajo emerged from the jungle.

CHAPTER 32

Something strange was happening to Herrith. Even as Isika and the others made plans to run and intercept the king, he found his mind drifting, daydreaming. Flashes of memories floated in front of him like cobwebs. Herrith tried to wave them away, but they tangled in his hair, in his eyebrows, around his shoulders.

But when Jabari said Herrith should wait at the village with Mara, Herrith woke up enough to refuse.

"I'll come," he insisted. "I may be behind you, but I'll get there." Fortunately, the Karee prince had enough respect for Herrith to agree. And Isika saw his side, too, because she loved Aria as he did.

Herrith needed to be there when Aria came with her army. He had to greet his new, strong daughter.

He started off running with the others, but it wasn't long before he slowed to a walk. The last days and weeks had been hard on his body—the insistent biting of insects, hard ground, and not enough sleep.

But, oh, they had been so good for his soul, he reflected, as he walked. Freedom was sweeter than Herrith had imagined. Here in the village, for the first time since he was a small boy in the shelter of his parents, Herrith hadn't had to fake a single emotion, hadn't needed to lie and pretend. He was absolutely free. This gave him a feeling of dignity that almost hurt.

He had lost so many years. The lost years were for the cause, for the resistance, so Herrith would be in the palace when the young ones arrived. He had sacrificed his days for the sake of the new tide of change that was coming.

But it still hurt.

And Aria. The daughter he wished he could have had. He had the honor of protecting her now. Herrith had thought he knew the girl, but when she was freed from the poison of the arrow, he could feel the change like the sun rising. He had never really known the real Aria. She was strong and sunny, like a bright day with a promise of a short rain and a cool evening.

And her freedom gave him pain, as well. She had spent so many years in the fog of the Great Waste. *How much potential did Mugunta crush—all around the world?* Herrith cowered under the sorrow of this loss. He stayed quiet, even while the others rejoiced to feel the difference in Aria. Herrith felt the truth of the hope the others felt and the fact that they just might win this battle, that all these years of resistance might be fulfilled. But he also felt the sorrow of Aria's stolen joy. There were days that could never be given back, and Aria was the one who had paid.

Herrith felt weighed down by grief, barely able to hold up his head, but he continued on. He needed to see Aria in her power. After a while, he sensed, rather than saw, the Othra who flew above him. Eemia, that was the name of this one. Herrith wondered why she lingered with him, but the breeze from her wings gave him the strength to keep walking through the humid jungle, so different from the desert of the Gariah people. Herrith had always imagined that the jungle would be full of beauty and life, and it was. He was not disappointed. But it was also hostile, competitive, and overwhelming. He had been bitten by ants, stung by hornets, and swiped by more sharp branches and leaves than he could count. It was not a fairytale, this jungle. It needed to be known to be loved.

In the desert, there are snakes and scorpions, he told himself. But he felt that a breath of dry desert air and a sky that revealed more than it hid would be welcome right now. He paused in his tracks, trying to beat back panic, the feeling that he couldn't breathe in the humid air, that he was trapped.

Eemia landed on a branch in front of him.

"Have courage, elder," she said to him. "Why are you so far behind the rest?"

"I have no strength to go faster," he told her.

"You are in danger if you are separated from them," she said.

"Oh, but I, and those I love, have always been in danger," he told her. It was true. The resistance didn't have the comfort of peace. They never had.

The Othra gave a long, mournful cry. "You are right, elder," she said. "I sense that you are tired from the constant danger, but keep on. Today is a day of hope." She opened her wings, and a feeling of bravery expanded Herrith's chest and straightened his spine. He began to walk again.

She was trying to support him, he realized, flying above him and sending waves of hope and comfort. They did help him to keep walking, but still, his mind wandered. He felt as though he was half in a dream.

Amani, the children's mother, appeared in this dream,

shimmering in the air in front of him, smiling at him hopefully. She held out a hand when he felt that he couldn't walk anymore, that he might just sink to his knees on the jungle floor. She seemed to walk in front of him for some time, so lovely and full of light that Herrith was smiling when the king found him.

He didn't have much warning. One moment he was alone in his plodding stupor; the next, the king had burst out of a side path. Ikajo was flanked by several of the sea people and two men with scraps of red cloth on their backs. Red robes.

The king stopped in this tracks, holding up a hand to keep the sea people from attacking. He seemed puzzled, staring at Herrith as though he didn't recognize him.

"Herrith?" the king asked. "Cousin?"

At that moment, so many things happened inside Herrith that it was like a sandstorm in his skull. He reflexively began to put on the face that he had worn his whole life. His father had taught him this face. It was the mask of someone who has everything to hide, who lives in deception in order to create a better future. But as he reached for the face, for the fawning and the lies, Herrith found that he could no longer access that part of himself. He couldn't locate the skilled manipulations that had kept up the deception for so long.

So, though he sensed his sudden and overwhelming danger, he felt an immense relief, like a sunrise, break through the fog in his mind. He was finished. Around him, the jungle leaves quaked, and he heard Amani's laugh echoing through the sky. *Come to me, love.*

"Where is your robe?" the king asked. His face was still faintly puzzled, not yet angry. Herrith took two breaths to compose himself and then said, "I took it off while I was still in the water, hoping I never needed to put the detestable thing on again."

The king's face shifted alarmingly but slowly, as if he couldn't quite believe what he was hearing. He leaned closer, his dark, handsome face still full of power, though the clothes he wore were torn and faded.

"Sorry?" he asked.

"I do cherish the fact," Herrith went on, sealing his fate, "that while I wore it, you never guessed how much I hated you. You never knew that I double-crossed you again and again, that I hated everything you loved and loved everything you hated."

Now the king's face clouded with a sudden fury, and he backhanded Herrith so swiftly and so hard that Herrith's head whipped back, and he crashed into a nearby tree. The pain was overpowering. Herrith felt as though he would vomit, but behind the anguish, he felt a sudden exuberance. His whole life had been spent trying to assuage the king's anger. It felt so good to finally just make him mad.

"Kill him," he heard the king order in a flat voice, and as Herrith waited for the sword to fall, he reached out to Eemia.

Tell her I love her, he said in his mind, hoping she would understand. Amani was close by again, gazing at him with tenderness. But she already knew that Herrith loved her. He had sent her away out of love, after all. But he needed Eemia to tell Aria, his daughter.

But then the king spoke again. "Actually, no, wait. We will bring him with us. The girl should see him die before she dies herself." There was the sound of a sword clinking back into its sheath.

Herrith hadn't realized he was holding his breath, but when air rushed into his lungs, it was like a revelation. He would see

Aria. He didn't want to cause her pain, but he was so happy that he would see her again.

They forced Herrith to his feet and bound his hands. Blood ran down his face from the cut that the king's ring had gouged into his cheek. They made him walk at the front of the group, and as he walked, the man behind him struck him on his shoulders with a rod of wood at whim. Herrith didn't know when the rod would fall, and his shoulders and neck were tense from expecting the blows.

They walked faster than Herrith wanted. He tried to take comfort from the fact that Eemia was still somewhere nearby and that he would never have to wear the red robe again, but he also struggled with the pain. His misery seemed to awaken in him an awareness of all the suffering of the earth. All the times Herrith had seen Ikajo beat a slave, that person had been feeling something like this. This horror of violence profaned the Uncreated One. And so, as he walked, Herrith wept.

After what seemed a very long time, Herrith stumbled onto a beach. There, in the water, facing them, were Isika and Jabari, Abbas and Ben, and all the others. Through the blood and sweat that ran into his eyes, Herrith saw the panic on their faces when they realized Herrith was a captive.

He couldn't speak, but he wanted to tell them to attack before the king realized what he was facing and gathered his strength. His voice was gone, though. Herrith watched as the knowledge of his captivity stopped their attack. Oh, the futility of the world. He despaired.

"You rotten, wretched worms," Ikajo said, laying a hand on Herrith's shoulder and squeezing so that Herrith cried out. So he did have a voice to shriek in pain. He was weak and dizzy. "You left an old man for me to find in the wilderness," the king went on. "You have stolen the loyalty of my closest servant, and for that, you will die."

There was a sudden commotion, and Herrith lifted his tired eyes to see that Isika had rushed forward, but Jabari had caught her and was holding her back.

"You never had his loyalty," a deep voice said, and Herrith smiled, thankful that someone could tell the truth. It was Abbas, the Karee prince. "This man has always been against your line, and his father, and his father's father as well."

"Abbas!" Isika said, her voice a wail, and Herrith knew that she wanted Abbas to stop talking out of fear for Herrith's life. But Herrith made a sudden motion, and Isika stopped. He tried to look brave, to communicate to her that this needed to happen. It was so clear to him now. He wanted the king to hear the truth. Abbas continued. The four Othra circled overhead, giving little cries again and again, and as Abbas spoke, the beach began to vibrate under their feet.

"Who helped Azariyah to live and not die? Who loved Amani all her life? Who protected Amani's children from your hatred, Ikajo? Who comforted Benayeem after you beat him? Who helped Amani escape? Who kept Aria safe from you?"

Tears were streaming down Isika's face now, and Ben's eyes were locked on Herrith, as though he could not bear to hold himself back. Ikajo's hand spasmed near Herrith's neck, and Herrith knew he had only a few moments left in this life. As he saw this true thing and accepted it, he had more visions.

Amani's face again, her hand touching his briefly. Amani as a child, playing with him in the palace. And then the Shaper, singing the sorrow of the world, holding it in his heart, spinning it into the gold cord that Herrith wore around his hair.

"Herrith should be king," came a clear voice, and the hand

that held Herrith in its unforgiving grip loosened and fell completely. "He is my true father." Herrith nearly toppled but forced himself to stay upright as Aria and an army of the runaway slaves marched out of the jungle and onto the shore. They were armed, and the magic surrounding them was so clear that it was visible. Herrith could hear Isika and Gavi calling Aria's name, but Herrith only had eyes for her. This strong, upright young woman, his daughter by choice. She held his eyes, and there was so much love for him in her gaze. *Father,* it said. She knew that he would die today, he saw, and then he saw a vision of Nenyi running through the sea toward him, taller than a mountain, splashing the water so high that it splashed his shoulders. The Shaper was smiling, the color of night, with skin filled with stars, and he held out his hands just as the king ordered, "Kill him now."

Aria cried out and stretched out her hands. She began to run to him, but Herrith knew it was too late. He blessed her again and again, waiting for the sword to fall. The last thing he saw was Amani's face swimming in front of his, her hands outstretched in welcome. And then pain, an explosion of pain, and then peace—peace that bloomed into the sky and never stopped blooming.

CHAPTER 33

As Herrith's song emptied out of the world, Ben staggered and nearly fell. Herrith's music was gone. He couldn't believe what had just happened. The king had just had his own cousin killed. Any hope Ben had held that Ikajo might have mercy on his family disappeared. What kind of monster killed his family in cold blood? *That's right,* he thought. *My father is that kind of monster.*

It felt as though despair and evil would press them into the ground. Ben looked around and saw faces as shocked and bleak as his heart felt. But then a voice rang out in the air, stirring the fronds of the trees, lifting a little of the fog.

"This is no victory for you, Ikajo," Aria called, and her voice was strong and clear, even joyful. "You can't take life from someone who gave it up every day of his life. It wasn't yours to take. My father, Herrith, was so powerful that he couldn't be killed unless he allowed it."

"He wasn't your father, ungrateful witch," the king spat out, his face a mask of rage. "And the world doesn't work that way. Those with power take life whenever they want. This is what I have been trying to teach you. And Herrith was my servant from the day he was born."

Ben couldn't pull his eyes away from the sight of Aria. She glowed, feet planted in the earth like a tree, a wooden staff in her hands, her eyes full of light. Ben had never seen his sister look so strong and whole. He had memories of a laughing little girl in the worker village, but they were nothing like this.

"I chose him as a father," she said. "And I have proven hard to teach." And then she laughed, and several things happened all at once.

The king made a sudden lunge at Aria, but her army closed in front of her and drove him back. Ben had a brief impression of dozens of women and men, their eyes full of anger and joy. Then Isika, Jabari, and Nat ran toward Benayeem. "We need to get Herrith," Isika said.

"Herrith is dead," Ben said, despairing. Maybe they didn't understand because they weren't able to hear that his song had gone out of the world.

"We know," Isika said. "Benayeem, we must send him out to sea, properly, so his body doesn't get trampled."

Ben wondered if it mattered, if anything mattered, but Jabari grabbed him by the shoulder, and Ben stared at the older boy, his friend.

"Brother, the king is spreading the poison of despair," Jabari said. "Pay attention to Aria. How is she fighting it off?"

Ben looked at the spot he had last seen Aria but couldn't find her in the tangle of fighting people.

"Come on, Ben," Nat said. "They need our help. Let's help Herrith and then join the battle. This must end here—like Herrith said."

Ben followed behind Jabari and Isika as they headed to the

clump of trees where Herrith had fallen. What did Jabari mean by paying attention to Aria? What had she done? She had spoken.

They found Herrith lying in a crumpled heap. Grief threatened to overwhelm Benayeem. He tried to do as Jabari had said, as Aria had done. He spoke.

"Herrith did not die in vain," he said, as loudly as he could. "No one can be killed who gives his life daily."

Isika squeezed Ben's arm, and Jabari glanced at him. "Good work, little brother."

Ben felt courage come to him like a gentle breeze. Despair lifted.

Three other men drew near. "We came with Aria," one of the men explained. "She asked us to come help carry this great man. She said he spent his life saving the lives of the enslaved whenever he could. We can give you one of the rafts we brought with us, so you can send him into the sea. Wait here."

As they waited, Isika stroked Herrith's hair out of his eyes and gently brushed his eyelids closed. Like this, he looked peaceful, like he was sleeping, except that he had no song.

"They stabbed him in the back," Ben said. He tried again, tried for words that hurt less. "He loved our mother."

Isika smiled at him with tears in her eyes. "It has been good to know that she was loved so much, even in that terrible place."

Ben, Jabari, Isika, and Nat helped gently place and arrange Herrith's body on the raft. Ben longed for Herrith to come back and say, "I'm here, I'm not really dead," but he didn't. His beloved body stayed as it was, lifeless. And so they carried the raft to the sea and waded out with it until they could push it past the waves. All of them were weeping. Isika called the Naia, who came and nudged the raft until it was adrift in the endless ocean. While they worked, there was a bubble of space and quiet around them, despite the seething battle.

As they waded back to shore, Isika remarked on this circle of calm. "This is magic," she said.

"It has a sound to it," Nat said, "like the Othra. I think they made a safe place for us."

"Thank you," Isika called, and they heard a trill of birdsong from overhead.

"That was Eemia," Jabari murmured.

"She says she had grown to love Herrith," Isika said.

"That is done," Jabari said. "I wish we could go and cry for a hundred years, but there are pressing matters. What is our plan?"

Isika gazed at the shore in front of them. Ben opened up the room in his head to listen to a bit of the battle. Most of the fighting was taking place on the beach, but there were skirmishes in the jungle as well. He heard Aria's loud song within the action and a web of music made of the many songs. Ben could hear unfamiliar music within the web, but he also heard Gavi, Ivy, and Deto. Brigid was in there too. And Abbas.

"They have formed a web of strength," Ben said, "with the peculiar magic that Aria brought with her. I think the best thing we could do is link into it."

Isika nodded, but Jabari shook his head. "You two do that," he said. "But I have another idea. I'm going to run this way and see if I can pull it off."

Isika gazed at him for a moment and then murmured her agreement. "Be careful," she said. Jabari grinned at her, irony all over his face. "Nothing safer than this place and time! It's as easy as eating Auntie's flatcakes, staying safe here."

Nat shook her head, rolling her eyes, but Isika smiled. Ben looked away for a moment as Jabari leaned in and kissed Isika.

"Come," Isika commanded Ben, and he ran after her and Nat, muttering, "Yes, Majesty," under his breath.

They raced into the fray. Ben dodged blows from fighting bodies around him. There didn't seem to be any rhyme or reason to what was happening. Many people didn't even have weapons, so there was a lot of hitting going on, but there were some spears, and Ben took a moment to yank a spear out of a sea person's hand just before it came down on the neck of an older woman. This was ugly. Many people caught up in the machinations of power, not people who actually had any gripe against each other. The despair threatened to choke him again, but he screamed out, "We will win this, we will stop this," and it ebbed a bit.

They found Aria. She stood with her eyes closed, protected within a circle of people while she formed large sheets of ice out of the water in the air, and dropped them on the heads of their enemies. *Oh, dear,* thought Ben. *So many powerful sisters.*

Isika waded into the circle, flanked by the Palipa, and grasped her sister's hand, and there was a massive explosion of sound that nearly deafened Ben. But others had heard it too, crying out and covering their ears. The web that had been invisible glistened into existence, made of threads of gold with stars at the places where they crossed. The web rose and then dropped over all of them. Spears glanced off of arms and backs. Nothing could penetrate this web. Not even the king, who threw himself at it when the arcs of light from his hands made no effect. Ben heard Jabari's voice, magnified, calling and then what seemed like every animal in the jungle rushed out and surrounded the king and his servants.

There was a long time of scuffling that ensued, and when the dust settled, the scene that appeared was almost comical. Ben smiled, despite Herrith's death, lodged like a stone in his heart.

The king and his red robes and a few captains of the sea people sat on the ground. Guarding them was a group of people who had come with Aria, those the king had enslaved. Birds pecked at the heads of the king and other prisoners while they tried to push the birds away or protect their faces with their arms. Ben saw a monkey gently pawing through the king's hair, in search of insects to eat.

Isika drifted over to stand beside Ben. "They don't look very impressive at the moment, do they?"

Ben spotted a group of caterpillars crawling over the king's neck. Ikajo felt them, shrieking and trying to brush them off.

"Not at all," he said. "What is this?"

"This is Jabari," Isika said. "He has located his power."

A jungle cat strode up to one of the sea captains and stared at him in the face. The man's face lost color.

"It's surprising," Ben said. "Not what I would have expected his power to be."

"Me neither. That's why I love Jabari. He's surprising."

"Oh, so his handsome face has nothing to do with it?" Ben said, elbowing his sister.

Jabari wandered over just as Isika was elbowing Ben back. "What's that?" Jabari asked. "Did I miss something?"

"Nothing," Isika said. "What do we do now?" she asked, sighing. "I wish we could ask Herrith. What are we going to do without him?"

They stood in silence for a while, contemplating a future without Herrith. It seemed bleak.

"Where's Aria?" Jabari asked. "Let's ask her what she thinks."

Aria, Brigid, Ivy, and some other women sat in a little group in the waning sun, watching the king and his red robes trying to fend the animals off.

"This is oddly soothing," Aria said, but Ben could hear the sorrow in her song. He reached out impulsively and took his younger sister's hand. She looked surprised but didn't pull away.

Ben's eyebrows shot up. "I don't hear any magic from the king in you," he said. "It's as though he lost his power."

Isika nodded. "I think we broke the curse," she said.

"How?" Aria asked. "Neither of us died."

"We unified. The arrow is gone."

"I think it had something to do with Herrith," Brigid said softly. "When he adopted Aria, it redirected the curse."

Hera was pacing silently around the group of prisoners. It *was* strangely soothing to watch, Ben thought. Like balance had returned. The terror Ikajo had inspired was mitigated by the strength of the animals.

"I don't want to kill anyone," Aria said, suddenly.

"Me neither," Isika said. "But what do we do?"

"We banish him."

"That's a good idea," said Isika, "but we don't have Herrith to rule the Desert City or the Gariah people."

"This is true. But we have the Circle, and anyway, Herrith wouldn't have ruled. He told me what needed to happen if he ever died."

"What is it?" Ben asked, and Aria lifted her eyes to him.

"I am to be Queen of the Gariah," she said. "Warrior and Whisperer will rule side by side for justice everywhere."

There was a long silence.

"But you will be so far away," Isika said with a break in her voice.

"I will come back to Azariyah first," Aria said. "Some of the people who fought with us today will help to hold Gariah for my return. The others will go back to their villages." She paused. "Abbas?"

Ben looked up to see that Gavi, Deto, and Abbas had joined them. Gavi sat next to Aria, and she leaned on him. Deto and Ivy sat side by side, and Abbas squatted, watching the king with a smile on his face until Aria called him, and he looked at her. Ben thought that being in the company of friends felt like a long sigh of relief after holding his breath. He began to relax.

"Yes?" Abbas asked.

"Will you be a regent for me while I heal and find my strength in Maween?" Aria asked.

Abbas bowed his head. "I would be glad to," he said. "Can I bring Jerutha, Mesu, and the baby to the palace as well?"

Aria smiled. "Of course."

Ben could hear that Isika's music was full of conflict. She seemed to watch in awe as the mantle and responsibility of a queen settled around Aria. But Isika seemed full of sorrow, too.

"What is it?" Ben asked her. Everyone turned to look at the queen of the Maweel. Isika turned troubled eyes to Ben.

"It's just that I never envisioned this. Never imagined that we were doing all this fighting to continue to be separated. I wanted to be together."

Aria moved across the circle and embraced her sister while tears rolled down Isika's cheeks.

"We fought to liberate the Gariah people and to right the wrong of the kidnapping of our grandmother. We will be closer than ever, as ruling queens," Aria said. "You'll see."

Ben, looking at the sorrow on Isika's face, wondered if she would. Then Aria turned wary eyes on the king, still guarded by the people he had previously enslaved, now surrounded by large lizards who looked as though they would like to eat him.

"Now, what do we do with him?" she asked.

CHAPTER 34

A ria stood, arms crossed over her chest, gazing at the man who had imprisoned and controlled her for the last year and a half.

"It might be easiest just to kill you," she said.

"You won't," he said. "Or rather, you might, but your sister won't let you."

Aria glanced up at Isika, who also stood with her arms crossed and a scowl on her face.

"I won't stop Aria from doing whatever she wants with you," Isika stated. But, she did give Aria a look that begged her not to do anything too terrible in front of all these people.

"Even if she doesn't want to kill you," Nat, Isika's personal guard, said, "the rest of us do."

Ikajo stared at the powerful woman, dressed in rags but clearly a fighter. "You are a merciful child," Ikajo said to Isika, his eyes widening. "I know this about you."

"Well, you're wrong," Aria said. "Because she is not a child. She is a grown woman and a queen. I am still a child, though. And as a child, I can't be held responsible for my actions."

She was bluffing. She wouldn't kill the Desert King. Partly because she didn't want to start her life as a queen off with patricide. Partly because she still felt like she could see herself the way Nenyi saw her. And partly because she didn't want to be attached to this terrible man in any way, even as his killer. She only wanted to be free of him.

"I ask for mercy," the king said, still looking at Isika, which made Aria furious. Even now, he couldn't acknowledge her as anything more than the sister.

"The way you showed Herrith mercy?" she bit out. "Or have you already forgotten that you murdered your cousin?"

The only thing holding back the tidal wave of grief was the task in front of her—deciding what to do with the monster. As she watched the Desert King, she could feel the anguish of Herrith's death knocking on her skin, letting her know it was out there waiting for her. Suddenly, she was very, very tired.

A monkey scampered over to the king and rapped him sharply on the head.

"Ow!" the king yelped. "Call these animals off!"

No one moved to do it. Aria wasn't sure who was responsible for all the animals harassing the prisoners, but she wasn't in any hurry to stop it. She rubbed her hand along her jaw, feeling the scar from one of the times the king had backhanded her while wearing his rings. She thought that time had been punishment for protesting when he beat one of his slaves.

Yes, she felt weary. She felt the weight of the sorrow of the world. What was she supposed to do with all of this sorrow?

It was unbearable. It would consume her. Her head slumped forward, and she saw the king's eyes brighten.

Suddenly Isika was there at her elbow. She linked her arm through Aria's. "Are you well, sister?" Isika murmured.

Aria turned to look into her sister's eyes and was surprised to find that they were nearly the same height now. And the kindness in Isika's eyes was so unfiltered and lovely that Aria felt its power warm her soul.

"I don't know what to do with him," she whispered. "I don't think we should have his death on our hands, but then what do we do?"

"We make him promise to leave forever if we spare his life. We make a binding promise, one he can't break."

Aria looked back at the king. Her eyes were dry and aching. Ikajo's hair was wild, his eyes darting between the two of them, the guard they had on him, and the Palipa who sat nearby.

"He's slippery," Aria said. "He will search for a way out of anything we bind him in."

Isika nodded and sighed. "You are probably right," she said, "and so we will deal with that if it happens. Together."

Aria looked into her sister's eyes again. "Oh, Isika," she said. "I've missed you so much."

Isika leaned her head on Aria's shoulder. "Not anymore," she said. "You're coming home for Maweel food and warmth before you start ruling anything; I don't care what it is."

Aria took a deep breath.

"Very well, Ikajo," she said. "Hear me now. You are stripped of your throne and your crown. They are mine now, and you are banished. In return for your life, which we will leave for you to live miserably, you will promise to never return to the Desert City and to leave the Maweel and Gariah people alone."

Ikajo's eyes turned to daggers, and Aria nearly took a step back. She reminded herself that he had no power here, that the combined power of Aria and Isika, the enslaved, and Herrith's sacrifice had erased the king's magic. At least for the time being.

"Where am I supposed to go?" he spat out.

Aria shrugged. "Go with your sea people. I don't care. It is that or die here. Abbas won't hesitate." She glanced at Abbas and saw with apprehension that he really wouldn't hesitate for even an instant if Aria told him to kill the king. He was a warrior prince, after all, and his people had long been enslaved and oppressed by the king. The king looked at Abbas's face and agreed.

They made a ceremonial promise, binding it as well as they could, though Aria worried that it was just a matter of time before the king figured out how to unravel it. Then, she and the others marched the king and the sea people out to one of the smaller ships of the sea people. It was mostly intact, and it would hold them.

"We don't have anyone to row the ship," one of the red robes said.

"We'll give you a boost," Isika replied calmly, "and then you'll have to figure it out for yourselves."

As the king was stepping into the boat, he turned to give a parting shot.

"You are so simple-minded, Aria. I should have known not to bother with you. What do you know about promises and magic, anyway?"

Aria flinched under his malice, immediately angry with herself for showing weakness. She turned to walk away, but he raised his voice and yelled after her.

"You have crossed magic over magic. You formed a bond between us with your betrayal of your people, and you don't even know how deep that betrayal goes." He laughed, and as he did so, thunder boomed in the sky, which had turned stormy. "You'll be surprised, daughters. How young you are, how foolish. You really have no idea...you are cursed because of that the cord that goes back into times before..."

"Okay, that's enough," Isika said. "Unless you want us to reconsider and have you executed, Ikajo." The king scowled but got into the boat. After they had rowed out and boarded the big ship, Isika closed her eyes, and the sea hummed and began to move, making waves that sent the ship flying across the surface of the water.

Aria slipped her hand into Isika's. Together they stood at the shore and watched until the ship was just a speck, and then they couldn't see it anymore. Aria felt the presence of the king slowly fade away.

She took a shaky breath, so weary she couldn't stay standing anymore. Now that Ikajo was gone, now that she didn't have to show strength, Aria crumpled to the ground and pressed her face to the sand, weeping for the father she had only had for a short while. *Herrith.* She felt as though her heart would break.

She fell asleep where she was and only woke slightly when someone picked her up and carried her to a place near the fire. Her muscles relaxed when she felt the warmth of the flames. The stars were bright overhead, and Eemia was singing somewhere nearby. Aria sighed and fell back asleep, smiling.

When she awoke the next morning, the camp was already buzzing with activity. The beach was lit with the gentle light of morning. All around, people were talking, swimming, cooking, and cleaning. Aria felt the deep weight of sorrow that she thought she would probably always carry. But she also sensed the heady breeze of freedom. Not one person seemed worried that they would be attacked or captured. Aria smiled.

Gavi sat nearby, staring into the small cooking fire, a cup in his hands, and one more at his knee. He looked up and noticed her watching him, then handed her the spare cup when she reached him. She held her face over the steaming drink, breathing its aroma.

Next to her, one of the previously enslaved women was sharpening a spear. Aria took a sip of tea, watching her work. The woman glanced up and smiled. It was the woman who had been so angry with Aria the first days off the ship, the one who had called her "princess." Aria thought about names and how the king had always tried to call her daughter, but the name had eventually slid off of her. He couldn't hold her.

"What do I call you now?" she asked the woman. "You are no longer the enslaved, or slaves."

"We are from many places," the woman said, her tone friendly. You can call us by our names or separate the Gariah family from the Northern Tribes. You can simply call us family. Or, if you want, you can call us freepeople now. It gives power every time you say it."

Aria believed her. "Why are you sharpening a spear?" she asked. "The fighting is over."

The woman made a skeptical face. "You're naive if you think we'll have no more fighting," she said. Then her face softened. "Although you're probably right for now. This is for spearing fish."

Aria watched the woman wade into the water and stand waiting for an unwary fish to swim by, then she turned to Gavi. "Hi, friend," she said, finally feeling settled enough to talk to him. His eyes were steady on her face, but they swam with tears. "Oh!" she said, scooting close and putting a hand on his arm. "What is it?"

"You don't know what it has been like to feel how tortured you were," he said after a moment. "I've just been sitting here, absorbing your peace. It's wonderful, but it also makes me sad."

She understood. Gavi knew better than most what the last months had been like. It was sad. It would never not be sad. She felt the loss of Herrith again, like an ache under her ribs.

"What is happening?" she asked finally. "What are we doing today?"

He chuckled. "Good question. Isika has been hard at work, using the Othra and Naia to find the best ships to take us back to the mainland. A scouting and repair group has located several ships of the Hadem that are in good condition. Somehow," he glanced at Aria from under his eyebrows, "you managed to push them to shore nearby. We want to leave soon because there must be other sea people and Gariah on this island. If they stuck around, that is. We plan to stay with the Hadem to recover, and then we will begin our journey home."

Aria nodded. "And the freepeople?" she asked.

"They are making preparations as well," Gavi answered. "They've been waiting for you to wake up. They want to talk to you."

After finishing her tea and eating some food, Aria went to look for Rema. She found him sitting in the shade of a globenut tree, chatting with her brother. Aria held back, feeling shy, but they both turned toward her as she approached, and then Ben stood and bounded over to her, throwing his arms around her. Aria squeezed him back, feeling tears threaten again. Her whole self felt raw and exposed, as though all the colors were brighter and all of them liable to make her start crying at any moment.

She sat on the ground beside the elder.

"Thank you," she said.

"You are welcome, and I echo your thanks," he said, his face creasing into a smile. "I did not expect to find myself free again in my lifetime. And then the Shaper sent you our way."

"And I promptly shipwrecked you," Aria said wryly.

"And you promptly helped us get free," he said. He grasped her hand. "We have been waiting until you woke so we could speak with you, but many of us want to leave immediately. Once we reach the mainland, we have homes and families to get back to, those of us who can find them."

"Only 'many' of you? What about the others?"

"There are some who want to stay with you. Those who don't have families or are originally from the Desert City or Gariah lands. They want to pledge themselves to you."

"They don't find that too strange? After slavery?" Ben asked. The man's smile was like the rising sun.

"This one does not carry the scent of slavery on her. She has championed freedom and fought hard to gain freedom for herself and others. It will be easy to serve her freely."

Aria was quiet for a long moment.

"I will be honored to have the freepeople in the Desert City," she said finally. "Whoever wishes to go there right away can journey with Abbas, and whoever would like to remain with me can come to Azariyah. And the rest of you," she leaned over and kissed the elder on his forehead. "Go with the wind of the Uncreated One and the blessing of the Gariah queen."

She sat back to find Benayeem staring at her. He shook his head.

"You and Isika have queenly blood cells or something, and all it takes is for them to wake up, and poof! Royalty."

"You're royalty too, brother," Aria said, her voice teasing.

"Ah, I don't know about that," he said. "We'll see, I guess."

The sun was nearly at the horizon when the freepeople set

sail in the boat they had repaired. They had done an excellent job, and Aria could see that the web they had built was holding the repairs together. She cried as they left, with Gavi standing beside her.

"Am I going to cry all the time now?" she asked him.

"Maybe," he said, smiling at her, tears in his own eyes again. "There are different ways of being powerful. The king had you in a fog, which made you weak, so maybe your new ability to feel deeply is strength."

Aria thought about that and watched the ship disappear on the horizon, tears still coursing down her face. After a moment, she curled her hand into Gavi's and took comfort from the way he did not pull away, but curled his hand around her own and held it tight.

CHAPTER 35

After the freepeople left, Isika rounded up the rest of the company. She smiled as she looked at them—they were a scraggly, raggedy, ship-wrecked bunch. Jabari stood close to her, hair a mess, a few inches taller than everyone other than Abbas, who wore his long hair tied back with a strip of cloth he had torn from his shredded shirt. Nat stood beside Isika on the other side, alert as always. Isika had grown to know the older woman on the journey, and even if no one else could tell that she was more relaxed than she had been the previous day, Isika could. Nat clutched her spear with a little less intensity than the day before. Ivy was more stork-like than ever, and Brigid looked fierce with the black eye she had earned the day before. Gavi stood gazing back at Isika with shadowed eyes and Aria beside him, so intense and queenlike in her fragility. Ben, with his steady, haunted gaze, and the unflappable Deto, who was holding one of the children.

Next were the freepeople who had decided to stay, including many of the foundlings now in Isika's charge. Jabari had cleared his throat many times while the children pleaded their case to come back to Maween, trying to catch Isika's eye, shaking his head. Isika had given him one hard, squinty look, and he had raised his hands and backed away.

So, yes, Isika now had an assortment of urchins from a full spectrum of lands. The tallest, palest one had hair the color of a sunset and freckles like a star constellation all over his body. Isika tried not to stare, but it was quite remarkable. And the littlest one was the child who had attached herself to Deto, possibly because Deto reminded her of her parents from the Northern mountains. One of the other children had hacked her straight black hair off so that it stood up from her head in a halo.

Then there was the missing Hadem ship crew, who had finally found Isika, drifting by raft to their beach during the night, drawn to them by a force that told them where to go.

And there was a sharp, painful absence where Herrith should have been. Isika still couldn't think of the resistance leader without her face aching terribly. *Herrith.*

"All right, everyone," Isika said as she stood there. Yes, they were tired, dirty, and tangled, but to her biased eyes, they were the loveliest people she had ever seen. "You are remarkable people," she said. "Beautiful and brave. We have achieved a significant thing and won not only our Aria back but all of these freepeople as well."

"And freepeople into the future," Gavi chimed in.

It was true. Aria would be the queen of Gariah, which meant the massive and pervasive slave capture was coming to an end. Isika swallowed. Gariah's new queen was fragile and had been abused. Isika would help her at any cost.

"Yes," she said. "We won more than we dreamed we could. And now we need to go back to the village to say goodbye and collect Mara." Her voice nearly broke then. Mara's grief would be immense. Isika cleared her throat and composed herself. "Then, we will travel to the northern shore where this crew has the best of their ships." She gestured to the Hadem ship crew. "We will return to the Hadem village and rest before traveling home." Ivy started a cheer, which grew and grew until everyone was laughing, and then the people dispersed to prepare for the journey.

Jabari found Isika as she was scattering the coals from the cooking fire, and kissed her.

"What's this about?" she asked, flustered.

"I like you as a queen," he said, smiling at her. "It suits you."

"Well, that's good." She looked back at him steadily, feeling joy building within her at the clear look in his eyes. "Yab, you did it! You found your power."

His smile grew, his eyes still fixed on her.

"You don't mind that my power involves insects?"

She laughed. "Me? You know I love insects."

"It's hard to describe how much as changed," Jabari said, looking down at their entwined fingers. "Now that my magic has woken up, I can hear everything all the time. It's a jungle of sound, full of twittering, fretting, finding food, feeding babies. I know what Ben feels like now."

Isika made a face. "Be glad you aren't Ben. Animals are more peaceful than humans."

"That's true," Jabari said. "Poor Ben."

When they set out, Isika walked with Jabari ahead of her and Aria behind her. The cats were more annoying than usual, walking too close, nearly tripping Isika and Aria. Isika told them with strong words to find another place to walk. Hera gave her a long, level look and then moved a handspan away.

They walked for half the day, slowly because of injuries, until Abbas told them that they were close.

"I knew that," Isika muttered to Jabari, and he winked at her.

"Maybe we need to work on your tracking skills," he said.

She elbowed him, but her playing was half-hearted because she was terrified of seeing Mara. The elderly woman had given her life to the circle, and Herrith was at the center of the circle's activity. He had been her closest friend. Everything had changed now, and it felt as though the world had shifted into something unrecognizable without Herrith in it.

But when they walked into the friendly, familiar circle of huts, Mara was there, leaning on Neeva, and she was beaming at them through her tears. She knew, somehow. Mara left Neeva's side to go to Aria, holding her arms out, and Aria collapsed into the old woman's embrace. They held each other and cried, and Isika saw that Aria was beloved and wanted. Her people had waited for her for a long time.

That evening around the fire, Isika sat next to Mara, and Aria sat on the ground at the older woman's feet. The Palipa were sprawled anywhere they could find space. Jabari came with a plate of food for each of them. "Thank you," Mara said, and Aria wordlessly took the plate that was handed to her. Isika smiled her thanks into Jabari's eyes, and he left, perhaps feeling that the three of them needed to be alone.

"I have something to tell you girls," Mara said.

Isika could feel her heart beating in her throat. Aria turned around to look at Mara.

"Herrith knew very well that he might die," Mara said. "So, he gave me a message for the two of you." She paused as if wondering whether they were ready. Aria nodded, and Isika moved closer to hear Mara's quiet voice more clearly. Mara took a shaky breath and continued.

"For the last few years, Herrith has been living a breath away from discovery, knowing that at any moment he might be discovered and executed. He knew the king; he had seen sudden executions. He knew the danger he was in. The lake of evil in Ikajo is wide and deep." She shook her head and wiped at her eyes.

Isika found that she was holding her breath. She heard the crackle of the fire and felt Aria's hand in hers without knowing when they had clutched at each other. Firelight moved over the old woman's dark, beloved face, seamed all over with lines. For a moment, Isika thought she could remember this woman from when she was small. She must remember. But the memory faded like smoke before it even had a chance to solidify. Then Ben was there.

"Did you call me?" he asked Mara.

"You heard," she said, a single tear sliding down her cheek. "You should be here for this too."

Ben sat down beside Aria, and she scooted close to him.

"Herrith wanted you to know that he has always thought of you as being like his own children. That he loves you and trusts you and is so proud of you. That he wishes he could see Aria take her place as queen, but he knows that he did as Nenyi wished. He will be at peace with that knowledge. And Benay-eem, he wanted you to know that there is much more in your future."

Isika turned to look at Ben and found him gazing back at the elderly woman.

"It was the last thing he thought," Ben said. "Just before he died, he sent out a great wave of song. Belief in me and my future. But I have no idea what he intended."

Mara only smiled. "It will be an adventure to find out," she said.

They were silent for some time. Aria turned to lay her head on Mara's knee. Isika pressed the old woman's hands between her own.

"Thank you," Isika said. "Thank you so much. Thank you for this gift."

The next day, they started for the northern shore, offering farewells to Neeva and Makree and the other villagers. Telling them thanks over and over again. Aria gave a short speech saying that she was sorry they had brought trouble to the island, and they were happy to be able to leave them in peace. Isika beamed at her sister as she spoke. How did she know exactly what to say? Her love for Aria bloomed more every hour.

The journey north took three days. The crew welcomed Isika and the others into the Hadem ship that awaited them and got to work preparing to set sail.

They camped one last night on the beach. Isika felt exhausted and full of grief to her very bones, but catching glimpses of Aria gazing at the night sky soothed her soul. In the morning, they boarded the ship and clustered on the deck, watching the island fade from sight.

"Do you think they are sad to see us go?" Isika asked Jabari, leaning on the rail beside him.

"I think they are in their village doing dances of joy," he told her, and she burst out laughing.

It took two days of sailing to reach the Hadem village, and at the familiar, beautiful white cut stone cliffs, the whole group let out a cheer. Isika cheered until her throat hurt, doing a wild dance with Ivy and Jabari on the ship deck. The prospect of a real bath and delicious food made her giddy with anticipation.

When Isika and the others disembarked, the Hadem and the Karee warriors who had stayed in the village to help cheered so loudly the cliffs rang with their calls. Suddenly, the reality of what they had accomplished broke through to Isika. She staggered, and Nat caught her arm.

"Hey there," she said. "You okay?"

"We dethroned a tyrant," she said.

"You did," Jabari said. "You're just now noticing?"

"*We* did," Isika said, correcting him. "And what I'm just now realizing is that the Hadem don't need to hide anymore. The Karee can move freely. Deto's people don't need to be worried about their children being taken in the night."

"That's true," Jabari said. "We did well. I think we're only beginning to see the effect this will have on our lands."

Then they were enveloped in a crowd of brightly colored, dancing people, and conversation had to wait.

The feast that night was everything Isika could have desired. There were mounds of the special whipped bean paste of the Hadem, piles of fresh fruit, and bowls of the tiny golden grain that Isika had been dreaming about. Isika bathed in the hot pools with Aria, Ivy, and Brigid, then sank into a dreamless sleep.

The next days were a blur of pleasant things. The Hadem insisted on keeping them for at least seven days. Reluctantly, and after a few intense words from Gavi about Mara and Aria's need for rest, Isika agreed. She was eager to get back to her city, and she didn't love the delay, but she was soon calmed by the rhythm of the following days.

Each morning, there was an enormous breakfast of fruit and

healing herb infusions. Then, hours at the baths, where they soaked in the mineral waters and were rubbed with mud and oils by the Hadem healers. Even Nat submitted herself to the healing power of the pools, as well as all the other people in Isika's company. The Hadem knew what it meant that the Desert King was gone, and they channeled their gratitude into their healing care. The Palipa slept all day, waking only to eat and direct heavy-lidded stares at Isika.

"What?" she asked, one day, annoyed.

"They're just making sure you don't leave without them," Nat said. "I'm watching you, too."

"I'm not going anywhere!" Isika exclaimed. "You can all just relax."

After the time at the baths was singing and dancing. The Maweel taught the Hadem and Karee their songs, and the Hadem taught their dances. Isika's foundlings entered in with gusto, dancing until their legs were a blur. Isika, who had no clothes of her own anymore, began to get used to the loose scarves and ribbons of the Hadem and found that after a session of dancing and singing, she was boneless and tired, spent and happy. She could tell that Aria felt the same way and that these days were taking her toward health in great leaps. She laughed all the time now, mostly at things that Gavi said.

One night at the fire, Isika was watching Gavi and her sister when Jabari came and plopped himself down beside her.

"What is it?" he asked. "You look like you're searching for a single grain of sand on the beach."

Isika tried to smooth her forehead out. "It's nothing. Just...what do you think is happening there?"

"Where?" Jabari asked, and when Isika pointed at Aria laughing up into Gavi's face, Jabari looked for a few breaths, then turned to stare at Isika. He burst into laughter so loud that it drew Ivy and Brigid to them.

"Share the joke," Ivy demanded. "We need to know funny things too. My muscles ache so badly from all that dancing that I need to laugh, or I'm going to cry."

"Isika is just now noticing that Gavi and Aria seem to have a preference for one another," Jabari said.

Isika glared at him, but Ivy stared at Isika.

"That's obtuse, even for you," she stated, and Jabari laughed even harder, holding his sides. "Did it not occur to you that Gavi left his home to protect your little sister?"

"I didn't think it was like that!" Isika said. She chewed her lip. "It's just...is it weird? Too symmetrical?"

Jabari stopped laughing. "What, my little queen? You mean two brothers and two sisters? That's what you find weird? Out of all of this? Two sisters under a curse, lizards that do as I tell them, double queendom, and the fact that you have a servant who is a grumpy bird?"

"Jabari's right," Ivy said. "We're all a bit weird. Brothers paired with sisters is the least of it."

Isika watched Aria's face in the firelight as she smiled up and Gavi, and she had to smile as well, because brothers paired with sisters was indeed the least of it.

CHAPTER 36

J abari ran every morning, starting before the sun rose, setting off along narrow paths between the towering white stone cliffs. He began in the intricately carved corridors, then left the canyons behind and ran in the open desert-like coastal trails. He inhaled sea air and ran as though he was free from everything, free from the heaviness that plagued him. For a few moments, during those runs, he felt free.

Now that his senses were open to his gifting again, the whole great world wanted to make itself known to him, pressing on him from every angle. High above, the hunting birds wheeled in the sky, curious about this young two-legged creature they could feel and hear. Jabari ran hard and fast, trying to come to terms with his new way of being. Everything alive, everything pressing in. The world and all its life. He ran.

He turned around once his muscles were shaky and burning, his mind quieted by love for the sky and the road. Sometimes, when he reached this state, his gift seemed to click into place, as though all the birds in the sky were singing with him, urging him on, as though they were in it together. Sweat streamed down his face and hands, trickling from under his hair. He felt at peace. And he was able again to think of the future without panic.

When he returned to the Hadem village, it was usually to the sight of Isika making trouble—urging Ben to learn to dance, teasing Gavi into a smile, begging for more spice in the morning's food. She was alight, the happiest Jabari had ever seen her. The weight of Aria's loss had been lifted, and she was absolutely captivating and without guile.

On this day, he left the village while it was still dark. He ran for a long time. The rising sun cheered him on, the sky could have made him weep, and the lizards seemed to agree with him. So, on his way back to the village, he made up his mind.

When he turned the last corner, arriving in the gathering space in the heart of the village, there was Isika, sitting beside the well, apparently waiting for him. Nat was sitting close to her, but when she caught sight of Jabari, she winked at him and slipped away. Isika's borrowed Hadem clothing looked different on her black skin than it did on the pale-skinned Hadem villagers. Crafted of strips and loops of colorful cloth, it swung around Isika's long arms and legs, creating shape and motion with every step.

Jabari soaked the sight of Isika in before she saw him. Her hair was wound with strips of colorful cloth, her face serious as she sat gazing into the well, but Jabari knew how easily her mouth flashed into a smile, how he could always tease her into happiness. Her long neck and the strong, elegant lines of her face were like a painting. She looked up as he approached, and her eyes widened.

He grinned, knowing she liked how he looked after coming back from a run, and suddenly, suddenly, he couldn't be away from her for even a second longer. He ran to her and pulled her into his arms, burying his face in her hair, then bowing in half before her, one hand on his heart. She was laughing at him, but he was dead serious.

"Marry me, Queen," he said, still bent at the waist. At her silence, he unbent himself and looked at her.

She stared at him with wide eyes, her mouth open slightly. He smiled.

"You had to know I would ask," he said.

She swallowed, cleared her throat, and finally spoke. "I thought there would have to be something more formal or that you would have to ask Dawit or..."

"I asked Dawit ages ago. And I don't mean right away; we're both still young. You can decide when you're ready." He stepped closer and took her hands in his. She shivered slightly. Isika's eyes were trained on his, and in them, Jabari suddenly saw all the men of her childhood; men who had harmed her, beat her, or wanted to own her.

Jabari realized what it was that he was asking of his friend. Isika's trust was a gift that couldn't be given lightly. The sorrow of the world seemed to beat down on Jabari as he thought of the things that had hurt his beloved, but behind the grief, there was the teeming life of Nenyi's creation, the life sparks of all living things. Jabari's eyes filled with tears.

"I love you more than you can know or imagine," he said. "Your name has somehow become saturated in every beat of my heart so that it echoes in me all the time. I don't know how you managed it." He felt his breath coming quicker. What if she said no? "Here's what I imagine our life will be like. A peaceful little nest where we can escape the heaviness of the world and find ourselves again, together. We can rest, run away, ride our horses, run along sunny roads, tear down walls. I want to be a place for you to rest, my queen, and to be as kind to you as Nenyi is."

Now there were tears on Isika's face. She leaned forward and buried her face in his neck.

"Now, you have to say something to tease me, or I won't believe this is really you," she said. Her voice was muffled against Jabari's skin.

"You still haven't answered me," he said, horrified to hear his voice shaking.

She leaned back and looked at him.

"Yes, Jabari, yes. Yes, to a lifetime of swimming in Lake Ayo, or lying under the stars." She smiled, and the look in her eyes turned hazy. "You are so beautiful to me—" but then she stopped talking because Jabari leaned close and kissed her.

After a few moments, he broke away. "Can I tell people?" he asked.

She looked a little fuzzy around the edges, and he inwardly gloated about the effect of his kisses on her.

"Um, yes," she said, and he pulled away to run into the village.

"Right now?" she called after him.

"I want everyone to know!" he shouted, and behind him, he could hear her laughing.

He tore around the village, yelling. "The queen has agreed to marry me!"

He grabbed Nat and danced around with her, to her dismay, then hugged Ben, who would be his brother. He came face to face with Gavi.

"Can you believe it?" he asked Gavi.

"I knew it would happen," Gavi said. "Ever since we found

305

her on the shore, and she made you more furious than anyone ever had."

That night was their last night with the Hadem, who were satisfied with the health of the travelers. It seemed fitting then that a feast was already prepared because the villagers and guests were beside themselves with joy. Their difficulties seemed far behind them, the haze of fear had lifted, and now the queen was marrying someone everyone generally agreed was below her but still likable and maybe okay.

Jabari took the insults and jokes in stride, agreeing affably with everyone that Isika was far too good for him, but she got angry, and they stopped teasing. Jabari loved that about her. She didn't find the idea that one person was too good for another funny, even as a joke.

The food, dancing, singing, and drumming seemed to match Jabari's inner world as they celebrated all that night. The people shook off the fear of the past years, and every day that passed solidified the knowledge that those days were behind them. When Isika made the official announcement that she would marry Jabari, a great shouting and ululation was the response, as the people stood and picked her up, dancing with her until she begged to be put down. That night the Maweel, Karee, freepeople, and Hadem celebrated everything they had won. "The Hadem have long danced to express the Shaper's joy in the whole created world," Mara said. "They have been sad for too long, and new magic is coming to them, now that they are partially freed from that sadness. They will dance and dance now, more and more." The dance went into the morning, when finally the people slept, remembering they were starting a journey the next day.

. . .

THEY WOKE late but decided to leave that day anyway.

"We can camp early if we need to," Isika said to Abbas and Jabari. "But I don't want to wait even one more day to start the journey home. I want to tell everyone what has happened. I want my bed."

But first, the companions needed to say their farewells to the Hadem, who had given them so much kindness, thousands of small services.

"How can we thank them enough?" Isika had fretted to Jabari, "for feeding us and caring for us in this way?"

"Not to mention giving us ships that your sister wrecked," Jabari added. She shot him a glare. "Thanks, Yab, you're so helpful," she said.

"Dear one," he said to her. "The Desert King has been trying to destroy the Hadem for years. They are thanking *you* with their kindness. You have set them free. Don't worry about repaying them."

The group of companions set out for Azariyah. Many would break off along the way, to travel to the Desert City, a thought that was only slightly less strange than the fact that they would be in no danger there. Abbas would begin the task of settling the city and the people into the new realities of life under a new ruler. Aria and Mara would be traveling back to Azariyah to rest.

It was a long journey, but they took it slowly and rested often. When the company reached the place where the paths diverged, they spent two days telling each other stories of their sorrow and joy before they parted. Many of the Gariah freepeople and the Karee warriors went with Abbas, but the foundling children stayed with Isika and Aria. They were theirs now, Jabari realized. Isika couldn't go anywhere without tripping over the Palipa and the children.

Jabari's happiness seemed to exist without limit, a great pool of joy that he swam in daily. But as they traveled, he noticed Isika and Aria often in murmured conversation. At first, he thought it was only remembrance and grief that troubled them, but over time, he began to suspect there was more to their talks.

He asked Isika late one afternoon, as they walked down the roads lined with grain fields. The sun cast soft-edged shadows, and the sky was a rich blue. He walked on Isika's right, and Nat walked on her left.

"Is something wrong?" Jabari asked.

She glanced at him. "Maybe something will always be wrong," she said. "Are you sure you want to marry a queen?"

"I am. I am very, very sure. What do you mean?"

"I'm beginning to realize that I've been holding out hope that everything will be fixed completely, one day, and that we'll be done. I won't have to tend to so many struggles. But now I see that I will be pushing against the specter of injustice forever."

"That is all very dramatic," Jabari said. He leapt out of the way when she tried to shove him. "But I want to know, specifically, what is wrong?"

She held a hand out. "It isn't raining."

"But it did rain," Jabari said. "Don't you remember? We were just walking in it yesterday. You got wet? You complained when I jumped in a puddle and splashed you? Nat hit me because I pushed her into a puddle?"

"It's not enough," Isika said.

Jabari looked around. How could he have missed it? In his joy, he had been unaware.

"Aria and I are worried about what the king meant when he

said we did not understand. It could have been only bluster, or it could have been sincere. Maybe there is something we missed." She sighed. "I miss the wisdom of our brother Herrith, and Aria misses him even more."

Jabari's stomach tightened with nerves. "Maybe the elders will have some wisdom when we get home."

"I hope so," Isika said, and though she smiled at him, her forehead remained lined with worry.

* * *

THEY ARRIVED at the city two days later, and as they walked in on the tree-lined road, Jabari felt his own worry grow. There were so few people out on their porches, and though many people called to them, a strange hush lingered in the air.

They didn't have to wait long to find out what the problem was. Jerutha appeared in the distance, running toward them, her hair flying out behind her.

Nat walked very close to Isika, who gasped and staggered as Jerutha drew near. "Please, has something happened? Is it Mesu?"

Jerutha shook her head, her face even paler than usual. "It is not Mesu."

"Kital? Ibba?"

No more kidnappings, Jabari thought. It would be ridiculous. It must be over now. It must be.

"No...no, Isika. It isn't the children. It's the elders. Many days ago, there was a loud boom, the sound of an explosion. I heard it, but when nothing happened, we just went about our days. The next morning, though, there was panic because they all—Andar, Laylit, Ivram, Karah, Dawit, and Teru—they all disappeared. We haven't been able to find them anywhere."

The world spun, and Jabari staggered and nearly fell. It hadn't been bluster, he thought. They had got it all wrong. The Desert King hadn't been bluffing.

Want to know about World Whisperer 6 as soon as it comes out? Sign up here.

What is the most important ingredient for a book's success? Besides, of course, the book itself?

It's what you, the Reader, says about it. Social proof. Reviews.

When people are out there, in the wilderness of the book jungle, looking for something to read, the main question they ask is, "Have other people read this? Did they like it?"

So if this book is your kind of book, and you think it might be someone else's kind of book, I will be over the moon if you leave a review on whatever site feeds you your books. Reviews can be the key to a book's success. Thank you!

* * *

ACKNOWLEDGMENTS

This book took longer than I thought it would, but I am glad because I don't think I could have written the same book any sooner. So thank you for your patience, dear ones.

I am so thankful for the beautiful people who read my books and love them. I hope you know how lovely you are, and how kind and supportive you have been.

I am so incredibly thankful for my family, the ones who inspire me to write stories and more stories. Thank you Chinua, Kai, Kenya, Leafy, Solomon, and Isaac. I honestly couldn't have imagined a family that would bring me more joy.

Mom and Dad, Tj and Mark Chapman, Diane Brodeur, Rowan Keyzer, Alicia Wiggin, Annie Laurie Nichols, Bob Kohlbacher, Carrien Blue, Verena Berndt, Wenda Friesner, Julie Winslow, Stephanie Donnelly, Karen Engel, Elisha Pettit, and Kathleen Andersen, you are so radiant, how are you like this? You trail stars everywhere you go. You light up the sky. Thank you for being my patrons.

ABOUT THE AUTHOR

Newsletter

If you want to join Rachel Devenish Ford's newsletter and learn about books and new releases, sign up here. Your address will never be shared!

* * *

Bio

Rachel Devenish Ford is the wife of one Superstar Husband and the mother of five incredible children. Originally from British Columbia, Canada, she currently lives in Northern Thailand, inhaling books, morning air, and seasonal fruit.

* * *

Works by Rachel Devenish Ford:

The Eve Tree
    A Traveler's Guide to Belonging
    Trees Tall As Mountains: The Journey Mama Writings-
Book One

Oceans Bright With Stars: The Journey Mama Writings-Book Two

A Home as Wide as the Earth: The Journey Mama Writings: Book Three

World Whisperer : World Whisperer Book 1

Guardian of Dawn : World Whisperer Book 2

Shaper's Daughter: World Whisperer Book 3

Demon's Arrow: World Whisperer Book 4

Azariyah: A World Whisperer Novella

Writing as Rae Walsh

The Lost Art of Reverie: Aveline Book 1

A Jar Full of Light: Aveline Book 2

* * *

Reviews

Recommendations and reviews are such an important part of the success of a book. If you enjoyed this book, please take the time to leave a review.

Don't be afraid of leaving a short review! Even a couple lines will help and will overwhelm the author with waves of gratitude.

* * *

Contact

Email: racheldevenishford@gmail.com

Blog: http://journeymama.com

Facebook: http://www.facebook.com/racheldevenishford
Twitter: http://www.twitter.com/journeymama
Instagram: http://instagram.com/journeymama